# MORRIESON'S MOTEL

# MORRIESON'S MOTEL

*Edited by Gordon McLauchlan*

TANDEM PRESS

First published in New Zealand in 2000 by
Tandem Press
2 Rugby Road
Birkenhead, Auckland
New Zealand

ISBN 1 877178 72 1

Cover design and artwork by Donovan Bixley, Magma Design
Text editor: Jeanette Cook
Text design and production by BookNZ
Printed in New Zealand by Publishing Press

# Authors

Barbara Anderson
Catherine Chidgey
Tessa Duder
Maurice Gee
Kevin Ireland
Stephanie Johnson
Graeme Lay
Sue McCauley
Gordon McLauchlan
Owen Marshall
Vincent O'Sullivan
Sarah Quigley
Elizabeth Smither

The above authors are listed alphabetically and not in
the order they appear. We leave it to the reader to decide
who wrote which chapter.

# Introduction

This book is the result of a collaboration between the New Zealand Society of Authors (PEN Inc) and Tandem Press. I have attended a number of International PEN congresses in recent years and learnt that some centres, particularly Canada and Japan, have added to their funds and their prestige by publishing anthologies of members' stories. So first I would like to thank some of the best and busiest fiction writers in New Zealand for generously putting aside other work and joining this project with enthusiasm. The writers donate half their royalties to NZSA PEN.

Next, on behalf of our organisation, I would like to thank Bob Ross at Tandem Press for his quick and positive decision to support us, for the gusto that has helped ignite so much interest in this book, and also for his suggestion that we adapt to New Zealand the Irish idea that inspired *Finbar's Hotel*. It was so successful a book there that it was followed by *Ladies' Night at Finbar's Hotel*.

One author I approached replied that he was not interested because it was a second-hand idea and he was interested only in original concepts. I tried to persuade him to join us — because he is a brilliant writer — by suggesting that William Shakespeare never, to my knowledge, managed an original plot idea in his career and he wasn't half bad with the second-hand stuff. To no avail.

I think we've made the idea our own. Morrieson's Motel is in a semi-mythical South Taranaki town. I provided the names and rudimentary descriptions of the moteliers and some staff, and the authors have seized these poor people, fed them through their imaginations, and transformed them and their guests into genuine Kiwi characters. I hope you'll forgive us if some members of the staff, Laura Blowse in particular, are very close to being in two places at once with different people. Laura, you will notice, leads a rich and lusty life.

We decided not to put the authors' names with their chapters and thus give literary buffs the chance to demonstrate their skills in identifying style. On publication, only I know exactly who wrote what, and I wait, intrigued, to discover if anyone can match up all the authors with their work.

Perhaps we should dedicate this book to Ronald Hugh Morrieson, the man who hardly ever left the small town he was born and raised in. I'm sure he would have contributed a dark and richly funny story to this book were he still alive and writing.

*Gordon McLauchlan*

# Contents

# Friday March 26, 1999

# On Teevee

**4.00: Jed and Harriet have a delivery problem.**

'When she *be* here,' says Jed once again. Not, this time, to his mother, whose turned down mouth tells him her patience is stretched. Instead he speaks to the window, so close that his breath leaves a faint mist on the pane. In this mist he draws a square. Then he adds four legs, though these remain invisible until he delivers a second breath and then they appear, as he knew they would. It disappoints him that this trick works every time; magic should be unreliable.

'I'm waiting,' he says through the glass to the driveway, where the car would already be if anyone cared. Jed wants a world where everyone does what they said they would do and does it on time. He screws up his eyes in an effort to make the car appear between himself and the fence. A greenish, brownish car with scratches and dings and an inside that smells like a puddle of water. A car of no interest except that Jed and Harriet sometimes get to ride in it and today it is bringing them everything Jed has been missing out on.

'How big?'

Her look says he's asked that already.

'This big or thaaaat big.' Stretching his arms out and staggering beneath the invisible weight.

It works. The edges of her mouth strain to go up though she's trying to stop them.

Plays me like a violin, thinks Harriet. No, not a violin, something you pluck at – a mandolin perhaps or a balalaika. Each single note resounding in her cavities. Chest, womb, throat, eye-sockets. How can someone so small be so cunning?

He has old eyes. A number of people have said so. At the Three Lamps end of Ponsonby Road a woman in a leopard-skin hat had looked into the pram and said, 'This one has made many journeys.'

And only last week, watching Jed bury a matchbox full of dead flies, Ginny had said, 'That boy's been through some heavy shit in one of his past lives.' Harriet had stifled a groan. She'd hoped all that stuff had been left behind her in the city where it belonged.

Nevertheless there are moments when Harriet watches her son and wishes she'd never seen *E.T.* There wasn't much about Jed's father, Hughie, that was arguably terrestrial. Nothing that would, for certain, connect him to this planet.

And now Ginny, who she'd thought of as sharp and as down-to-earth as a spade.

Is it that Harriet attracts weirdness? Twelve thousand people in this town and Harriet chums up with Ginny, who should've been here by now but may just have forgotten. Or has been waylaid by unfinished business from one of her past lives. Harriet allows herself a grin at Ginny's expense.

'Pingu,' cheeps Jed, still at the window. 'Pingu. Pingu. Pingu. Pingu…'

It's a competition. If she admits to irritation he will have won. Harriet remembers the company of adults, weird or otherwise. The kindness, the tact, the lack of repetition. Her brain throws in choral music and sunrays in beatification of the childless past.

'Pingu…Pingu…Pingu.' He is winding down, or perhaps just giving her false hope. *Pingu*, the penguin, is on every afternoon before *Teletubbies*. Jed watches both on those glorious times when he is invited after play group to the home of his friend Charlton. Harriet goes too, like a handmaiden or personal secretary. She sits at the kitchen table drinking instant coffee with Charlton's mother, Lisa, and sometimes also with Charlton's grandmother, Laura.

Harriet isn't entirely comfortable with these friends that Jed has thrust upon her. Lisa is very young and her mother seems… 'smug' is the word that offers itself, but Harriet sets it aside and chooses 'provincial'. Which cannot be a criticism since people like Lisa and Laura, who – unlike Ginny – belong in this place, are the kind of people Harriet wants Jed to grow up amongst. 'Real' people, she'd called them when she made that decision.

Poor Jed, already the children's programmes are over, and those are all she plans to allow him to watch. It's important to mark clear boundaries. They will both be bound by rules. In this house there will be no mindless channel surfing. Programmes will be selected in advance. To this end Harriet has bought a *Listener* – in fact she has bought two, although she could probably have gauged tonight's programme from the following Friday's and put the extra $3.20 towards the next power bill.

Jed lived in channel-surfing houses for his first two and a half years, but seems already not to remember. Rather to Harriet's relief, as it's impossible to monitor the programmes – the fragments of programmes – watched when it's someone else's TV.

Then came the months with just the two of them in an ugly overpriced unit. They went out a lot, for obvious reasons, to the playground or to visit Harriet's friends. There was no need for TV. Harriet had thought it would be the same here. She didn't believe in all that grabbing at things you didn't really need and couldn't really afford.

She wasn't aware that she was depriving her son. Even when she'd stood down the back of the cluttered shop staring at the dead black screen jammed between the vacuum cleaners and a tangle of skis, she'd thought just of herself. Had imagined the relief it would surely be to have Jed's attention diverted away in programme-length chunks. Seen herself curled up with a book and a mug of tea. Or, better still, taking a bath.

She'd envisaged Jed on his belly, the way he likes to watch TV at Lisa's place, with Charlton – who is several months younger – sprawled in carefully observed imitation. Chins propped, eyes fixed, mouths open. That last was the bit that excited Harriet –

Jed's mouth gaping and, for considerable stretches of time, motionless.

An extra eighteen dollars, the man had told her, to have it delivered. He said this after she'd been up the street to the ATM machine and returned clutching the price of the TV and a slip of paper saying her balance was now $3.65. She told the man she'd arrange to collect the set tomorrow.

On the walk home from play group she told Jed. She knew he'd be pleased but she wasn't prepared for deliriously ecstatic. 'Our teevee,' he shrieked over and over, running, skipping, laughing all the way along Gordon Street. 'Our teevee. Our Pingu. Our Teletubbies.'

They detoured to walk past Ginny's place, but no one was home. 'No big truck,' said Jed, but was unable to manage his customary disappointment. Once, when they'd called on Ginny and Mac was home he'd swung Jed up into the passenger seat and driven around the block.

Harriet rang Ginny that night. No problem, said Ginny. She'd pick the set up in the morning.

Jed has been waiting, now, twenty-nine hours. It isn't fair. 'Where is she?' he asks the ceiling. 'What she doing?'

Harriet hates to nag when it's a favour and everything but she rings anyway, and after quite a long time Mac answers. Not Mac himself but his voice saying in a dopey American accent, 'Little Ginny and Big Mac are missing you already. Y'all just leave us a message after the beep.'

So Harriet rings the man at Good Deal Traders, who tells her a girl with a ring in her nose came and got the TV some time after lunch. 'Now you're gonna tell me there's a problem with that!'

'No,' says Harriet bleakly. 'No problem.'

In the *Listener* she looks up what they could be watching right now: 'Justine and Susie squabble over Tom and Fisher learns a secret.' 'Marcus whips up some guacamole and what's on at the movies.' 'The Huxtable family prepares for Theo's graduation.' For a moment Harriet feels as bereft as her son; the unaccessed airwaves are full of people she's missing out on.

## 5.30: Ginny feels sure she's on a roll.

When Ginny ran into Corin outside Video Hire, he claimed he'd summoned her there by transmitting beams of intelligence.

'Intelligence?' Ginny queried. 'I'll buy the transmitting, but intelligence?' She saw the uncertainty of his smile and felt ashamed of herself. 'Testosterone,' she invented quickly. 'You're transmitting testosterone, babe.' Then she wet her lips with her studded tongue, because he liked to think she was dangerous.

'Actually,' she said, 'I was looking for you.' His smile settled in then, narrow-eyed and knowing. Not at all a Corin smile. He's been practising, thought Ginny and she imagined him at his blue-rimmed shaving mirror teaching a magnified mouth to leer.

His hands kept inching towards her, though they knew that touching wasn't allowed – not in High Street and especially not on a busy Friday afternoon.

'It's been five days!' Corin bleated, close to her ear. At the same time a woman stepped out of the pharmacy next door to the video shop and said, 'Corin dear, how's your Mum? And Dianne? Tell Janet I haven't forgotten about the pink chrysanths.' And Ginny had smirked up at a poster of Harrison Ford with his tie unknotted, as if she was trying to decide, while Corin was mumbling, 'Fine, thanks. Fine. Right,' and smiling like the nice boy he didn't want to be.

But Ginny was also replaying Corin's voice so full of indignation and blame. Five days! She pressed her forearm against her inside pocket to be sure the money was still there, crisply folded. Her decision was made. The idea had come to her just like that, and her instincts today are in very good form.

Earlier, heading back from Good Deal Traders, she'd detoured past the old pub, telling herself just the ten dollars she had in her pocket, just that and no more. Ten dollars and – why not? – one rum and cola, and then she would leave.

But she had to use her EFTPOS card for the drink, and it's economic to take out some cash when you make a purchase. That's what they say, so she did.

And when the pile of coins was gone, Ginny had a feeling, a

very strong feeling, that she'd been almost there. It was like when you're searching for someone who's maybe been taken hostage and you try all these houses but they're not the right house. And then you go in a gate and up a path and you get this feeling. You just know that this is going to be the one.

So she asked for ten twenty-cent pieces – which really didn't count because two dollars was next to nothing – and fed them into the machine. She'd always felt that this particular machine was well-inclined towards her, though it had so far shown her no favour.

Three coins played was all it needed. The machine sang its song and the money came tumbling out in such numbers that Joeleen rushed in from the bar with an empty glass tankard to catch the spillage. Only then did Ginny notice her company. Some old geezer in a Rasta beanie. Guppy Brown and a handicapped woman. It didn't seem proper, somehow, for a middle-aged woman in a wheelchair to sit in a pub playing the machines.

Joeleen weighed the coins. Two hundred dollars. The old geezer clapped and Guppy raised his fist and shook it, presumably on Ginny's behalf.

Ginny spun the Cortina around and drove back through town. Parked out the back of Paper Plus. She was trying to remember things she wanted but never had the money to buy. Must be hundreds, but not one came to mind. Something for Mac then? But Mac hated her playing the machines and he'd want to know where she got the money.

So Corin then. Corin has no problem about the machines; in fact that's how they met. He told her later that he had chosen the one next to her on purpose. Corin likes her skinny, foxy looks. He likes the stud in her tongue and the rings in her nose. Admiration is hard to resist, and besides there were things they had in common, like too much time on their hands.

You could say that was Mac's fault for being on the road days and nights at a time. Plus, Ginny was wary of making friends because of being on the benefit – you never know who you can trust. In a town like this everyone has a cousin or mother or aunt working for Income Support, and Ginny has signed the form to say she's just Mac's boarder, someone to look after the place and feed the cat when he is away. One stray word about where she sleeps and it wouldn't be just them stopping her benefit, they'd expect her to pay it back. A whole two years' worth. Thousands and thousands of dollars.

And if there's one thing Ginny was always good at it's making friends. 'Linking with people' they used to call it when she was going to Group. 'You have a real talent for linking with people, Ginny.'

You were supposed to find positive stuff to say at the beginning, and again at the end, since the last words were the ones people usually remembered. So there may have been other good qualities that they mentioned, but 'linking' is the one that Ginny remembers.

She'd linked with Mac the day he stopped his truck just north of Bulls to give her a lift. And she'd linked with Ashmita and Joe at the local dairy. And she's linked with Harriet, who can be trusted since she's also on the benefit and knows how it is for a woman.

And she'd definitely linked with Corin.

'Follow me,' Ginny told him, then walked up the street towards Paper Plus with Corin a couple of metres behind. She walked through the shop and out the back door to the council's wildly optimistic car park. So much space and so few cars that each time she parks there it makes Ginny grin. Corin had got waylaid between stationery and the Easter bunnies. He has lived in this town all his life.

Now, while she waits in the car, Ginny tries to imagine how it must feel to have so many linkages in a place before you were even born. Trapped, is how it must feel.

When Corin climbs in beside her, she shows him her winnings. 'Got anything planned for tonight, Babe?'

'Like what?'

'Motel.' She watches his eyes expand.

'He's away?'

'No. Well he is, but he'll be back later on.'

'So just for an hour or something?' He's disappointed.

'Don't be tacky. I mean all night.'

'Yeah? Really? So...you've told him 'bout us?'

Ginny sighs and shakes her head. They've been through this before. At first Corin was wildly happy just to have got what he wanted, but now he objects to sharing. A small part of her is flattered, but it's a very small part.

'But he'll know,' Corin insists. 'If you're away all night. He might not be very smart, but I think he'll manage to figure that out.'

Ginny is offended on Mac's behalf. 'Actually he's a whole lot smarter than you. And he's an adult. And he earns a living.'

Corin is grinning as if somehow this puts him ahead on points. 'So what's gonna happen? He finds out...and then what? I mean, is this some kind of game?'

Ginny doesn't answer. She sees no need to. Instincts cannot be expected to explain themselves, and hers are not on trial here. But if they were her bones would defend them. 'Sometimes,' her bones would say, 'you just have to chuck the cat amongst the pigeons, or the flaming aerosol can into the hen house.'

### 6.00: Mac calls home.

At that sentimental stretch of road just outside Bulls, Mac allows himself to ring home. He limits his calls but it's still a shock each month when the bill comes. Sometimes he'll hold off ringing until he's almost there, maybe fifteen minutes away. Then he hits the town belt, and the bad years after Beverley left come back and have him grabbing for his mobile. Those days when the closer Mac got to home the colder and deader he would feel.

She used to complain − Beverley − that he took her for granted, and Mac won't be making that mistake again. Too many calls are costly but too few would be false economy. There's a delicate balance, which Mac hopes he's achieving. In Beverley's time there were no cellphones or it could've made all the difference.

Mac gets himself on the answerphone and has to chuckle. He doesn't bother about a message. She'll have just nipped up to the dairy for smokes. She likes to make out she's quit, but he knows she hasn't. He can feel the grin still hanging around on his face. These coming-home calls always make him feel like an astronaut who's worried that, in his absence, earth may have changed orbit, or even galaxies.

## 6.30: Ginny follows her instincts.

Corin has never before stayed in a motel. Ginny finds this remarkable. It's twelve years since she was nineteen but, as far as she remembers, she had at that age done almost everything it was possible to do. His delight peeves her.

'I've stayed in much better places than this,' she tells him, as he empties sachets of coffee into the white cups he has carefully placed in their saucers. He makes no response. He may not have even heard her above the racing cars that scream at them from the over-coloured screen.

They'd driven around considering possibilities. Ginny had in mind Camellia Lodge because of the windows, which were criss-crossed into diamonds in a Shakespearian way. But the sign said 'No Vacancy'. And this one, at least from the outside, had looked new and rather important. In the interests of discretion they'd driven on past and left the Cortina under the big tree behind the picnic table at the reserve, where they used to sometimes go when the days were longer and warmer.

Corin kept out of sight while Ginny booked in. He was worried about being recognised and word getting back to his parents, and anyway why pay for two if you don't need to?

Ginny said she was Andrea Horne, a name she'd used once or twice in the past. She wrote her address as 15 Hakanoa St, Herne Bay, Auckland. She'd lived for a while near Hakanoa Street and had liked its name.

'A friend will be calling later to drop off my gear,' Ginny said, and the face of the woman behind the counter took on an unconvincingly inscrutable look that said, 'It's none of my business but don't think I'm fooled.'

'Betty Claridge' said the name on her lapel. She put on glasses to study Ginny's immaculate writing.

'Do you know, Andrea, that you have a double in this town? I've seen her a couple of times at McGregor's Garage.'

'My sister,' said Ginny, waving her hands to show that life's little coincidences never failed to delight her. 'Everyone says we're peas in a pod.' She pulled the notes out of her pocket, getting in first. 'I expect to be leaving early so best I pay you now.' Seeing the little glow of relief as the key was handed over. Unit three. Three is one of Ginny's lucky numbers.

Watching Corin spoon sugar into their cups, Ginny thinks, for a moment, of Mac at the kitchen bench boiling and pouring. Mac who wants a big rig and a couple of sprogs and Ginny at the stove stirring the rice risotto. A great furry spider binding her up in his dreams.

Corin sets the cups on the bedside table and lies down next to Ginny. The bed is vast, a prairie of possibilities. Up until now they've made do with the confines of the Cortina or the remarkable squalor of Corin's sleep-out. This second option entails creeping like robbers between heavily scented roses and parental windows. Ginny won't take her lover to Mac's place, despite what he's going to think, she does have scruples.

Corin's arm runs across Ginny's thighs. *All night,* she thinks. The prospect tastes like peppermint cremes. In the morning light he will see that her bones show and her neck has more skin than required. He will feel, if not revulsion, at least a tremor of distaste.

Smiling, she turns her body to align with his and gropes for his hand. The channel is changed. East Timor is the cause of growing concern. Corin's hand is exploring possibilities other than Ginny. He has a TV in the sleep-out, but it's a fourteen-inch screen and has only three channels. No continuous sport, no uninterrupted movies.

Ginny remembers the TV in the boot of her car. Ooops, she thinks. Sorry Harriet. But what difference can one night make?

'I'm starving,' says Corin. 'When are we gonna eat?'

## 7.30: Harriet succumbs to self-pity.

'I'm really pissed off,' says Harriet to the bathroom taps. She finds that she does this quite often – conversing with household utensils and fittings. Is that a cause for concern?

If she'd known Ginny wouldn't turn up before dark, Harriet and Jed could have walked into town. Maybe gone to McDonald's to share a sundae. Something to keep his impatience at bay.

While Jed was having his bath she pressed redial, and the real Mac answered on the very first ring. Harriet asked to speak to Ginny.

'I thought you were going to be her,' Mac said. He'd only just got in and no sign, no note.

'She can't have gone far,' said Harriet.

If she sounded snappish, Mac didn't seem to notice. He seemed, in fact, reassured. He'd take a stroll up town. Bound to find Ginny there being led astray. Should he give her a message?

'Tell her I rang.' Harriet knew she needed to keep it brief. Even with the phone cord carefully extended she could only just see the tap end of the bath and half a blue duck.

'Sure thing,' said Mac. His confidence was clearly restored, and was so contagious that Harriet let Jed stay up way past his bedtime playing Snap.

Now Harriet sits on the edge of her son's bed and reads aloud, but she's aware of both of them listening to every passing vehicle. She's aware, too, of what a small family unit they are, she and Jed.

When one book is finished, he hands her another and she reads that too. Her voice is a bulwark against the night, against the urge to ring her sister in Oamaru or one of her flaky friends in Auckland just for the feeling of being connected to something and someone. An adult.

'Ginny might be home,' offers Jed. 'She might be home now.'

So Harriet rings again, but there's only Mac's silly cowpoke voice. He had evidently found Ginny and now they are eating at a café. A couple. Free to spend a Friday night however they please.

Harriet's envy appals her. She has a sweet smelling son with bristling hair and a scab on his nose. Who could need more?

In the absence of lollies she mixes cocoa and sugar in the bottom of a mug and takes it to him.

### 8.00: Mac has growing cause for concern.

Mac went straight to the Central Hotel. Which once really was, but the town has grown, like a plant, towards the sun and the Central is now at the south end. It has Mac's respect for having largely resisted fashion. Except, that is, for the regrettable refurbishment of the former office into 'The Casino Room' – as dim and glitteringly icon-filled as any cathedral.

Mac had reckoned on finding Ginny there among the sacramental losers. Near enough rubbing shoulders yet oblivious to each other, their concentration so private and intense – like each of them was perched in a cubicle crapping.

He did the circuit: Cora Petrie, Davey Collin, Guppy Brown, and no one at the other machines. None of them even looked up, and Mac was on his way out when Guppy spoke.

'Mac, the man. Bet you're gonna get a slap up meal tonight.' Then he shot a hand over his mouth. 'She hasn't told you. Gonna be a surprise. I din' say a word, okay.'

His neighbours looked up.

'Yeah. She's a good little one, your missus,' said Davey Collins.

'One out of the box,' endorsed Cora.

'Right,' said Mac agreeably. Ginny the hero. Someone wins and it's like an achievement – that person's beaten the odds, proved that winning is possible. They don't even have the nouse, this lot, to feel envious.

She's smarter than them so why does she do it?

Mac walks along High Street peering into cafés and bars. He wishes he'd brought his phone; she's probably home by now. And pleased with herself. Mac doesn't approve but he does like to see her happy. He turns for home, his legs in a hurry – strides so big he's almost skating.

There's a call on his answerphone. Constable Shane McKinnon, and would Mac give him a ring. Mac's fingers shake a little on the dial buttons, but Shane sounds relaxed. 'Evening Mac. Would you be missing a Ford Cortina?'

Mac thinks of the car he passed yesterday, curled in on itself like a foetus. Policemen and firemen doing their thing. Though, as always, he'd barely glanced. Stuff like that on your mind could be asking for trouble. Shane's still waiting.

'What is it?' Mac blurts.

'No panic,' says the cop. 'It's parked in the reserve, kind of hidden away. Know anything about a TV set? Like, has yours gone missing?'

Mac has to check in case he'd walked right past an empty space. But it's there the same as it was two days ago when he left. 'No, it's here.'

'And your car. You knew it was there?'

'No. My...friend uses it, but she's... You think the car was nicked?'

'What d'*you* reckon. TV in the boot. Your boot doesn't seem to lock by the way.'

'No,' says Mac. 'Never did.'

**8.30: Betty's suspicions may be confirmed, and Lisa is discontented.**

'That's her in three.' Betty holds the curtain aside so Lisa, balancing plates, can peer out. 'And there's a chap. Staying the night you can bet, only she didn't bother to mention.'

Lisa waits until the woman, dangling plastic bags, triggers the intruder lights. 'Yeah, I know her. Drives around in an old Cortina. Jenny someone.'

'I knew,' says Betty with satisfaction. She lets the curtain fall. 'Sister my eyebrow.'

'She's been here maybe a couple of years. That's definitely her. She gets round a bit. You've seen that little fulla Jed that Charlton likes so much? Well his mum is friends with this one.'

Betty follows Lisa into the kitchen. 'Takes all sorts,' she says, opening the big fridge, 'but she doesn't look much chop to me.'

Lisa grins down at the dishes she's scraping. Doesn't look much chop. She can take Betty off to perfection saying that sort of stuff. But this time Lisa feels inclined to agree. She's seen that woman with Harriet, the two of them all palsy-walsy. Maybe because they're about the same age. But what does age count? Lisa's friends, the ones her age who are still around (and that in itself says something about them) – they all seem like kids.

It's not easy to make new friends when you still live at home with a mother who really should take a good look at herself. Who thinks she's Tina bloody Turner, spilling out the top of her dresses and flashing her thighs. When the fact is that, unleashed from their pantihose, the flesh on those thighs looks like custard that's been baked on a tilt.

'I can find out for sure if you want,' she tells Betty. 'Would just take a call.'

Betty nods towards the dining room. 'When you've finished in there.'

### 8.45: Ginny is feeling a trifle short-changed.

Ginny studies her Junior Whopper, which is the size and shape of a powder compact. She holds it up on the palm of her hand.

'Are we talking junior mouse or junior ant?'

But Corin just throws her a tender smile. He's intent on unpacking his Double Whopper Meal (with fries and a drink of your choice) without missing any crucial action at Athletic Park, where the Hurricanes are playing the Brumbies.

Ginny had been the one to walk alone to McDonald's and the bottle store, because the match had already started and is of no interest to her. Luckily there had been time to use the motel bed in the manner to which it was accustomed before the game kicked off in Hamilton. All the same there's a lot of night still to go, and Ginny finds herself wondering about her chances of a partial refund if they left right now.

### 9.00: Mac fears the worst.

Shane McKinnon popped around to pick up Mac and his spare key just as soon as the sergeant had got back from his dinner. Shane's wife, Leanne, is the cousin of Mac's ex-wife, Beverley, and this makes for a little awkwardness between the two men.

There was, Shane insisted, no cause for worry. If a woman was in some kind of trouble, why would she bother to lock the car?

Mac had no answer to that, but he found the question less than reassuring. He didn't want to argue with the 'law' but his own unspoken reasoning went: if you stole a car to carry your stolen TV, why would you lock the car but leave the TV in the boot that didn't lock?

'Not like the big city,' Shane had said, sounding relaxed and knowledgeable. 'Here it came down to just a handful of youngsters with too much time of their hands.'

'Mind you,' he added, 'I do think TV is part of the trouble.'

And Mac suddenly remembered that when cops on TV said 'Don't worry' they were every time proved wrong.


Beyond the beam of the police car lights, the reserve is a restless inky black. Mac's mouth is dry. Shane McKinnon shines his police issue torch into the boot and Mac peers over his shoulder.

'I don't get it.' His voice is hoarse. 'Why would they leave it here? And where's Ginny?'

'My guess,' says Shane, 'is she'll be waiting when you get home.'

He unlocks the boot of the police car. 'Okay with you if I take that TV back to the station?'

Mac helps the cop transfer it from one car boot to the other. Who, he wonders, would steal a TV as old and ugly as this?

He doesn't believe that Ginny will be back home waiting. He suspects the policeman's judgment has been clouded by the Leanne-Beverley connection. Shane is probably convinced that Ginny, too, has done a runner, that somehow Mac has that effect on women.

So Mac says very firmly that they must take Shane's torch and search the dark corners of the reserve. Shane shrugs, then leads the way, and in the light's beam, ferns, tree trunks, milkshake containers and a couple of used condoms spring to life.

'Remember those magic books?' Shane says. 'You just added water and bingo the colours are there.'

Mac thinks that isn't the kind of thing he'd go saying if he was a cop. But he likes Shane the better for having said it.

'Happier now?' asks Shane when every shadow has been explored.

Mac has a picture of Ginny somewhere above them, her body wedged between branches. But how can he suggest that they start over again, beaming skyward?

'If you haven't heard anything in, say, a couple of hours, give us a bell,' the cop says.

**9.15: Harriet finds out more than she needs to know, and Mac is getting desperate.**

Jed has finally fallen asleep and, any other night, Harriet would be reading or listening to the radio – possibly both at once – and feeling happy because this was her time and hers alone. But tonight she frets and paces. Tonight, had Ginny not been so totally bloody selfish, Harriet could be engrossed in 'Ruth is worried about her stomach pains, and John and Sarah are further estranged;' or 'Jarod matches wits with a group of students;' or 'Prue's dreams are filled with images of a strange man.'

When the phone rings she snatches it up, but it's only Lisa, mother of Charlton.

'This may seem a strange question,' says Lisa, 'but your friend with the nose rings…'

'Something's happened?'

'I just wondered if she was at home tonight?'

'I wish. I need to get hold of…'

'I know where she is,' Lisa's sounding so pleased with herself. 'She's here, Morrieson's. Booked in for a night with some bloke. Only she gave us a phoney name. If you want I could put you through.'

'No,' says Harriet. Now that she knows, she's happy to wait. 'Thanks Lisa, but it doesn't matter.'

There's a silence.

'Okay. Gotta go now,' says Lisa and hangs up in Harriet's ear.

Harriet goes over the conversation to see if she inadvertently dropped Ginny in it. She knows that her friend is worried about nosy parkers getting her cut off the benefit. All the same she feels a bit resentful. No one's given Harriet a slap-up night in a motel. Somehow it doesn't seem right – renting a bed when you already have one only three or four kilometres away. Not when the State is paying you.

Mac and his Cortina have done a slow crawl up and down every street. His cellphone is on, the light on his answerphone waits for him, unblinking. He thinks he'll have to go back to the reserve, look up in those trees, but he's putting it off. Ginny has a raggedy doll look and he knows the fate of raggedy dolls, has seen enough of them in the local tip with their leaking seams and partially severed limbs.

## 10.00: Ginny reflects on balance.

Ginny wakes to the flickering light of TV and a room she has nothing to do with. The boy Corin has fallen asleep on top of the duvet. The bedside clock tells her she's slept no more than an hour. Corin must have changed channels – men with guns pop up like sideshow rabbits, shoot, then disappear. Ginny can feel herself smiling. She remembers how the group used to talk about balance. 'You're aiming for balance.' 'We all need balance.'

Well, Ginny's just put her life on one end of the seesaw and dropped a shitload of bricks on the other. Everything's flying about in the air, and it feels great. Feels, in fact, like she's been underwater holding her breath for at least the last two years and now she's resurfacing.

### 10.30: Harriet needs to make a decision.

On his way back from the reserve Mac calls in at Harriet's place. He's been thinking about why Harriet needed to get in touch with Ginny on this particular night. Whatever the reason, he has to know. Besides, he doesn't want to go home and be there alone.

Harriet comes out when she hears the car. 'Oh, brilliant,' she says, 'At last!'

Mac is confused. 'Ginny's here then?'

It takes a few moments to get this sorted out and for Mac to explain about the TV being in the hands of the police.

'I'll take you to get it. Right now if you want,' says Mac.

Harriet declines because of Jed being asleep and she offers to make Mac a cup of tea. She's tempted to suggest he could go to the police station on his own, but it might be unwise to consign her TV once again to that Cortina.

She feels sorry for Mac. He's in a terrible state.

'I've looked all over,' he mumbles into his oversized hands.

Harriet doesn't know what to say. After all it's nothing to do with her, none of it is. She should not have to be the one to tell him. And she's Ginny's friend, not Mac's, and there's always more to this kind of thing than meets the eye.

'I guess she's told you about Beverley?' he tests, weighing the sodden teabag on the raised spoon. 'How she took off?'

'Only…briefly.' Amusingly.

'It's the job,' he says. 'Too much time away from home. Women don't like being left on their own. Isn't that right?'

Harriet gives it some thought. 'I wouldn't mind,' she says. 'Some women might think it's the best of both worlds.'

If she doesn't tell him soon she won't be able to tell him at all, because she would then have to explain why she hadn't told him right away. Perhaps they'll mount a search – policemen and dogs and volunteers, all for nothing.

What's the right thing to do? How is she supposed to decide? She'll look for a sign. If Mac stirs his sugar clockwise she'll tell him where to find Ginny.

But Jed now comes to join them, in blue pyjamas and sweet with sleep. He remembers Mac. 'You come in your truck?'

'Next time,' says Mac. 'I promise.'

Jed smiles at Harriet as he drapes himself over Mac's knee.

Mac forgets about sugar. He takes off his cap and drops it over the little boy's head. It covers him right to his mouth and ears. Jed laughs.

In front of Jed's eyes is an arm fluffy with fur, all of it going in one direction as if a big wind has been blowing. But when Jed reaches out to touch that fur he feels only the crinkled skin beneath it. If he tips his head right back he can see his mother's face, the way she's watching him with her mouth soft at the corners.

# Dawson Falls

She always drove with her chin out, as if it were a navigational instrument helping her to guide the car along the road.

'Did you know you always drive with your chin out?' he said to her. There was a tautness in his voice but she couldn't tell if it was impatience or laughter, and if it was laughter she couldn't tell if it was with her or at her expense.

'Maybe it comes from learning to drive before I could see over the dashboard,' she said. 'I had to sit on a pile of cushions.' She flicked her indicator and tooted the horn in a lighthearted way, letting the driver behind know it was safe to pass. She was capable of being capable, she could be carefree.

'Oh yeah, your farm girl upbringing,' he said. 'You should have kept the braids. Braids are sexy.'

It was probably because of his different nationality, she thought, that often she couldn't interpret him. Over the past three months she had spent a lot of time trying to work out things he had said: more time than on work, more than she should.

'I learnt to drive in a Landrover,' she said. 'With dust pouring in through the floor and an old army map unrolling from the roof.' She liked creating pictures, it was all part of where she had ended up and why. As she spoke she tasted the hot Taranaki backroads under her tongue and heard her father's instructions roaring along with the gears. But before she could go far down that road of nostalgia, Dawson had already stopped listening.

'Would you look at that roadhog,' he said as the Mercedes roared past them. Yes, that was definitely admiration in his voice.

'I'm driving at a hundred,' she said, slightly defensively. 'Which is probably too fast in weather like this, anyway.' She took a sharp corner without changing down, stepped on the brake, realised her chin had crept out and quickly pulled it back in. Rain hit the windscreen hard like the flat of a hand.

'You're doing great, sweetie,' said Dawson. He put his hand up and held the back of her neck, lightly and firmly as if it were a golf club. At one time he had been a pro on a driving range near Palm Springs, being paid big money to stand close to the wives of plastic surgeons. 'Taught them how to wiggle their rich asses,' he told her, as he stroked hers. 'Sweetest job I ever had.'

They could hardly see the sea as it lay to their right, a horizontal sheet of water behind vertical ones. 'Bloody rain,' she swore. 'Bloody mist and rain.' She had taken the coastal road to impress him with views of the ocean and now the ocean was invisible.

'It doesn't matter,' he said, laughing at her. 'I've seen the Pacific before, from the other side.' He was definitely laughing this time, and definitely at her, but his hand stroked up and down her neck. The skin behind her ear flushed where he touched it, a red tide following his thumb.

At Opunake they stopped for petrol and a pie. She stood tilting her head back, the huge roof of the forecourt like a substitute sky, and she filled her mouth with pastry and a warm rush of meat. Dawson ate an apple one, checking the wrapper to make sure there were no animal products. Once, back in New Plymouth, she had taken him to her favourite Chinese restaurant. They had had to leave without ordering because all sixty-six dishes included pork or chicken stock.

'It sure is hard to be vegetarian in this country,' he said now, looking at the wet cars leaping past them like flying fish.

'There used to be twenty sheep for every New Zealander,' she told him. 'And now we only have twelve each.'

'Yeah?' he said. 'What happened?'

'I guess we got hungrier,' she said, waving her half-eaten pie in his face. He laughed but she kept her face serious. She had been working on her deadpan humour.

As they flew out of Opunake, he checked the map. 'Seems to me you got a lot of places beginning with O round here,' he observed. 'Didn't we come through two earlier?'

'Oakura,' she intoned like a tour guide. 'Okato.'

'Ohhhh-klahoma!' he sang, 'Where the wind comes rushing down the plains.' He had a great voice. When he was seventeen he had won a medal in a song quest, and it appeared that only a combination of lethargy and restlessness had prevented him from pursuing a career in opera.

When he had finished his song, he asked her for one. She felt the beginnings of a sweat between her shoulder blades. 'What do you like?' she asked quickly.

'You *know* what I like,' he said suggestively. 'But it might prove difficult in a moving car. So a song will do for now.'

She laughed. Her mind was blank: a road without markings, giving her no information as to where or how far she should go.

'Well, come on,' he said, sounding a bit impatient.

'My wife and I lived all alone,' she sang desperately, 'in a little old house we called our own.' Her stomach tightened under the seatbelt, and her fingernails dug into the wheel.

'Hey, look,' he said. 'Thank God. A little invention called a radio.' He bent forward and turned it on. The back of his neck was smooth and brown, and she wanted to bite it: out of humiliation, out of hunger.

As the car slipped on towards Manaia, she threw her mind back like a net. She caught the echoes of a conversation between someone who might have been herself several months ago and someone who had once been a friend. 'He's staying with you for… how long?' Grizelda (or someone like her) was saying incredulously.

And ninety days later here they were, sliding down wet shiny roads to Wellington where she would leave him at the ferry terminal. He would explore the south, but he would come back again. And by then she would be ready, or sufficiently bold, to ask certain questions. Then there would be 'time to sort themselves out in the wash', as her mother used to say.

'The sea,' she said. A huge relief flooded over her, so that her hand floated off the gear stick towards him. 'There it is. See? Look!'

And there it was: silver, crumpled, thrown out to their right like a survival blanket. The sun and the rain glanced at each other, challenging, bright. And she had been saved from dismalness, from all things drab and commonplace.

'Yes, I see,' he said. 'I look.' His voice was droll.

'This is what we call the South Taranaki Bight,' she said. Reproof had crept into her voice without her noticing and she bit her lip, because this was not the way she was. Not her, not with *him*.

'I'll give you bite,' he said. He undid his seatbelt and shimmied over to her, and started sucking on her neck, just below her ear. His teeth and the strength of his tongue made not only her neck wet. It was all she could do to keep her eyes on the road.

'Air!' he said suddenly, dramatically, emerging from her hair. 'Give me air.' He wound the electric window down and lit a cigarette, so that the smoke mingled with the rain and the mist in front of her eyes. He moved his mouth sideways and blew a smoke ring at her.

'Put the window up,' she said. 'It's freezing.' But her voice was faint. No one had given her this in a car before: a near orgasm, a song, and a perfect smoke ring.

'Problem,' he said. 'It seems to be…' He pushed on the button, pushed again. 'Stuck,' he said.

'Shit,' she said.

They drove on. Long streamers of rain trailed into the car; it was as if they were being sent off on an ocean liner. They pulled rugs from the back seat and spread them over their knees, retracted their necks into their collars like tortoises.

'That's what you get when you buy a French car,' said Dawson, sounding annoyed. 'Crap electrics. And why is it so cold in March anyway?'

'It is pretty cold for autumn,' she said. She was finding it hard to see through the drizzle on the inside of the windscreen.

'Coald for or-tum,' he mimicked. He turned away from her as if the open window was less irritating than her accent. 'I think we should stop,' he said to the moving grass verge. 'Get someone to fix it.'

'Next town,' she agreed. She pulled her hands inside her sleeves.

'I can't believe this is a main route,' he said, pronouncing it *rowt*. 'In the States there would be gas stations all the way along here.'

And suddenly, through the mist, there was a huge bright flare. She stepped on the brake, saw orange traffic cones and danger tape, swerved to avoid the site. It was an oil tanker on fire. It lay on its side in a ditch, blazing.

'Cool!' said Dawson. He sat up in his open-air seat, craning his head out the window. 'Great smash!'

They drove on past but in her rear vision mirror the flames still burned. It was like a Russian folktale, she thought, brushing her cold hand over her eyes. Obstacles being thrown down as they fled through alien countryside, combs turning to forests and scarves into burning trucks.

'Up ahead,' she said, and she was too tired and cold to put any kind of emotion in her voice. 'I can see a sign.'

'Civilisation?' said Dawson. 'About time.' He stroked her hair as he said it, though.


They found a garage on the main road into town. The garage was flanked by a dairy on one side, and a dairy factory on the other.

'We're in cow country, all right,' she said, a trifle despondently. Suddenly she wanted traffic lights and shops, even though she had spent most of her life trying to escape these.

A radio was blaring out the back.

'Anyone home?' called Dawson. He was energised again,

though his hair was still beaded with rain. Without waiting for an answer he strode into the workshop. 'Anyone, anyone?' he called, sounding like a school teacher chivvying answers out of a silent class.

A large pair of boots stuck out from under an old Holden. The ankles were shaking slightly from unseen effort.

'Hang on,' a muffled voice said. A minute passed. Then a low trolley shot out from under the car with a figure lying on it, propelling it like a luge expert.

'Yes?' the guy said, rolling to a stop at their feet. He sat up, stood up, and was suddenly towering over them. He wore navy overalls, was tall and unshaven – but in the middle of the dark stubble, all down one side of his face and neck, was a long stretch of shiny scarred skin.

'We need our window fixed,' she blurted out, not looking at his face, looking somewhere out past his right undamaged cheek to the Playgirl calendar on the wall.

Dawson looked directly at the guy. 'Hi there,' he said with a smile. 'Steve, is it?'

Why could she not say hello like a normal person – like Dawson? And how did he know this garage-man anyway? He had only been in New Zealand for a few months. Though certainly he struck up conversations wherever he went, could be president of the Instant Friends Club. (Only twenty-four hours after meeting him in the gallery back home, she had already been to bed with him.)

'What's wrong with the window?' said the guy unsmilingly. He looked at her, not at Dawson, which was as it should be because it was her car, after all. He wiped his hands on the front of his overalls. His name was written in flowing italics on a white fabric oval over his heart.

'I won't be able to look at it until tomorrow morning,' he said.

'Saturday?' said Dawson. 'No rest for the wicked, huh?' He laughed and his teeth were almost luminous in the dim grey garage. She had thought he would be impatient, wanting to get to Wellington, but then he hardly ever reacted in the way she expected.

'Can you recommend a good place to stay?' he asked.

They left the car at the garage and got a silent lift into town with Steve. He only spoke when he pulled up outside Morrieson's Motel. 'I'm no electrical engineer,' he said. 'You could probably do as good a job on the window yourself.'

'Oh, hey,' said Dawson easily. 'Sure, I used to drive taxis for a living, but I'm not into maintenance.'

The front lawn of the motel was covered in a thin sheet of water so that it looked like a small dull-green lake. Red brick walls curved around them in a horseshoe. It reminded her of a rehab institution.

'I hope there's a spa,' said Dawson. 'We'll have to have something to do – apart from the obvious, that is.' He caressed her left breast as they stepped into the office, the buzzer went off, and her cheeks flared.

The woman behind the desk shook her head in sympathy. 'Cars,' she said, her tight perm quivering with every shake of her head. 'They're the pits. You just never know what's going to go wrong with them. People on the other hand – well, people are much easier to figure out. People are my thing, Clarry always says.' She paused for breath, filled up the space with a laugh. 'Clarry's my husband,' she went on. 'He's a born and bred local. Me, on the other hand, well, I come from Wellington.'

'Is that right?' said Dawson affably. 'We're headed to Wellington.'

'Oh, you'll love it!' the woman exclaimed. 'It's so full of culture. You're certainly not from around here, are you! Canada, is it?' Her eyes darted over them and her fingers flew over the keyboard.

'Canada! I should be offended at that,' said Dawson. 'No, lady, I'm from Noo York.' He put on the accent he always did when people asked him where he was from: direct from Downtown, green from Greenwich, brought in from the Bronx. In fact he was from upstate, from a place called Saratoga, and in the middle of quiet nights he told of shovelling snow off sidewalks and wearing padded jackets to school. These were the times she loved him most, when she could see the small core of him.

'You don't say!' said the woman, bobbing behind the desk, filling in forms and gathering up brochures. 'And what about you, dear?'

'She's from New Plymouth,' said Dawson. 'Which makes her almost a local herself.'

'You don't say,' said the woman again.

'I *do* say,' said Dawson solemnly.

'Clarry!' the woman called. 'Clarry, dear, would you get these people's bags?'

'I suppose Betty's been talking your head off, has she,' said Clarry, as he escorted them through the drizzle. His grey head was the colour of the sky, but there was a wry twist to his mouth as if he could tell a good yarn once he got started.

'Check-out's at ten,' he said. 'If you want breakfast you have to order it tonight.'

'What are the highlights round here?' said Dawson. 'Apart from milking time, that is.' His face was perfectly serious.

Clarry looked at him levelly. 'Plenty to do here,' he said. 'We've got cafés. And an Elvis Presley Memorial Collection that might interest you – the best in Australasia, they say.' There was an odd note in his voice: part pride, part something else.

Once he had disappeared, pulling the ranchslider closed behind him, Dawson exploded with laughter. He lay on the bed and laughed until tears trickled out the side of his eyes. 'Elvis the Pelvis, here in town!' he said. 'The King himself! *That* old guy's a king. He's a real prince.' Once he stopped laughing he sat up, kicked his sneakers off, and patted the bed. 'Speaking of pelvic thrusts,' he said persuasively, 'how do you feel about taking a mid-afternoon nap?'

She stood beside the kettle, fiddling with the tea bags, arranging the sugar sachets into squares. For some reason she didn't feel like lying down on the floral apricot synthetic and having her clothes removed, not right now.

'Don't you want to go out and take some photos?' she said, sidestepping the issue. 'It looks like it's clearing up a bit.'

'I should have shot that burning tanker,' he mused, staring past

38

her for a minute. 'Change my whole angle to car smashes, maybe – a sort of J. G. Ballard focus.' Then his attention was back on her as quickly as it had left her. 'Come *here*,' he wheedled. 'I need servicing.'

And that was it. It was just as it had been when he had come into the Govett-Brewster. He had asked her for directions, then for a coffee, and two weeks later she had asked him to move in with her. Swept away by a sweeper of sidewalks. In that first month he had made love to her several times a night, with the strength and stamina of a gymnast: lowering and raising himself on his arms, lifting his body off her as if it were the Double Rings event. Mount! Dismount! She had never known such vigour existed, outside the frames of the paintings she hung.

'How long am I staying here?' he said one night, as they walked up her steps. 'I'm gonna be an illegal alien soon.' Was he asking her or himself? She didn't know and so she said nothing, just opened the door into the dark living room and heard the sea sigh once outside the window.

'You're so mysterious,' he had said, shoving his face into her neck like a horse. He fumbled at her collar with his lips. 'Sometimes I think you don't care if I stay or if I go.'

She laughed. A laugh was good, said things that would be too definite in words, and often implied the exact opposite of what she was feeling. Her face was hot but she held it away from him, and the room cupped her careless laugh in the way a shell cups the sea.

For dinner, they ate in the restaurant adjoining the motel. It was early: only about five thirty, but they were hungry from bed. When they walked in there was no one around, though they could hear a faint clattering out the back. So they picked up slightly sticky menus from the front desk and showed themselves to their seats. They were the only ones there and empty tables stretched about them like islands on a paisley sea.

'I'll have fish in a basket,' she decided. It seemed just right for this room, with its brass curtain rings and its imitation wood beams.

'How could you,' said Dawson, making a face. 'God only knows what my options are. Coleslaw and fries, probably.' He looked around for service. 'Excuse me!' he called loudly. He didn't approve of the way New Zealanders hung around for things, took what they got, and apologised for no reason at all. 'The meek shall inherit the earth, my ass,' he would say.

A woman came bursting out through the swing doors. 'Sorry, loves,' she said, smoothing a tight nylon skirt over her hips. 'My daughter was supposed to be here at five, the little shit.' There was pink lipstick on her front teeth and her neckline plunged to an ample tanned cleavage.

Dawson looked interestedly at her. 'Are you the waitress?' he inquired.

'No, my daughter Lisa is,' she said. 'But I'll take your order and get things on the road till she gets here. Call me a pushover.'

Dawson glanced across the table, his eyes flickering and alive, then looked back at the woman. 'I'd rather call you by your name,' he said.

'Eh?' said the woman. 'Oh, the name's Laura. I'm the general dogsbody round here. I clean the loos, straighten the towels – I'll even turn your bed down if you're nice to me.' She raised her plucked eyebrows suggestively.

'Beds, huh?' said Dawson, equally suggestive. 'Are you saying we'd better tidy up after ourselves or you'll spill all our secrets?'

'I've seen more than dirty sheets in my time,' said Laura with a broad wink. She leant over Dawson so that her breasts almost touched his face, flicked open his serviette, and then straightened up and looked across the table. 'I bet he's a handful, this one,' she said. 'Lucky you're young enough to keep tabs on him. He'd be beyond me.'

'You,' said Dawson, straight-faced. 'You wouldn't be a day over thirty-five, would you?'

'Get off,' said Laura, looking flattered. 'Wrong side of forty more like it.'

'Are you behaving yourself, Laura?' said a voice, and there was Clarry looming up behind her. But now he had a striped apron knotted round his thick hips so that he looked a bit like a benign butcher.

Laura laughed. 'Not on your life,' she said, and she pinched him on the cheek. 'Clarry loves it when I misbehave,' she said.

'Lisa's just arrived,' said Clarry. 'So get down those orders and then get down to the pub where you belong.' His lined cheeks had a slight flush to them.

'We'll have one fish in a basket,' said Dawson, grimacing. 'One vegetarian burger. And two of your finest house whites.'

'I'm on my way,' said Laura. She swung her hips in an exaggerated manner as she walked back to the kitchen. Clarry watched her until the doors swung shut behind her, and Dawson watched Clarry.

'You're cooking?' said Dawson to Clarry, once Laura had disappeared from sight. But he sounded as if he meant something else altogether.

'Chef's late,' said Clarry absently. 'I've done a bit before.'

'Haven't we all,' said Dawson.

Their meals, cooked by Clarry, were brought to them by a blonde girl with her hair in a ponytail. Her figure was nowhere near as showy as her mother's.

'The tardy Lisa, I presume,' said Dawson, lifting the top off his burger and peering inside.

'Tardy?' said Lisa, in a pale flat voice. Her face was pale too, and there was a sheen on her forehead as if she wasn't quite well.

'Never mind,' said Dawson. He looked across the table. 'How does your fish look?' he said. 'Long dead, or just recently slaughtered?' He laughed at her, momentarily shutting Lisa out.

'Battered,' she said. 'Like my ego when you ignore me for ten minutes.' She took a huge swig of her wine.

'Oh, honey,' said Dawson, and he raised his glass to her. 'A toast to you and your beauty and your goddam car which has landed us in this godforsaken place.'

'Dawson!' she hissed, and she raised her eyebrows in the direction of Lisa who was setting the table next to them. 'This is her home, remember.'

'Sorry,' he said. 'It's such a long time since I had one. A home, I mean.' There was a reproachful note in his voice, and then there was silence.

She put her hand out across the table. 'No, *I'm* sorry,' she said. 'You know my place is yours, for as long as you want it to be.'

He pulled his hand out from under hers and loaded his fork up with chips and tomato sauce. He filled his mouth, chewed deliberately, looking away across the restaurant. His shoulders rose and fell in a slight shrug.

It was time. She took a deep breath and another mouthful of cold tasteless wine. 'Are you going to come back?' she said. 'After you've been down south?'

There was a huge crash. Two wine glasses had flown off the next-door table and collided in mid-air. 'Oh fuck,' said Lisa into the silence. 'Fuck.' She sank down on her knees, started picking the shards off the purple and red swirls. 'Excuse my French,' she said over her shoulder. Her ponytail snaked across her back, making her look about sixteen.

Dawson pushed his chair back and got down beside her. 'Bad day?' he said sympathetically.

'Yeah, it's my son,' she said. 'Charlton. He's only three and he's had a cold so there hasn't been a lot of sleep in our house this week.' She sat back on her heels, blew her hair back from her face because her hands were full of glass and paper serviettes.

'Kids,' said Dawson. 'They sure can be hard work. I've got a four-year-old back home.'

The world rocked. The carpet swirled.

'Have you?' said Lisa interestedly. 'Boy or girl?'

'Girl,' said Dawson. 'Her name's Charlie, actually. How's that for coincidence.'

The chair stayed still under her, but she had to put her knife and fork down carefully in case she stabbed herself in the hand. 'Excuse me,' she said, but the others didn't look at her so she thought perhaps her voice hadn't worked.

'You know what?' said Dawson, giving Lisa a hand up off the floor.

'What?' Lisa said, and as she looked at him her face looked less sick and empty, more alive.

'Your eyes,' said Dawson. 'You've got the most amazingly blue eyes.'

'Oh,' said Lisa. 'Thanks. To tell the truth, I was just thinking that about your friend there.'

'Really?' said Dawson pleasantly. 'Coincidence number two.'


Outside, the rain had started up again, but lightly and easily, like crying caused by a movie rather than by life.

'I can't see why you're so upset,' said Dawson casually. 'It's no big secret. You never asked, was all.'

'How am I supposed to think of every possibility?' she cried. 'Do we have to play twenty questions every night after dinner?' She was caught on a see-saw of anger and a wry hilarity that had always grounded her – saved her – in the past.

'What?' he said, starting to sound angry himself. 'You want me to fill you in on every little detail now, is that it?'

'If you think having a kid is a little detail,' she said, 'then maybe we shouldn't be together.'

'Together,' he repeated, as if he wasn't quite sure what the word meant. He stood against the drab evening with the wet horseshoe lawn behind him, his hands in his pockets and his legs apart. He was a cowboy in white tennis socks and sneakers. 'We get on pretty well, don't we?' he said.

'I guess so,' she said grudgingly. 'But where are we *going*?'

'To Wellington!' he said. He always joked when she was most serious, and missed her puns when they flew like juggling balls.

She needed to know if she would see him after tomorrow. She needed a definite answer. An answer, was all.

'Dawson?' she said, stepping up to him in the white glare of the motel sign.

'Just take us for what we are, why don't you,' he said. He breathed on her, blew all over her cheeks and her forehead, and she felt something unclench inside her.

'That's better,' he said, as if he felt it too.

'Did you enjoy your dinners, then?' said a voice behind them. They both jumped, stepped apart, looked over their shoulders. It was Laura, complete with reapplied mouth and high strappy sandals. 'That daughter of mine look after you all right?' she said.

'She sure did,' said Dawson. 'She's a doll. Obviously takes after you.'

Laura laughed, turned her ankle in the wet gravel, and grabbed at Dawson's arm. 'Bloody heels!' she said. 'Hey, you don't fancy coming down to the Central for a drink, do you? I can't be too long. I have to get back, but you'll love the Central.'

Dawson looked indecisive.

Say no, she thought. Please say no.

'Well, all right then,' said Dawson. He turned away from Laura, raised his eyebrows. 'Feel like a beer?' he said.

'No thanks,' she said. She watched, waited for his eyes to change. He shrugged.

'Suit yourself,' he said. He walked away with Laura, past the red-brick curve of the motel, onto the slick road.

So he's failed, she thought. She should have felt exultant that he had finally lived up to expectations – or should that be lived down? But she only felt immensely tired.

She looked at her watch. It was time for the most popular soap in the country to start. This was a constant at least, whether you were in an alien town or not. She would watch too, and then she would go and get some cigarettes. And then she didn't know what she would do.

The dairy on Waipahu Street was all out of her brand.

'Try the superette on High Street,' the woman said helpfully.

But the main street was full of Friday night shoppers and teenage girls in midriff tops sitting on planting boxes, and she knew she couldn't walk the length of it. Turning the other way, she trudged several blocks to the outskirts of town. If she just kept going she could walk to Wellington, she thought, but she stopped at the Mobil station and went in.

'And then I told him to lay off or I'd deck him,' the guy behind the counter was saying. He was talking to Steve from the garage on the other side of town, and the sudden recognition was almost like relief.

'Hello,' she said politely. She thought this was possibly only the second thing she had said to him; she remembered the window comment, and after that Dawson seemed to have done the talking for both of them.

'How's it going?' he said. He still didn't smile but he nodded to her in a friendly kind of way and stepped back from the counter to let her pass.

'What can I do you for?' said the other guy cheerfully.

'Pall Mall Extra Mild, please,' she said.

'In that case,' said Steve, 'it's hardly worth smoking.'

'I do it for stress release,' she said defensively. 'If you're getting ulcers, you don't want to be landed with lung cancer and a sore throat as well.'

The guy behind the counter laughed and went out the back to answer the phone. Steve didn't laugh, which she was pleased about because she had been serious.

'Why are you stressed?' he said. 'Not the unwindable window, I hope.' He had changed his overalls for a white shirt and his scarred neck looked impressively red, soaring out of the collar.

'Oh, God no,' she said. 'It's only a car.'

'Don't talk like that,' he said. 'I never met a car I didn't like.'

'Ha!' she said.

And the next minute, there was a gun at her head.

Her legs stayed remarkably steady. She looked over at Steve and saw his face so clearly that she could have shut her eyes and drawn it.

'What do you want?' she said, feeling the cold metal mouth against her temple.

'Who's in charge here?' said the gunman loudly. He was wearing a balaclava and an overcoat, and it was only the cliché of it all that reassured her nothing would happen.

'He's out the back,' said Steve. He didn't move and he kept his eyes fixed on the gunman, and the gun, and her. 'Andy?' he called, still not moving. 'You'd better get out here.'

At the sight of Andy, the gunman moved his weapon away from her head and waved it at the till instead. 'Open it!' he ordered. 'Open it now or the lady gets it.'

'Let her go,' said Steve. 'We'll give you the money but you should let her go. She's got a medical condition.'

'Yeah?' said the gunman, staring down at her. His lips looked strangely pink, moving in the middle of all that black wool. 'What's wrong with you?'

'I'm suffering from stress,' she said. 'And it just got worse.'

Andy shoved a Burgen bread bag full of notes and coins over the counter. 'That's all we've got,' he said. 'Now get out of here.'

'Don't you call the cops,' said the gunman threateningly. 'Get down on the floor, all of you, and don't get up till I've gone or I'll take you out.'

Andy's eyes flicked once, twice, below the counter. Then he came out onto the shop floor and lay down on the lino like a dog.

'Shall we?' said Steve, and he gestured to the floor so that it wasn't impossible after all. She lay down beside Andy, and Steve lay beside her, so she was flanked by two backs.

'Stay there!' the gunman ordered. They watched his steel-capped boots walk away out the automatic doors. There was a swish as the doors closed behind him and, suddenly, in the distance, there was a siren.

'Oh shit,' said Andy. 'I pushed the alarm button. I didn't think they'd get here so fast.'

'You fucking idiot!' said Steve.

There was a huge crack and a roar. A bullet whined past her head. Glass splintered and fell around them like a waterfall. And this was all she could think: that she was thirty, and she had good legs and blue eyes but no one to save her.

Glass continued to fall like water and the fridge exploded. Bottles of juice toppled and lemonade spurted like severed arteries, but then she could see nothing because Steve was on top of her, pressing her into the floor. She felt a slight crack of ribs – his? hers? – and after that could hear only her own breathing, because his hands were over her ears. Her head rang in the sudden vacuum. It was like swimming slightly too deep, with immersion infinitely preferable to surfacing.

After a while the hands moved off her ears, and the weight lifted from her body. She could hear voices, though they seemed a long way away.

'He's gone,' Steve was saying. 'You're okay.'

She got up off the floor and brushed herself down. The floor was a shining lake of glass and lemonade, and she started picking splinters out of her hair.

After they had all made statements they were allowed to go home. Except her home was too far away to go to, so she went back to Steve's garage and sat in her car.

'I hope you don't think this is weird,' she said politely.

'It's fine,' said Steve. 'Take your time. I might as well do the window now.'

'But weren't you going out?' she said. 'You'll get your shirt dirty.'

'I was only going to drink beer I don't need, with people I see every day,' he said. 'They'll all be there tomorrow night.'

She sat in the driver's seat facing straight out the windscreen, and he took the panel off the inside of the passenger door. Underneath, the metal was concave and bare like the roof of a mouth.

'Are you feeling okay?' he said after a while. He had an extra eyebrow of grease on his forehead, and he looked over in a concerned way.

'Oh yes,' she said. 'Thank you for saving me from certain death.'

'I liked your stress joke,' said Steve. 'I don't think the gunman got it, though.'

'It's gone now,' she said. 'My stress, I mean.' She pulled the packet of Pall Malls out of her jacket pocket. They were squashed flat. 'Want a two-dimensional cigarette?' she said politely.

'No, thanks, I don't smoke,' he said, wrestling with a pulley. 'Why were you feeling so down, anyway?' He released a bolt and started winding the window up by hand.

'I invested too much time in something,' she said. 'I was filled with the waste of it.'

'Nothing's ever wasted,' he said, 'as long as you learn one thing. Even if it's a small thing, like, I don't know, not to wear white socks or something.'

She looked over at him but he was taping the window up with duct tape. His shirt was smeared all over with the black shapes of gulls flying.

'I haven't fixed it,' he said, 'but it'll stop you getting cold. You can drive it away tonight if you feel up to it.'

After they had had a cup of tea, she gave him all the money she had in her wallet, which he said was too much but didn't seem nearly enough for someone who had thrown himself in the line of fire. She left him washing his hands under the naked bulb and she reversed out into the dark yard. Just as she was about to drive onto the street, she looked in the rear vision mirror and saw him jogging up behind the car. He arrived at the passenger door.

'Hey!' he said, through the glass.

'What?' she said, leaning over and opening the door because she couldn't open the window.

'I just realised,' he said. 'I don't know your name.'

'Oh!' she said. 'Well, it's Libby.'


When she got back to the motel, Dawson was sitting inside with his feet up on the table, watching television.

'Hi, honey,' he said warily. 'Had a nice night?'

'It was okay,' she said. 'Yours?' But she had no particular interest in what he had or had not done, and she walked to the fridge and drank some milk from the carton.

'Look at you, you gorgeous thing,' he said, coming over and putting his hand on her stomach. 'I'm sure going to miss you.'

'Yes, it'll be different,' she said politely.

'What is it?' said Dawson, stepping back.

'Nothing,' she said. 'Nothing at all.' It was the truth.

'Look,' said Dawson, and he sounded defensive. 'I didn't kiss her, if that's what you're worried about.'

'Kiss who?' she said. 'Will you excuse me for a second? I just have to get something from the car.'

'Sure,' said Dawson. 'Don't be long.' He settled back at the table with the remote in his hand.

The car was parked around the back, and the motels curved in front like a dark solid band of hills. In the faint gleam from the curtained kitchen window she could see fingerprints on the passenger window, beside and below the strips of tape. She pulled the map out of the glovebox and laid her thumb along the roads to Wellington. She estimated 250 kilometres. Two-fifty ks, was all.

Walking back around the side of her unit, she was seized with a vision of her plain white room. The vision was so strong that she had to sit on the front steps for a while, thinking about it: the sea, the white walls, her low bed. She smiled. Tomorrow was just a sleep away.

# The Killing Fields

He flew back to his old province, catching the plane from Wellington to New Plymouth, then renting a car at the airport and taking the coastal road to the town where his grandparents used to live. It was a slightly longer route, but he took it because he had grown up on the coast. The road had often made him carsick as a child, but now, at the age of forty-eight, the drive brought on quite a different set of feelings. He hadn't been back to the province for thirty-three years.

Easter would be late this year, actually overlapping into Anzac Day, he remembered. But today the weather was kind, the sky clear, the temperature mild. He drove unhurriedly, absorbing the landscape as it unfolded before him, along with the memories he associated with it. Neatly rounded volcanic hills bulged from the paddocks like green breasts, and between the hills dairy cows with amputated tails munched diligently on the khaki pastures. The road rose and fell like a gentle roller-coaster with each crossing of the small streams that cut through the paddocks at irregular intervals after pouring down from the mountain that formed the core of the province.

The route was much as he remembered it, although in sections it had been straightened (or 'realigned', as the road works signs insisted). Though undulating, the land was elevated too, so that there was a sense of its height in relation to the sea that lay just a few kilometres to his right. Across the paddocks, lines of swells could be seen rolling in from the Tasman. What he could not see but remembered well from his boyhood was the place at the edge of the plain where the sea met the jutting cliffs and there fought an unending battle against the land. Rocks, reefs, gales and headlands made this a treacherous coast, a graveyard for vessels and for men, women and children in the days of the sailing ships.

As he drove he passed few other cars, saw even fewer people, even in the occasional settlement he drove through. Now and again he passed billboards entreating former students to enrol for impending school reunions. Passing one for his own school's centenary next Labour Weekend, he thought, *fuck that*, recalling the trauma of his adolescence. He would only attend such a reunion if he could somehow first make himself invisible.

The buildings he passed were mainly farmhouses, either weatherboard, iron-roofed and featureless except for the odd brave attempt at a garden, or low sprawling brick veneer with aluminium joinery. Not a single building was in any way distinguished or possessed of aesthetic appeal. What every farmhouse – even the meanest dwelling – had in common was a small grey satellite dish attached to its roof or side like a semi-detached limpet. Digital satellite television had obviously come to the coast, connecting this most insular region directly with the outside world. The global village all right, he thought as he passed yet another humble weatherboard house with its satellite dish add-on.

And he wondered, then, what did the locals think as they sat in their houses in the evening and watched the war in Chechnya or another famine in Africa? Probably they munched and watched but stayed as insensible to the outside world as the cows whose milk sustained them. And would they even bother to watch the television series that he was here to research, documenting an aspect of their own lives? Or would they switch quickly to another channel, preferring instead to beam into different, otherwise unreachable worlds?

He came to the most exposed and bleakest part of the coast.

Here the hedges, he noted ruefully, were still boxthorn, the tough, unforgiving shrub whose thorns could penetrate a gumboot sole, then through to the bone of a foot. In half a lifetime of travel he had seen boxthorn growing nowhere else in the world. It was the only hedge bush that could withstand the briny southerly winds that blew almost constantly across this part of the province. Now the hedges had been hacked back by machine cutter, shorn of their covering greenery, exposing the vicious brown spikes like a brutal number one haircut.

The only trees that could survive on this blasted heath were a few pines and macrocarpa, which had been twisted into unnatural shapes by the wind. Like the boxthorn, they sheltered the cows and kept some of the salt-laden winds from the pastures. He knew that stands of native forest once covered the cape, but they had been clear-felled with axe and saw, left to dry and burned, then grass seed had been cast into the ashes. His own forebears had taken part in the business. In one sense it was an heroic achievement, and yet the scruffy pines and macrocarpas which had replaced the forest were completely lacking in distinction or nobility.

The ugliness of the landscape made him downcast, and he increased his speed to put it behind him. Then his progress was held up for a couple of winding kilometres by an articulated stock truck. Following it closely, he caught the pungent, ammoniac odour of dags, urine and wool, saw the green shit and piss slopping out onto the road. He was relieved when the road straightened again and he was able to overtake the rattling wagon and its condemned steerage passengers.

The road dipped and crossed another stream. In the hollow was another abandoned cheese factory, its windows and doors boarded over, concrete walls tagged with meaningless graffiti. Built beside the streams so their effluent could be flushed directly and without cost into the natural watercourses, the factories had been a series of little communities for half a century, their workers processing the milk that the farmers sucked from their tractable herds twice a day. Now, the closed-down factories punctuated the road like the relics of a war. The war that had destroyed them was amalgamation. Just as the farmers sucked the milk from their cows, the factories sucked the production from each other, swallowing each other up, growing larger and ever larger, leaving the small factories useless and abandoned.

Occasionally he passed one that some courageous entrepreneur had tried to convert into a useful enterprise – a toy factory, a craft collective, an independent brewery – but mostly they remained ugly remnants of the era when each factory was a small community in itself. He also remembered that the little dairy factory settlements and their cluster of workers' houses had been rumoured to be hotbeds of wife-swapping and incest. Certainly the dairy factory workers were a breed apart, pale from spending their working life indoors, like plants deprived of chlorophyll, and with lean and hungry looks. They always wore white overalls and gumboots, even when not working.

Passing yet another derelict factory at a tiny dead settlement, he recalled the episode of the worker from there who, to express a grudge he had against the factory manager, collected a dead opossum from the road and slipped it into one of the cheese vats. A few weeks later the flattened marsupial, embalmed in mild cheddar, was sliced up in a posh delicatessen in the West End of London. The irate proprietor had the offending product traced by its serial number all the way back to Otakeho. There its batch number incriminated the worker, who was sacked. After punching the manager in the face and fracturing his cheekbone, he was jailed for six months.

This was not an unusual occurrence. Violence, like the gas and oil for which the province was now renowned, oozed up from the depths of this green and apparently placid landscape. Before the coming of the Pakeha, the inter-tribal wars of the Maori had involved much butchery. The land wars between Maori and Pakeha in the nineteenth century introduced a new technology of slaughter. Thus, for centuries now, blood, butterfat and oil had lubricated the history of Mike Simpson's old province.

And it was that very theme – violence – that had brought him back.

Two years ago, while doing research on homicide patterns for a series that the current affairs magazine *Issues* was running, he had stumbled on the fact that his boyhood province in general and his grandparents' town in particular held the national record for murder. Not only had there been more violent deaths per capita in the area, but the murders had been exceptional in their ferocity. During the 150 years since the town's inception, there had been a spectacular parade of bludgeonings, strangulations, disembowellings and poisonings, along with many straight shootings.

The first recorded murder was that of Constance Partridge, who while painting the local landscape one Sunday afternoon just outside the town, was beheaded by a local Maori in a totally unprovoked attack. The year was 1867. This killing was followed by the public hanging six weeks later of the convicted murderer, named only as Hepi in newspaper accounts of the time.

So began the grisly catalogue of killing. Wives had stabbed husbands, mothers had murdered their children, children had shot their parents, lovers had slain each other. Stunned by what he had uncovered, Mike had calculated the town's murder rate, compared it with the national figure and shown it to a statistician friend. She looked at the figures, made a few swift calculations, then gave Mike a startled glance. 'That town,' she concluded tersely, 'is not a safe place to be.'

When the story appeared in print, it had provoked an irate response from the townsfolk. The magazine received an unusual amount of hate mail, most of it from the local area, accusing Mike of maligning the town and sullying its reputation at a time when it was striving to promote itself as a tourist destination. Local tourism was based on events as varied and imaginative as the giant pumpkin-growing contest, the Ronald Hugh Morrieson imitation writing competition, the Elvis Presley Look-alike Festival, the race to the top of the water tower, and re-enactments of a key 1868 battle between the local Maori and a regiment of Forest Rangers. The latest drawcard, cleverly combining two attractions, was to see who could run fastest from the bottom to the top of the water tower, carrying the heaviest pumpkin.

Most interesting of the responses to Mike's story was the man who called him on the phone two weeks after it appeared. 'That story you wrote about the murders,' he began. Mike took a deep breath, preparing to defend himself. The man went on. 'You got it wrong, mate.' Mike drew another, even deeper breath. Another shit-kicker. The caller continued. 'I used to be the police constable there. From 1965 until 1987. And you missed at least five killings. You didn't mention the teenage girl who hacked her father in half with the boxthorn hedge-cutter, or the wife who poured petrol over her husband's girlfriend and set her alight, or the boy who drowned his father in the cow-shit pit, or the...'

'Hang on, hang on,' Mike blurted out, holding the phone with one hand and picking up his pen with the other. 'Start again so I can get all this down.'

And so the idea for the television series had begun. Mike had contacted Barry Lawson, the television producer, who had enthused over the *Worst Murders of New Zealand* concept and had contracted Mike to do further research. It seemed to him only logical to begin the series with his grandparents' town, because of its unrivalled record of inventive and gruesome slayings. He had booked an air ticket to the province and a unit in Morrieson's Motel for the next three days, to use as a base for a deeper delving into the district's impressive history of killing and to video relevant locations. The opening episode was to be called 'The Murder Capital'. But aware that many of the townspeople would be sensitive to his name as the author of the infamous article, and conscious of how quickly news spread in a small town, he had decided to use an assumed name during his stay.

The road ducked into another hollow, passing another abandoned dairy factory. Along its unpainted concrete wall someone had sprayed in black the words THIS IS MAORI LAND. Underneath these words someone else had sprayed in red, AND THIS IS PAKEHA WRITING. Chuckling at this small war of words, Mike drove up the hill and emerged onto an expanse of level land. As he glanced ahead he saw on the horizon an enormous white building, bigger and higher than anything he had ever seen in the province. The result of all those small factory amalgamations and dairy company mergers, the building loomed from the landscape like one of the huge power stations one came across unexpectedly in Europe, dwarfing not only every other building in sight but the trees and surrounding hills as well. What would the next development be? he wondered. A mega-mega dairy factory? The road was straight now as it crossed the elevated plain, passing large and more tastefully designed farmhouses surrounded by mature exotic trees whose leaves had turned brown and russet with the onset of autumn.

He reached the outskirts of the town, where there were a few agricultural machinery displays and a sign directing southbound traffic away from the main street. He turned left, entering a long flat street lined with nondescript bungalows. A few minutes later he came to Waipahu Street and drew up on the forecourt of Morrieson's Motel.

'I'm Clarry, Clarry Claridge.'

'Perry Campbell. Pleased to meet you, Clarry.'

As they shook hands, Mike wondered where he had heard the name before. Claridge…Claridge. Then, with a jolt, he remembered. One of the letter-writers, after his *Issues* story had come out. And the most threatening. It had concluded with the words, 'In one foul [sic] swoop, by his accusations of violence, Mike Simpson has slandered the reputation of our district. If he ever shows up in this town, I'll break every bone in his face.' How right he had been to come here under an assumed name. Founded on violence, the place was still addicted to it.

'The missus is just getting some milk for you,' the proprietor was going on. 'She'll bring it over. You're in number ten. At the end. You can park right next to it, under the oak tree.' He tugged at a cluster of dark nose hairs. 'Here on business or pleasure, Perry?'

'Holiday. Having a break from the city.'

'Yeah, right. I never liked the rat-race meself. Stick to this place. Great little town we've got here. Pity you weren't here last week, you could've seen the giant pumpkin contest.'

'Really?'

'Oh yeah. The winner was over a hundred kilos, what a beauty.'

'What do you do with a pumpkin that size? Make pumpkin pies?'

'Jesus no, you can't eat the things, they're mostly water. No, cattle food, mate. Keep a whole herd farting for a week, a pumpkin that size. What sort of work do you do, Perry?'

'I'm in real estate.' *A giant pumpkin contest. Jesus. Pumpkin, bumpkin.*

'Oh yeah. Well, we've got some pretty nice properties round here. Conservatories, ensuites and that. Swimming pools too, some of them.' He picked up a key attached to a blue plastic tag and handed it to Mike. 'There you go. Unit ten. Oh, hang on, just fill in the book here.'

Mike carefully wrote the fiction, 'Perry Campbell, 8 Highland St., Karori, Wellington' in the book, conscious of Clarry's eyes following the words as he did so.

'Karori, eh? Not a bad place, went to a funeral there a while back. Mate of mine who'd given up farming and gone to the city to live. They said it was heart failure but I reckon it was the city that killed 'im. Never had any trouble with his heart while he lived round here. Okay Perry, there's yer key. Room's cleaned between ten and eleven in the morning, Laura's the cleaner's name. You going to be eating here?'

'Yes, I think I will.'

'Okay, I'll book you in. Seven all right?'

'Fine, thanks. What time does everything close today?'

'Five o'clock.' He closed the registration book. 'Have a good break then. See the town, do some shopping. We've got a Warehouse in High Street, a real big bugger. There's a television in the restaurant, so you can watch the Super 12 while you're having your meal. Reckon the Hurricanes can do it?'

'Yes. I think so. They're having a good run.'

'Sure are. That Christian Cullen, eh? Used to know his uncle, he was a share-milker out Normandy way in the sixties. There you go then. Have a nice day.'

He was unpacking when the knock came at the door. Opening it, he saw a short, plumpish woman in a dark blue trouser suit standing there, holding a carton of milk. She held it up. 'Hello,' she said, 'I'm Betty Claridge. Here's your milk.'

'Thanks,' said Mike.

'You're Perry Campbell, is that right?' The way she stood there, it was almost as if she expected to be invited in. She was peering past him, into the unit. What did she think? That he had a girl in there? A *man* even? People in this town had always been good at minding other people's business.

'Yes. Thanks for the milk.' He took the carton, nodded, and shut the door. Nosy cow. People here didn't have enough to do; that's what made them prone to poke their noses into other people's business. He put the milk in the fridge and looked around the nondescript room. At least the place had a desk. Checking the time, he saw that it was after midday. Time to get to work.


The office of the *Daily News* was in the middle of the main street. Mike sat in the room at the front, the high pile of papers beside him. He already had the approximate dates of the killings that would make good television; it was just a matter of obtaining the details, then researching the locations. He had selected five for the first episode: the slaying of the landscape painter and the subsequent execution of Hepi, because in a way that began it all; the boxthorn hedge-cutter killing because of the unique instrument involved and the motive of the girl, who had been raped regularly by her father from the age of ten; the murder of two young children by their God-bothering mother, using a concrete block, because they couldn't recite their prayers correctly; the drugging and pushing over a cliff in a car of a young wife by her husband and his massage parlour girlfriend; and the mysterious suicide of a twenty-year-old share-milker who was found hanged in a cow-shed. The latter was a little out of the ordinary because the coroner's report stated that his death had been one of 'misadventure'. He had been due to marry, but at his stag party the night before the wedding certain indecencies had occurred between the groom-to-be, his rugby team-mates and a bobby calf. The element of mystery, Mike and his producer agreed, added a definite frisson to the case.

'How're you going there? Finding what you want?'

Mike nodded, instinctively sliding his arm over his notepad. He'd told her he was researching the history of property prices. 'Mmm. What time do you close?'

'In twenty minutes. Will that be long enough?'

'Yes, thank you.'

Ten minutes later he left the office and walked back to the motel. The main street of the town had obviously been face-lifted, the ugly power poles removed and paving stones laid. At each junction roundabouts and humps slowed the traffic. It was a definite improvement, although he found himself seeking out the shops that he remembered from his holidays with his grandparents: the milk-bar whose fifteen-year-old assistant he had fallen in love with; the bookshop, now a Lotto outlet, where he had bought comics; the cinema where he had watched Elvis Presley musicals; the old pub whose windows he had peered into, intrigued by the mystique of male drinking – his grandparents and his parents had been teetotallers. Mostly, though, the shops as well as the street had changed. On one corner there was now an open square where a collection of gawky youths in jeans and back-to-front baseball caps were doing brainless things with skateboards, flicking and jumping and jerking around the space. Rather than walk past the gormless group, he crossed the street.

Back at the motel, Clarry stopped him to enquire about his afternoon. Mike made up a story about going for a walk in the countryside, then spent the two hours before dinner refining his notes and studying a detailed map of the district in preparation for tomorrow's research. At seven he walked across to the dining room and had a meal of snapper, chips and salad. At least the menu claimed it was snapper, but by its texture he suspected it was actually hoki. But he wolfed it down all the same, being hungry after his journey. The waitress was a rather attractive but harassed young woman who introduced herself as Lisa. After every directive Mike made to her, she replied, 'Not a problem', repeating the statement so often that he was tempted to suggest, 'How about a blow-job in unit ten after dinner?' just to see whether that would not be a problem either.

There were only two other tables occupied, one by a group of elderly women who were hunched over their plates, and two young couples who drank sparkling wine and whose behaviour became unruly.

'Tea or coffee?' asked Lisa, her pad at the ready.

'Coffee please,' said Mike.

'Not a problem,' she replied, writing it down, then hurrying away.

By eight-thirty he was back in his unit, making more notes and planning his second day. A strong wind had blown up after dark, and it howled around the unit and rustled the dying leaves of the oak tree. At nine-thirty he switched on the television to catch the end of the Super 12, saw with some disappointment that the Hurricanes had been well beaten by the Brumbies, then climbed into the double bed. The wind had grown stronger, and with it came a squall, with raindrops driven against the window like gravel. But he was weary, and in minutes was asleep.

The noise woke him just before two o'clock. Louder than the wind, it was a light metallic rattling, coming from the front of the unit. He lay still. It had stopped. But with another gust of wind, it came again. A light, rolling, rattling noise. He recognised what it was. An empty beer can being rolled across the deck by the wind. Again it stopped, but half a minute later it came again. Rolling, rattling, clanking. *Shit,* he thought, and got out of bed. Opening the door, he peered out. On the deck, no noise, no beer can. Must be on the next unit's deck. He walked down the steps, the wind tearing at his hair, and approached the next unit, staring into the semi-darkness. No beer can there either. Puzzled, he returned to his unit's deck. Black clouds were scudding across the moonless night, and the boughs of the oak tree were waving wildly in the wind.

He climbed back into bed, but even as he laid his head on the pillow the rolling and rattling came again. The sporadic noise was starting to madden him. He put the pillow over his head. Rattle, rattle, *clang*. Rattle, rattle, *clang*. At some time after three o'clock he drifted into sleep, the intermittent metallic noise accompanying his uneasy dreams.

He woke at seven. The wind was still strong, but a weak sun was shining through the curtains. Irritably Mike dragged himself from the bed, shaved and showered. Every few minutes the beer can rolled, rattled and clanged again. He dressed and went out onto the deck, peering about for the can. There was no can, on his deck or the next one. Baffled, furious now, he stood on the deck and waited. Another gust of wind, then the rattling. Coming not from the deck, but...he listened and waited for it to come again...above. Looking up, he saw the oak-tree branch buffeted by a gust, watched as it was blown across the corrugations of the iron roof, heard the metallic rattling and clanging, and saw the cause of the infuriating noise – acorns, being dragged across the iron. *Jesus.* He would get that bloody hayseed Clarry to saw the branch off before tonight.

He spent Saturday morning at the *Daily News* and in the afternoon drove into the country, pin-pointing old murder sites for when the shooting started, noting details and picking shots with the video camera. That night he ate and drank too much in the White Hart Hotel, to make sure he slept okay, acorns or no fucking acorns.

On Sunday morning the town was utterly dead. Even the skate-boarders must still be in bed, he thought. A few real beer cans, along with chip wrappers and milk-shake cartons, lay in the gutters. Mike continued looking for locations, this time in the town, so he could get a shooting script clearly in his mind. Late in the day he drove slowly down the street, around the succession of little roundabouts and out the other end. Here there were a few colonial buildings, including a bank and the library, which had been tastefully restored, their fancy facings picked out in bright colours. It reassured him to see that someone valued the history of the town enough to care for the old buildings.

His attention was soon diverted from them, however, to the town's most conspicuous landmark, the water tower. Stopping the car across the street, he stared at it. Unlike most objects remembered from childhood, it had not shrunk. Indeed, it seemed even bigger than he recalled. Its height, solidity and proportions were pleasing, seeming more like something from Europe than this province. Whoever had designed it had combined form and function pleasingly. Form even more than function actually, as he remembered that the tower had never fulfilled its designated role of increasing the pressure of the town's water supply.

But it was undeniably appealing. Small windows and balconies in its sides relieved the severe lines and the greyness of the concrete. His eyes went to the top, to the encircling balcony, which was also built of concrete and cantilevered out from the superstructure. And he remembered the wide steps inside the tower, spiralling upwards, seemingly forever, when he had climbed it as a boy. And the breathtaking vista from that balcony.

The tower would make the perfect viewpoint for the opening sequence of the series: a lingering shot of the town from its highest point. They could pan across the town and the surrounding plain, then zoom in on the specific murder locations. He envisaged the voiceover: 'The killing fields, extending as far as the eye can see.' Perfect. He got out of the car, and walked across the street and through the small park surrounding the tower. Then he saw he could go no further. Encircling it was a temporary fence of orange plastic mesh and a large sign declaring 'Water Tower Closed for Repairs – No Admittance'.

Mike stopped at the fence. Still unable to take his eyes from the tower, he cursed the fact that he wouldn't be able to climb it again, to savour again that panorama of town and country. He looked at the big wooden door, closed and no doubt locked, and the first line of windows, several metres from the ground. Maybe, maybe…

Still deep in thought, he returned to the car and drove out west of the town, to locate and video the cliff over which the drugged young wife and mother had been pushed to her death three years ago.


Using the master key, Laura Blowse opened unit ten and went inside, the parcel of clean sheets and cleaning gear under her arm. Inside the room, she stopped and looked around. A few papers on the desk, the bed unmade, an opened overnight bag on the suitcase rack. She went to the bed and pulled back the bedclothes. Peering at the sheets, she noted with some disappointment that there were no fresh stains, then stripped the bed and remade it with clean linen. Perry Campbell, the guest's name was, she had already checked in the register. Strange that he was here by himself, without a wife or a girlfriend. Why was he here, she wondered, at this time of the year? If it'd been last weekend, when the pumpkin contest was on, she could understand it. People came all the way from Wanganui to see that. But now, the weekend before Easter, there was nothing special on in the town, unless you included the cage bird show.

Lifting up the papers on the desk, she gave it a perfunctory wipe with her damp rag, then put the papers down again. She looked at the top sheet of paper. A copy of a hire contract from a rental car company, with the renter's name and address written on it. 'Mike Simpson,' it read, '112 Anzac Square, Lower Hutt.' Puzzled, Laura picked up another sheet of paper and scanned it. A list of dates and the names of people, handwritten. 'Beth McGuire, Seddon Road.' Laura drew a quick breath. Beth, the girl who had been drugged and pushed over the cliff to her death. The next name on the list: 'Gavin Harding, Lonesome Creek, R.D.' Gavin, the guy who was killed by his daughter, using the hedge-cutter. What was going on here? Collecting up her cleaning gear, Laura went quickly from the unit and over to the office.

'There's something funny going on, Clarry. That guy in number ten is using a false name. His name's not Perry Campbell, it's Mike Simpson. I saw it on the rental car sheet.'

'So? He can call himself Alamein Kopu, long as he pays his bill.'

'And he's got a list of names. Of people round here who've been murdered.'

'What d'you mean?'

'Beth McGuire, Gavin Harding, those poor Clement children. On a list.'

'Yeah? That's weird.' Clarry pulled at a stubborn nose hair. 'Mike Simpson... *Simpson*... Jesus, I remember. That bastard...'


It was mid-afternoon when Mike turned the car into Waipahu Street. He'd traced and located all the murder sites and taken video film of them, even the one where Constance Partridge was doing her painting on that afternoon in 1867. He was particularly proud of that bit of sleuthing. Constance's almost finished painting had survived, was still in the family, and using a photograph of it he'd been able to locate the approximate place where the decapitation had occurred, beside the small lake a couple of kilometres outside the town. He could already envisage the presenter, actor Peter Gifford, striding through the grass, brow puckered in feigned concern: 'It was a Sunday afternoon in February, high summer, when Constance Partridge made her way across the paddock to the side of the lake, easel and water paints under her arm, utterly unaware that Hepi was trailing her, tomahawk tucked under his belt and murder on his mind...'

As Mike drove up to the motel unit, he braked suddenly. His suitcase was on the deck, his unpacked clothes lying on top of it. What the hell was going on here? He got out and began to walk across the forecourt. Just before he reached the unit, the office door of the motel burst open and the proprietor strode across to meet him, his face like a gargoyle's.

'What's my case doing...?'

'Just take it and leave. *Now.*'

'Hang on, I've booked in here for tonight as well. I'm not leaving until...'

'Wrong. You're leaving. We don't want your sort in this town.'

'*My sort*? What are you on about?'

'I know who you are, *mate*. It's Simpson, isn't it? Mike Simpson?'

So, he'd found out. How? He nodded. 'That's right.'

'And you're the bastard who wrote that story about our town. The one that was in that filthy Wellington rag.'

'I wrote it, yes. And everything in it was true.'

'You…little turd. We've spent years building up this town's reputation, and you destroy it in one foul swoop.'

'*Fell* swoop. The murders happened, I wrote about them. That's all.'

'That's all… You *arsehole*! And I'll bet you're here under a phony name because you're sneaking around doing something similar. Jesus I hate *outsiders* like you.'

For a moment Mike thought Clarry was going to hit him. His eyes bulged, his face had gone the colour of a boiled crayfish. Deciding there was nothing to gain by prolonging the conversation, he walked past the fuming proprietor and over to his belongings. He picked them up and began to walk back to the car. On the way he paused. Clarry was standing on the forecourt, hands on his hips, watching him closely. In the open door of the office he could see the wife, Betty, rubbing her hands together nervously.

'How much do I owe you?' Mike asked, putting his belongings in the car boot and trying to sound nonchalant.

'I wouldn't take a cent of your grubby, city slicker money. Just…fuck off!'


Well, that was that then, he thought as he drove down High Street. It didn't make that much difference. He wouldn't stay for the last night, he'd drive back to Wellington this evening, arrange to return the hire car there. He only had to attend to the last part of the assignment, to get video footage from the balcony of the water tower for that opening sequence. When he had that, then the series writers could use the video film of the locations to start the scripts.

'The killing fields. As far as the eye can see.' Mike chuckled. That would really set off that hillbilly, Clarry.

He parked a little way down the street from the tower. He picked up the video camera, locked the car and approached the tower from the far side, out of sight of the street. Sure, the main entrance was locked, but he knew there was another one, the one he and his mates had used when they were kids. The underground one.

Slipping through the park and around to the southern side of the tower, he stepped over the plastic mesh and came to the other entrance, half hidden by a camellia bush. There was a narrow set of concrete steps leading steeply downwards to a door under the base of the tower. He went carefully down the steps, which were cracked and covered in slime. Shouldering the video camera, he approached the small green door.

It had a Yale lock, but in the old days was never actually locked. He turned the knob. Locked. Shit. But as he turned it he felt its looseness, its flimsiness, and realised the door was coming away from the lock. One shove and it gave way completely. Mike crept in, ducking under the cobwebs which draped over the frame.

He climbed the spiralling concrete steps steadily. Round and round the tower's central core, down which the water was supposed to have dropped, so as to build up pressure to fight the fires that had afflicted the town. That had been the theory, anyway. Pity it had never worked. As a boy Mike had once counted the steps, but he couldn't now remember what the total was. Four hundred and something, he thought. The concrete of the steps was in good repair, and he wondered exactly why the tower had been closed to the public. Some town bureaucrat exercising his petty authority probably.

Moving on upwards, he saw the last of the afternoon sunlight slanting through the tower's side windows. The sky had cleared, so conditions for shooting the video footage were ideal. Chest heaving with exertion, he went around the last curve. The steps levelled out and there was an open doorway leading to the balcony that surrounded the top of the tower like a cowling. He walked out onto the balcony, and there, spread before him, was the vista he needed: the town, its veranda-fronted shops and iron-roofed houses surrounded by green patchwork farmland; the huge white monolith that was the dairy plant; the distant coast to the west and the swelling flanks of the mountain to the north, its cone capped in cloud. Superb.

Stepping right up to the concrete railing and unshouldering the video camera, he peered over. The main street led away to his left, straight as a lance, its tallest feature the spire of the Anglican church. At the far end of the street was an expanse of dark greenery – the big park where he had once played.

Then he remembered a building, the Masonic Lodge his grandfather had attended. He had often gone there with his grandfather to help him clean the lodge, which was somewhere up this end of the town. But it had been an old building, even forty years ago. Had it survived? He leaned over the railing, searching the side streets of the town for the old lodge. It had been near the community hall... somewhere... over there...

Beneath the pressure of his chest, the porous concrete cracked, crumbled, then gave way. As it parted from the rest of the railing, he and a short section of it fell forward into open space. Clutching wildly at nothing, he saw the video camera fly from his hands like a released falcon, felt the autumn air cooling his face, watched the slab of rotten concrete dropping away below him. Seconds later, the killing fields rushed up to greet him.

# Heartbreak Hotel

'You wouldn't believe it. They say there's an Elvis Presley museum somewhere around here,' said Bronnie. She stuck her hand out to feel the wind on her fingers.

'Pull your bloody hand in,' Cameron shouted. 'How many times do I have to tell you?'

Bronnie wound up her window, then complained, 'I was just cooling off. This car stinks of male body odour.'

For a few moments Cameron clenched his teeth. Even though Bronnie had said it was the car that stank, he knew she was trying to get at him personally. She was well aware how particular he was. He always used a deodorant.

'Wave your hand about and it looks like a signal,' he explained furiously. 'I could get pulled over for that.'

Bronnie raised her eyes and sighed but said nothing. It had been a long drive, and she hadn't been told they were going to have to change cars in New Plymouth because Cameron's BMW was too noticeable. The whole trip was obviously a con. Cameron was here on a job and he'd tricked her into coming. She looked straight ahead blindly and didn't notice the huge milk factory, the water tower, or even the sign in front of them that said there were only a few more kilometres to go.

'Anyway, what's this about an Elvis museum? Why Elvis?' asked Cameron.

He was satisfied he'd put Bronnie in her place, so he calmed down and changed the subject.

'You tell me why not Elvis?'

Cameron grunted, then suddenly slapped a hand against the back of his neck, as if he'd been stung. The tight curls of his newly permed hair didn't even flutter.

'Who bloody told you there's an Elvis museum?' he yelled. 'Come on – who've you been talking to? Why can't you ever…'

'No one's talked about nothing,' Bronnie cut in. 'It's printed on the back of the map. The one Bonzo Dog gave you in New Plymouth when you swapped cars. It may surprise you, but I can read, you know. Books, newspapers, Weetbix packets…'

'I keep telling you. Shut up about Bonzo and swapping cars,' Cameron said. 'We're nearly there, but you keep taking the piss. You're getting bloody close to your final warning – you know that, don't you? Eh?'

Bronnie looked about her and noticed they were travelling past houses. There was a shopping centre ahead. 'Don't tell me this dump is it,' she said.

'Make the most of it and enjoy,' said Cameron, suddenly delighted that Bronnie was definitely not going to like it here. That would punish her for provoking him. 'This place is all nightclubs, highlife and cocktails. It positively rock 'n' rolls. It's the hub of the universe.'

'What've they done with the rest of it?' was all Bronnie could manage to say. 'Buried it with Elvis?'

'Keep your eyes peeled for the Heartbreak Hotel,' Cameron ordered, then wondered if the reference might have passed completely over Bronnie's head, since she was acting so stupid. He added, 'It's actually called the Morrinsville, or the Morrison or something. It's written on that map you were looking at – if you haven't lost it already. Which wouldn't surprise me.'

'Up yours with a pineapple, too,' said Bronnie, though she reached down and picked up the folding map some moron in a Bonzo Dog T-shirt had given them.

'It's called Morrieson's, spelt 'ie' in the middle,' she announced.

'And it's not a hotel either. It's a motel. And it's on Waipahu Street. And that means, if we just came in from New Plymouth, we've driven right past it.'

'Shit,' said Cameron, slowing down as they entered the town centre, where some local lunatics seemed to have gone to a lot of trouble to think up ways to stop the traffic from getting through.

'Why would they do it?' he demanded. 'I don't bloody believe it. They've turned the whole town into an obstacle course.'

The car jolted on a judder bar, then Cameron was forced to drive cautiously past a series of parking bays and pull up at a pedestrian crossing.

'Christ, you wouldn't read about it,' he said. 'I'd like to drive a bloody bulldozer right through the middle...'

Bronnie cut in on him. 'There's a cop standing at the corner over there staring in our direction,' she said, with a grin. 'So just hold on to your permanent waves and try not to run anyone over. Then move off gently, take the next turn and double back without getting yourself dog-knotted, okay?'

'Bitch,' said Cameron, smiling viciously back at her. 'Just wait...'

'Let's not have another one of your nasty little mood swings, please. The crossing's nice and...'

Before she could finish, Cameron edged the car slowly to the corner and turned down the road. 'Not another word, okay?' he warned her. 'This whole town's gone mental, so I don't want to hear another bloody squeak out of a fruitcake like you. Get me?'

Bronnie gazed out of the side window and ignored him.

After a few minutes, Cameron turned again and was gratified to see a street sign that read Waipahu Street. His attitude changed completely.

'Skill and logic,' he boasted, drumming his hands happily on the steering wheel. 'Did you note how I drove right around to the exact spot I was looking for? It's natural instinct does that. It's the way my brain's programmed. Skill and logic.'

He drove into the driveway of Morrieson's Motel and pulled up at the office. After telling Bronnie to stop bloody sulking and look on the bright side of life, he stepped out, slammed the car door behind him and rang the bell.

Laura was walking sideways through reception, carrying a pile of towels, so she almost bumped into him.

'Was it you ringing?' she asked.

'No,' Cameron said, shaking his shoulders and stretching his arms back as if doing his daily exercises. 'The bell rang itself.'

Clever bugger, Laura thought, but she wasn't bothered. She knew the type. All needle and no prick. 'I'll get someone to help you with your problem,' she said, smiling. She wasn't going to let him get her down.

'Someone needing attention?' a voice called. Then Clarry appeared.

Laura stopped herself from saying some bastard certainly did.

'You've got a booking for Jensen,' Cameron said. 'I rang from New Plymouth. A unit for two. For the weekend.'

'Jensen?' Clarry said. 'I'll take a look.'

'I only rang an hour ago. I must've spoken to you. Don't you remember?'

'I'll take a look,' Clarry repeated slowly. City slicker, he decided. Just another know-nothing, up-himself townie. Probably from Wellington or Auckland. That was the main trouble with what Betty called 'the service industry'. You couldn't pick and choose. You took all sorts. Some of them desperately asking for the toe of your boot.

'Jen-sen,' Cameron said again, pronouncing the two syllables separately.

A voice behind Clarry said cheerily, 'Good afternoon, Mr Jensen. I can look after this, Clarry. You've got that garage stuff that needs… You know.'

Clarry nodded at Betty and went outside, where he saw a young woman sitting in the front seat of a parked car, pulling faces into the vanity mirror and applying lipstick. He shook his head and walked past.

'Your studio unit will be number four, Mr Jensen,' Betty went on. 'You're staying two nights. Is that right?'

'Two nights,' Cameron agreed, then added, 'Which means tonight and tomorrow.' It paid to spell things out in these godforsaken places. The people were probably inbred.

'That's a pleasure, Mr Jensen.' Betty passed him a form and said, 'All we need is a signature here and the usual details, and I'll get some milk and show you over. You'll be very comfortable here. We've made it as convenient as possible.'

Cameron copied down the number of the false plates on the car he'd 'borrowed' in New Plymouth. He'd taken the precaution of scrawling it on the back of the map he'd been given. It was bloody clever to have thought of that, he told himself. Then he wrote that his name was Jensen, added an equally false address and said, 'I'm paying cash on this holiday. All rooms and whatever. I don't want it getting mixed up with business expenses.'

'Oh, that's perfectly understandable, Mr Jensen. Whatever suits. But when it's cash, it's usually motel policy…'

Before she could finish, Cameron had stripped two Rutherfords off a roll and laid them on the reception counter. 'That's cool. I was told on the phone it's ninety-five a night,' he said. 'You owe me ten.'

Betty took the notes and returned the change. She didn't care for this Mr Jensen's manner, but his money was the same as anyone else's. And, after all, it took all sorts, didn't it? She took a key and the milk, then went out.

A tall, close-cropped brunette, wearing a loose, black pullover and tight, black leather trousers, was now leaning against the Jensen's car door. She was quite obviously not the shy type, so Betty wasn't at all impressed by the way she merely nodded at her cheery greeting. However, the woman somehow managed to push herself off the car and follow them into the unit, where she watched in bored silence as Betty pointed out the 'facilities'.

Betty knew when she wasn't wanted, but she wasn't going to let that affect her business interests, so she finished off by saying, 'If you'd like to dine in our licensed restaurant this evening, I'd advise you to make a booking. There's only a dozen tables and there's often a crowd at the weekends. Of course, that's the best possible recommendation, but…'

'Yeah. We'll give it a go,' Cameron said, cutting her off decisively. 'We'll stroll over about sevenish.'

He heard her begin to say something about making the booking, but he closed the door on her and cut her off again. 'I'll give her a minute,' he said to Bronnie. 'Then I'll fetch the car over and unpack. I can't stand any more of that "best possible recommendation" crap.'

'Nobody's making you eat here and get poisoned.'

'What?'

'We can always go somewhere else.'

'No we can't. And you know why, so bloody-well give up, will you?'

Bronnie shrugged as Cameron stood in front of her and stared threateningly, hands on hips. He was a nasty-looking bastard when he did that.

'I'm going to park the car,' he announced at last. 'But before I do, I want you to tell me what mustn't even cross your feeble bloody mind when I leave you alone.'

Bronnie groaned and flung herself full length on the double bed. Then she raised herself on an elbow and recited in a sing-song, lisping, baby voice, 'I'm not to be a wicked girl and touch the naughty telephone. 'Coz telephone calls can be traced, so we can only use prepaid cellphones. Is that right, daddy?'

'Try and act your age,' was all Cameron replied as he went to get the car.


'Why this place?' Bronnie asked at six that evening. They'd fallen asleep after a brief episode of what Cameron had described as his urgent need for 'a bit of nooky', but since they were city dwellers they'd woken as darkness fell.

'How do you mean?' Cameron replied lazily.

'I mean, why not stop somewhere else?'

'Same reason as that Elvis museum you were taking about, I

reckon,' said Cameron. He didn't feel like arguing. He'd given Bronnie the old male tranquilliser and she shouldn't be getting nosy about things that didn't concern her. 'It's a simple matter of why not this place.'

'I'm not silly, you know,' she snapped. 'There's always a reason where you're involved. All that business of maps, and swapping cars, and false names, and having to get my hair cut, and that freaky perm-and-dye of yours, and me having to wear leather when you know I hate it.'

'That's nothing. Do you want to know something really funny?'

'Try me.'

'That Bonzo guy told me that somewhere around here is the murder capital of the world. There's more bizarre killings here than anywhere else on earth.'

'That's not funny – especially coming from you. It's sick. I don't believe it.'

'Well, stop asking silly questions if you don't want silly answers.'

'But why come here? It's not your kind of territory.'

'*Territory*? I don't have any particular *territory*. That's a stupid word.'

'You know what I mean.'

'We stopped here because someone I know recommended it. And we changed cars and we're lying low because we're incognito – we're on holiday, okay?'

'That's bullshit. And how come, if we're incognito, we're going out to eat?'

Cameron was beginning to feel very irritable again. 'We're not *going out*. Because we're eating *in*. You heard what that fat cow said. There's only a dozen tables, so there'll only be a dozen people…'

'There could be four or more to some of the tables.'

'Okay, Einstein. So who cares? They work in milk factories and they're fans of Elvis Presley.'

'It's all right for some to break rules when they feel like it. But no one else can even put a hand out of a car window without someone jumping down their throat.'

'Take a bath and drown yourself,' he said angrily. 'I'm going to pour a little starter. I'm beginning to need it, okay?'

Cameron threw back the bedclothes and got up. He turned on a wall heater and poured a couple of small gins over ice, then added a lot of tonic. He was always careful about booze when he was on a contract. That was why he was the best in the business. It was all a matter of steel nerves and total control. Christ, just look at how Bronnie had been provoking him all day. Yet had he once lost his cool? No way.

Then the very moment he lifted the glass to his lips, his mobile played the opening bars of the *William Tell Overture*. 'Yeah... Yeah... Yeah...,' he said. 'No, we're not going out. We're not going anywhere, not even the Elvis Presley museum... What do you mean, we couldn't get in?... It's only by appointment? Really? Is that so?... No, it was a joke... We're not going to any museum. Okay, okay, keep your hair on... Yeah... Yeah... See you tomorrow.'

'Who was that?' Bronnie shouted from the bathroom.

'The Phantom.'

Bronnie opened the door and looked at Cameron hard. 'You've bloody conned me again, haven't you. You're here to do something to somebody, aren't you?'

He laughed. 'I've already done "something to somebody" – don't you remember?'

Bronnie ignored the remark. 'All this false name and disguise stuff. You're on a contract, aren't you? That's why we're here, isn't it?'

'Ask no questions – you'll be told no lies.'

'But you said last time was the finish. You nearly screwed up, didn't you? You got half pissed and you nearly lost it. You swore you wouldn't have anything more to do with it, didn't you? You swore on your mother's grave.'

'Listen,' Cameron said, whacking one fist furiously into the other. 'You've been driving me crazy all day. I've had a bloody gutsful.'

'That's the problem – it's your rotten temper. You can't hack it any more.'

'You know bloody nothing, okay?'

'You ought to see someone – for your own good.'

'Drown yourself, like I said. You look stupid standing around naked like that.'

Bronnie turned away. The shower was running. 'Try telling me the truth for a change,' she said as she slammed the door. 'I'm involved too – just by being here.'

'Fuckwit,' Cameron shouted.

When Bronnie came out again, Cameron was well into the gin. He watched her in angry silence from the kitchenette as she got dressed. Then she picked up her drink, sat on the far side of the bed, and glared back at him. For a full minute she didn't move, then she swept her free hand through the hard brush of her hair. It felt like she'd been turned into a hedgehog. She regretted allowing herself to be talked into coming. She'd been an idiot again. All that heavy hinting at getting married properly and settling down and this being a holiday trip, with perhaps just a secret look at a bit of property to outwit some two-timing Wellington type – when all the time he needed her for cover. It was so feeble, so bloody pathetic. She'd believed it only because she'd wanted to. She drained her glass and asked for another.

Cameron shook himself ever so slightly, as if he were waking from a trance. He smiled, took Bronnie's glass and poured her a large gin, then he helped himself to another of the same. 'Ordinarily, this wouldn't be on,' he said, patting his stomach and belching. 'You know my rules. But it so happens I've got a leave pass tonight.'

'What rules, for God's sake?'

'Take it easy,' Cameron said with a grin. 'Despite what certain people may think about me, it's still my rule number one – never mix alcohol and business.'

'You mean some poor bastard is going to live, for tonight at least, and never know how lucky he is.'

'I'll pretend I didn't hear that.'

'It's the same old routine, isn't it?' Bronnie persisted. 'You're here to do something bloody horrible and I'm the camouflage, aren't I? Doesn't it ever occur to you that I ought to be told what I'm letting myself in for?'

'You hear enough for your own good.'

'Oh yeah?'

'Yeah.'

'Well I don't think so.' Bronnie took a long swig at her glass then went on, 'For instance, why don't you tell me who that was on the phone?'

'It wouldn't mean anything.'

'I've driven all the way down here with you, so even if it doesn't mean bugger-all to you, I've still got my human rights. I've had my hair shaven off and I'm right in it with you. You've got to tell me.'

'Balls I've got to. It must be the gin – your brains are steaming.'

'That's right. I'm Daddy's stupid little baby doll, aren't I? Well, this time I've had enough.'

'Stick it, or I'll thump you right through that window.' Cameron could feel the rage inside him rising like boiling water. The silly bitch didn't know how close she was to getting the mother of all hidings.

'I'm not going to that restaurant.'

'Oh yes you are,' Cameron tensed and his face went red. 'If I have to break every bone in your body.'

'I'm staying here to phone my friends all over New Zealand.'

Cameron's mouth fell open, he blinked at the woman, then all his fury abruptly switched to laughter. She was mad. 'You haven't got friends all over New Zealand,' he spluttered.

'I have.'

'You haven't.'

'Well, I'll ring Directory Assistance and ask for anyone.'

Cameron laughed again and had to dry his eyes. 'Come and eat,' he said. 'I'll tell you all about the deal I'm on over coffee. That's a promise.'

'I know your promises.'

'I'll never know how I got tied up with such a crazy bitch, but this time it's a real promise. On my mother's grave. Honest.'

'Just like all the others? Some days her grave must look like a bomb's hit it.'

Satisfied she'd scored a point, Bronnie went to the mirror and adjusted her lipstick, taking a good long time, knowing it would secretly drive Cameron mad again. She was getting more and more brilliant at working on his moods. It was a gift. She knew exactly how far to push him – and no further. She smiled at herself and said, 'Okay, I'm coming. But one day I'll make you sorry.'

'That's my girl. I knew you'd see sense.'

'Huh,' was all she said.

They crossed to the restaurant, which Cameron was relieved to see had soft lighting. Some people might consider he ought to be lying low and sending out for Kentucky Fried Chicken, but Bronnie had been getting on his nerves all day and he needed a decent feed. And anyway, he always made perfect judgments. He was in total control and never got pissed, and he knew exactly what he was doing.

Betty met them at the door. 'Good evening, Mr and Mrs Jensen. It's nice to see you,' she said breathlessly. 'Just as well you booked. We're really busy tonight, but we've kept your reservation.'

Cameron stopped himself from asking if that was unusual only because they were being led to a table in a corner next to a large potted plant. Like the subdued lighting, it was exactly what he would have asked for. It meant he could see everyone coming and going through the door, but they'd only be able to get the vaguest impression of him, nothing more. It made him feel even more justified in deciding to eat here. Like he'd told Bronnie, it wasn't really eating out, it was like staying in their own room. No difference.

A young woman came over and placed menus in front of them. 'Good evening, I'm Lisa,' she said. 'Would you like drinks to start with, or would you care to see the wine list?'

'Yeah. Let's *care* to see the wine list,' he mocked, grinning to show he had a powerful sense of humour.

Lisa handed a folder to him with a forced smile, as though she was making an effort to pretend she thought him comical, too.

'Don't go,' he told her, as she was just about to leave. 'I can care to tell you what we'll choose to drink in exactly ten seconds.' He ran a finger quickly over the list and ordered a bottle of gewurtz. Lisa left, grimacing as soon as she turned her away. What a creep, she thought. I'll bet he swills his flowery white wine with a big steak, so overdone he could sole his shoes with it.

Which is exactly what happened. With only a few hums and hahs, Bronnie selected fish of the day – which meant fish and french fries, with salad – and Cameron asked for the biggest steak they had in the fridge, cooked till it was black. He was squeamish about seeing blood in his food. And he told Lisa she could forget all about lettuce leaves, tomatoes and garden slugs. He was strictly into real vegetables and he was particular about their presentation. They had to be properly cooked, not half raw like you got these days, with all the chefs trying to save gas.

Lisa congratulated herself secretly. She had got the steak bit right and she might have guessed the woman would have had the fish, just to be the opposite of the dickhead she was stuck with. She knew these types. City trash. Her mother had mentioned a bright spark who'd tried to put her down at reception early this afternoon. She'd bet this was him. They always thought people who lived in country towns were inbred hicks with hayseeds in their pockets.

Well, she'd spent quite long enough among them when she went to university, before she came home to have her boy – years she now referred to as BC: Before Charlton – and she'd got the measure of the lot of them and their bullshit and preening and strutting. Betty and Clarry might maintain that as long as customers paid up and behaved there was no real difference between them, except that some were a lot nicer than others, but as far as Lisa was concerned, you could take democracy too far.

However, Lisa was too busy to think any more about them, and they simply weren't worth the bother anyway – until, well over half-an-hour afterwards, something quite unsettling happened.

Just as she took the man his pavlova and the woman her apple meringue and ice cream (but 'without the custard please'), the man looked up and seemed to notice Lisa for the first time. His jaw fell slightly open and he froze for several seconds in mid-sentence. He had recognised her from somewhere. There was no doubt about it. But she couldn't recall ever having met him before. To her, he was a total stranger.

It was also disturbing to notice how, every time she went near him, he hunched. And he refused coffee, mumbling and not even looking up her. The last she saw of him was when she spotted him slinking out the door. He'd waited till she'd taken some plates out to the kitchen, then the pair of them must have shot over to Betty to pay, without waiting for a bill.

Lisa questioned Betty about the couple later that evening, after the last diners had gone, and Betty, as usual, hadn't missed much. She said that when she'd asked whether they'd enjoyed their meal and was their unit comfortable, they just said yes on both counts and cleared off.

'I'm really interested in all varieties of human life and I try to make allowances for all the people I meet,' Betty added. 'But this couple are a bit peculiar. The woman looks hard as brass, but she's definitely anxious about something. And as for him, let me put it this way: I don't care what men get up to so long as they don't interfere with others, it's just that I never trust a man who perms his hair. It's not exactly unnatural, but there's something *unnecessary* about it, don't you think?'

'What are their names?' Lisa asked. It was time to go home, but she still wondered if she could think of a possible connection. A name could make all the difference.

'They're called Jensen,' Betty said. 'That's if you can believe they're really married. Not that it matters to me one way or the other. As I always say, I'm broadminded, and their money's no different from anyone else's. Just as long as they don't disturb the peace or leave a mess.'

'Jensen. I don't remember anyone called Jensen. But I could have sworn, when I was serving them, that he recognised me from somewhere – or imagined he did. He looked quite shocked.'

'Yes, well, Lisa dear, you must have been to several quite risky places when you were up in the big smoke,' Betty said with a wink. 'Perhaps he remembers you letting your hair down somewhere.'

'As long as it was only my hair,' Lisa said, and both women broke into a giggle.

'Look. I can't stop here talking,' Lisa added. 'I'm holding you up and I've got to get Charlton home. You never know, this Jensen guy might give you a hint tomorrow about how come he thinks he knows me. That's if I haven't scared them off and they don't do a runner.'

'Don't worry. That's taken care of,' Betty laughed. 'Mr Jensen has paid in advance. In cash – just like his meal tonight. He won't run anywhere.'

Not at ninety-five bloody dollars a night, thought Lisa privately, though out loud she wished Betty goodnight. It was only in bed, later that night – after she'd wound down, and just before she fell asleep – that she was able to spend some time remembering all the details of the strangely disturbing encounter she'd had with the Jensens. She was curious about them and the peculiar way the man had behaved.

This pair were operators, she decided. They were the kind who were so tricky you couldn't think of them lying straight even in bed. There was something wrong about them – especially the man, though she wouldn't care to rely on the woman in any kind of showdown, either. They were up to something. And the thing that amazed her most was that she understood it from a single glance. All her life she'd responded to glances of one sort or another, and she'd read many of them wrongly. This time she knew she was spot on. She felt it in her bones.


'So what if you think you've seen the waitress somewhere?' said Bronnie. 'I get that feeling often. People see Elvis all the time. Millions of them. It doesn't mean it's real.'

'In this town it probably does,' said Cameron, pouring two big gins. He'd seen off a couple of very stiff ones already and he had a nice, warm, early-drunk feeling of total confidence. 'We must've landed in the world's capital of the Elvis industry. I mean, where would you ever think…'

He let the question fade away gently as he sipped, then fell back softly on the bed. 'Heartbreak bloody hotel,' he said suddenly. 'I wonder if that's where we really are. And who was that bloody woman? It's bugging me. I'm positive I know her.'

'You probably met her in a massage parlour with the rest of the boys, after watching the Super-12 with a gut full of beer,' Bronnie said bitterly. She drank deeply, too, then sat on a tubular steel chair, leaning it backwards against the wall. Her hair itched, but she refused to scratch it. Let it torture her. It was depressing having to look like a complete moron.

'I've got it,' Cameron said triumphantly.

'What's it this time? Crab-lice?'

'Don't be stupid. I'm talking about the waitress. It was somewhere in Auckland. She got pregnant. And the guy was in even worse trouble. I've forgotten his name. Anyway, there's nothing to worry about. She's a nobody. It's just a coincidence.'

Bronnie was only half-listening. The tinkle of ice in her glass seemed to suggest chill little words to her. Like, why did she keep going along with all the make-believe? Cameron had suggested a little weekend jaunt so they could talk about the future, and she'd fallen over herself to have her hair cut off and dress up in leather britches and be conned. Yet she knew bloody well that settling down and being normal wasn't ever going to happen. Not with him.

'She couldn't have recognised me,' Cameron assured himself for the third or fourth time, making Bronnie pay attention at last. 'But it has to be a consideration, doesn't it? I might have to make certain changes in the morning. Perhaps we'll shift to another motel.'

'Why wait till morning? What's suddenly happened to your world-famous logic and skill?'

Cameron sighed. 'I'm a very easygoing, tolerant man, Bronnie, but I think you ought to learn I've got limits.'

'You went out wining and dining. You took the risk and you screwed up. So stop moaning, will you? And do you want to know what else I think?'

'You need brains to think.'

Bronnie got up, grabbed her nightdress and went to the bathroom. 'I'm cleaning my teeth and then I'm going to bed – to *sleep*,' she announced. 'You can do what you please.'

'Thanks a million. That's decent of you,' said Cameron, pouring another drink. 'Thanks also for being looked after, thanks for a wonderful dinner, thanks for a comfortable bed, thanks for driving all day, thanks for wine and gin, thanks for spending a bloody fortune...'

'Thanks for a rotten fuck, too. You almost forgot that,' Bronnie yelled through the closed door.

'When you come out I'm going to be right here – just waiting. And then I'm going to take my time smashing your bloody face in,' came the reply.

The threat was nothing new, but Bronnie stopped and held her breath. The words had been spoken in a low and steady animal-like snarl. She'd never heard Cameron make a sound like it. There was nothing to compare it with – the way his voice seemed to claw at her skin. Suddenly, and for the first time since she'd known him, she was certain she was in danger. She'd just located the furthest, maddest boundary of his rage and she'd stepped across it.

Then the *William Tell Overture* started up again. She paused till Cameron's tone seemed to return to normal, then she came out of the bathroom and got into bed very quietly. Cameron was saying, 'Yeah... Yeah... But you said it was off tonight. You said it was tomorrow... I know... Yeah, I'm fine... No, I'm not upset... No, I haven't been drinking... Yeah, I've studied the map... No, everything's quiet here... Okay.'

Cameron slammed the cellphone onto the table and went to the bathroom. Bronnie heard him take a shower then get dressed again and leave. She had wanted to say something to the unpredictable, unstable prick, but she was too scared. His drunken rage was still everywhere in the room, like electricity. Yet the really weird thing – or so she thought later the next day – was how she promptly fell into the deepest sleep she'd had in months, perhaps in years.

She woke to a ringing and banging on the door. Still groggy with sleep, she pulled on a wrap, turned on the light and went to the door.

'Who is it?' she asked.

'Police.'

She opened the door on the chain. The courtyard lights were on and she could see it was the police all right. One was in uniform, the other in what they called plain clothes, though he still looked so much a cop he might as well have been wearing a sign. 'What time is it?' was all she could think of asking.

'Can we come in?' the plain-clothes man asked, then added. 'It's half-past-five. Let's keep it quiet. Release the chain, Bronwyn.'

They knew her name. That was a bad sign. It made her feel suddenly very much awake. Looking up, she noticed Clarry behind the two policemen. He was holding a torch, in his pyjamas and slippers, with a dressing gown tied with a tasselled cord. He was glaring as if he'd like to chuck her out on the street there and then.

The uniformed man turned to Clarry and began to say something about seeing him later, but Bronnie didn't wait. She opened the door and went to the bathroom, where she quickly splashed her face, put on some lipstick and brushed her hair. She came out knowing that she was going to have to be absolutely decisive.

'Okay? What's he done this time?' she asked without beating about. She waved the plain-clothes man towards a chair, then she sat facing him.

The uniform man closed the door, but remained standing, with a notebook in his hand.

'Well, let's put it this way,' the plain-clothes man said. 'Your friend Cameron is right in the sin-bin. In fact, I'd say he's not going to be playing again all season. He could be out for the maximum.'

'Has he got a lawyer?'

'He'll get one, because he'll need one, just to sort the charges out for one thing.'

'Like what?'

'Like possession of an unlicensed firearm, presenting a firearm at an officer in the execution of his duty, discharging said firearm… Oh, there's all sorts of interesting offences we're going to nail on him. With pleasure, I might add.'

The uniformed man wrote something in his notebook, though what it could have been totally mystified Bronnie.

'Is he hurt?'

'If you mean did he sustain injuries while resisting arrest – which, by the way, could well be another charge, though not the injuries, but the resistance, if you see what I mean – then the answer is yes. Though they're not of a life-threatening kind unfortunately. You see there's also a police officer who had to be flown to hospital in a helicopter. He has a bullet wound in the abdomen. And that's serious for him and it's going to look bad for your friend Cameron, too.'

'Will you stop calling him my friend. He's a rat,' said Bronnie, with a sudden surge of bitterness she could taste in her mouth. The bastard had gone mad tonight. She'd watched him building up to it for weeks. She'd been telling herself all day she was a fool. Well, she sure had been, but that didn't mean she was going to be dragged down with him. He'd made his choice. This time she'd look after number one.

'I'm glad you feel that way, because we'd like you to come to the station for a chat.'

She nodded. 'I want you to realise I've got no objection to talking – even if there's no real choice. I don't owe him anything and I've got nothing to hide. But, I don't know much. He might've gone mental, but he wasn't silly enough to tell me anything that could get him deeper in shit.'

'Oh, that's all right, Bronwyn. Every little helps.'

The policemen waited while she got dressed, then they all went outside. The uniformed man walked directly across to the office, where Bronnie could see him speak to Clarry, who came out and stared at them.

The 'borrowed' car was not there. Cameron must have taken it. The idiot must have been ten times over the limit.

'Don't tell me,' she said. 'There's drunk driving as well?'

'And a stolen vehicle and false plates,' said the plain-clothes man. 'It's the old scenario: speed, alcohol and the Wanganui computer. Cameron needed to be more circumspect if he was going to roam around Taranaki at night with a handgun. Especially since there was an armed hold-up at a petrol station earlier in the evening. Every officer in Taranaki was out on the roads checking on everything that moved. It just wasn't his lucky night.'

'Typical,' Bronnie said. 'He'd used up his luck long ago. But I never knew he had a gun with him. The bastard never told me anything.'

There were lights on in the police station and several cars were parked in the street outside. As they walked in, the plain-clothes man remarked softly, 'Cameron must have looked quite gorgeous in his perm, before it got messed up.'

'One thing's sure. He wouldn't have been mistaken for Elvis,' Bronnie said.

'Elvis?'

'It's that Elvis museum. Elvis has kept cropping up ever since we got here. Cameron called our motel Heartbreak Hotel. I guess he'll soon be joking about Jailhouse Rock.' She wasn't trying to sound funny or smart. Her voice was hard.

The plain-clothes man looked at her steadily for a few moments, then smiled and offered her the choice between tea or coffee.

So this is what it all comes down to in the end, Bronnie thought as she sat at a small table and the questioning began. What's it all amount to? You've wasted years of your life and what do you get? A choice of tea or coffee.

As she sipped and talked, and tried not to think of what

Cameron would do if he ever got his hands on her, Morrieson's Motel was just beginning to awake, though Clarry and Betty were already on the go with a couple of early breakfasts.

'The policeman said we'd hear all about it on the radio and see it on television soon enough,' Clarry protested, as he made toast. 'He said there's reporters and cameras flying in from everywhere. But you'd think they'd be obliged to tell us first what was going on, wouldn't you? After all, it's our motel. We're the owners.'

'I went in and had a look in number four. Just to make sure,' said Betty. 'Everything's there. And she's left the usual bags and things. She'll be back for them, I guess.'

'They're booked in for tonight, so I expect we'll see her,' Clarry agreed.

'Whatever happens, it's paid for.' Betty gave a small smile of triumph, then went on, 'It just shows, it pays to have rules and stick to them. The trouble with the world today is there's rules, but they just get broken.'

'I sometimes think it's a madhouse out there,' Clarry added. For a change he was allowed to have the last word. 'A proper bloody madhouse. There's no reliability. You can never predict what the bastards out there are going to do to each other next.'

# A Bad Business

Richard Nevington squinted between the horizontal slats of the venetian blind, across the expanse of concrete, over the sodden, manicured lawn to standard roses placed with mathematical precision along the high wooden fence. The drive and garden had that planned sterility, that tidy over-organisation left behind by landscape gardeners, with nurture geometrically triumphant over nature. His gaze swept around the courtyard but he couldn't see the ferret face of Mike Simpson. The car was still there, parked outside unit ten, next door to his own white Mercedes. Richard was angry with himself. The romantic notion of a tryst out of the limelight in Kelly's home town seemed idiotic now compared with a sensible assignation in a city hotel's anonymous corridors; except that Kelly wouldn't even talk about that.

He phoned her again and the quick switch to voice-mail revealed her phone was busy. Previously, it had been switched off. He put the electric wall heater on as the evening cool descended, opened a bottle of Moët under a towel to mute the pop, sat on the bed, poured himself a drink and kept hitting the redial button as Kelly, his obsession, took over his mind again. For a minute it seemed the call was going through, and then it went back to voice-mail. She had hung up and switched off, and he couldn't leave his phone live in case the media called. He threw the phone across the room and the battery flew off the back. 'Jesus,' he said aloud, looking around the room with its concrete-block outer walls, 'what the fuck's happening to me? I'm a prisoner in some goddamn excuse for a motel. I might as well be in Paremoremo.'

Twelve kilometres away, alone in the dusk on the veranda of her childhood home, Kelly ended her call to her father in the cowshed, flicked her hair back over her ear as she turned off her phone, and rattled the ice in her gin and tonic before taking a sip. Love as Richard understood it was a deal, she thought, reminding herself of when they worked together. It had the same complex components as completing a takeover or a merger. You targeted the desirable company, one which would complement your own, sussed out its principals and major shareholders, and pursued it with guile and tenacity. At forty-three she was impervious, she hoped with a sigh, to the romance of flowers and chocolates, to the pull of flattery and sexual attention. Now it would be a hard-earned trade-off between sex and companionship, excitement and comfort, between being herself and being a handmaiden, a balance she had hitherto found unattainable. It looked as though it had eluded her again.

She'd showered after milking, changed into a short black dress ready for the evening and pulled a cardigan over her shoulders before going outside. She tipped back slightly in her chair, put her feet on the veranda rail and looked towards the sea. The gusty wind from the west swatted the coastal trees and the long dune grass, always carrying with it rain or the promise of rain. The unrelenting wind, never a hurricane, and the rain never torrential. This is New Zealand, she thought, ennui by moderation. This farm was where she had been born and grown up and where she had felt more intensely the love of people and place than at any time since she left it exactly twenty-five years ago. Nothing that had happened since had excited her as much as the simple adventures and pleasures of her childhood. Nothing had gone as well since she'd left for university all those years ago. Tonight she had helped her father with the milking for the first time since her mother died. The smells of cowshit and silage and milk and the earthy musk of a cow's flank as she leaned against it, an amalgam of smells, always evoked her childhood. She'd started to tell her father about Richard, but after a while he said simply, 'Tell me only if you absolutely must, Kelly. I can't help you.'

'I'm sorry, Dad, but I need to hear myself say it.'

'Ask me about which calves to sell, ask me what's wrong with your car or what you should do with your money and I'll try to help with advice you'd no doubt ignore. But don't ask me about your personal affairs or anyone else's because I won't know what you're talking about.'

'It's not help I want, just an ear. I have things I need to hear myself say.'

'Say them to yourself, Kelly.' He loved and admired his daughter but he was living in suspension. He had suddenly been left alone by his wife and was engulfed by the turmoil of having to sell up and move away for the first time in forty-odd years.

Kelly had never been able to think internally, running something abstract through her head, weighing it up as she went and coming to a rational conclusion. She suspected it was a female need to talk and consider, with someone there to give purpose to the talk. Her mind otherwise slipped and slithered from one emotional point to another. She had to either say out loud or write down an audit of how she thought and felt, an exhausting process. She had only ten minutes or so before her father returned from the shed, so she reached for the phone again to make a start with her sister, Audrey.

Audrey had taken the kids to drama class and wouldn't be back until seven o'clock.

He drained his glass, refilled it and threw the phone across the room again; making sure this time it landed on the spindly-legged couch. 'Jesus,' he said aloud as he looked around the room in the crepuscular gloom, 'this place is nouveau-1950s. It's dedicated to discomfort,' he thought, scanning the floral bedspread, the mid-grey carpet flecked with darker grey so you couldn't see the dirt or the marks, the creamy walls flecked with several shades of blue, and the bench with stick-on wood grain. Three large pictures of daubed trees and hills and paddocks and skies and streams were by someone called Janice Janes, according to a signature in the corner in stiff letters like an oriental script.

The family genes had been generous to Richard. They'd given him the gift of height – he was six foot one – a lean but robust body and a well-shaped face marred only by patches of skin that had never recovered from the depressing eruptions of schoolboy acne. The pustulating had long ago ceased but the craters remained, extinct but ineradicable like the mountains of the moon. Some women found that attractive.

He went back to the window, looked through the blinds again and there was ferret-face fossicking around in the boot of his car. Richard instinctively pulled his head back but kept watching. Simpson slammed the back door of the van and paused a moment, and then looked at the Mercedes, peering into the back seat. Richard's car stood out like a Friesian's udder. He stepped further back from the window. Why hadn't he brought a rental car? Simpson was the sort of creepy nosy bastard who would do a licence-plate check for the hell of it.

He opened a second bottle of Moët in the toilet, using a bath towel to muffle the pop that never happened anyway, spilt some of it down the front of his trousers and began to burn with suppressed anger in a way he could never remember experiencing before. He felt like crying with the anguish of it. What had happened to the man of even just a week ago, the man with the ruthless opportunist's eye who had become what he had always wanted to be – rich and inordinately pleased with himself?

At eight o'clock, after her father had gone to bed, Kelly settled down in the lounge with the landline phone and called her sister in Napier.

'How's Dad?'

'He's a bit upset and confused by it all. But then so am I.'

'What?'

'I'm upset and confused as well.'

'For God's sake, Kelly, you're supposed to be the steady one helping him.'

'I know, but it's Richard Nevington. You know, the guy I used to work for.'

'The rich one.'

'I knew you'd say that. I like him. I might even love him. And I'm supposed to be having a romantic dinner with him tonight at the Dairy Shed followed by a night at Morrieson's Motel.'

'And he's not turned up?'

'He's holed up in the motel under a phoney name.'

'Well, go and hole up with him.'

'Look, don't make it sound so simple, Aud. I don't know what's happened, but there's been a blow-up in the company and he's resigned. From what I understand, he pulled out because of some scandal or something that he says he desperately wants to explain to me. All a bit ominous. He rang me from the motel this afternoon and left a message that I was to park my car out on the road and walk in through the exit to unit eleven and tap on the window. He babbled on about not letting anyone see me arrive.'

'Sounds exciting.'

'Not to me, it doesn't. He's tried one-night stands with me before and I'm past that sort of carry-on. I slept with him once and it was great but he can be an arrogant shit and I'm not just going to do what he says.'

'I think you need to make your mind up about him.'

'Yeh. You see, I always had him in perspective. He's fun to be with, but I used to mix with his type of guy and you feel you're a sort of distraction from the real things of life. Their shop's never shut in their minds. Business is life; life is business. And then when I run into him again, I sense he's softened. I find he's dropped a lot of his hyper mates and seems more real. I think I'm trying to say I've started to love the guy.'

'Phone him back for God's sake, Kelly, and ask him what it's all about.'

'I've tried and tried. His phone's on voice-mail. I left him a message saying I wasn't going.'

'Call the motel.'

'I don't want to embarrass him.'

'So it's Friday night at home with Dad and the cows?'

After she'd hung up from Audrey, Kelly decided to call the motel.


Most conspirators do not recognise themselves as such; and though the men gathered in the small Central Properties Ltd boardroom in the capital might have been briefly thrilled by that label and its echoes of backroom bravado, they would not have been distracted by it. They had a sense of destiny, an undiluted belief that you create your nemesis and don't just drift towards it.

Except for George Poore, who, before Richard arrived, said sardonically as they gathered around the table, 'Approaching the dénouement now. Dénouement is something you only enjoy when you've written the plot' – which hit the air like an onioned fart. Corporate businessmen do not talk in tropes but in words like cash, words with a hard intrinsic feel to them. They speak in numerals, analyses of numerals, of manoeuvres engineered by those numerals, in figures as precise as they could be honed, and in ideas that sprang from those figures, and in the outcomes – not in the concept of triumph but in the particular triumphs themselves. They leave metaphor to artists, philosophers, orators and other ineffectuals. George Poore's laboured maxim was one of the reasons they now averted their attention from him and avoided eye contact with each other, shocked that one of their own should continue using the language of losers. No one said anything, nor would they, but each thought back to other recent signs of decay in Poore's concentration, symptoms of emotional bleeding. When Richard went, George would have to go with him. Reform, they knew, was impossible once the weakness of dreams set in.

The boardroom was well-appointed but not sumptuous, and as the acrid aftermath of Poore's remark dissipated, Richard arrived and they chatted with that muted bonhomie of men whose purpose is so mutual it doesn't need stating, and moved quickly on to business. What they had in common was money and commercial power, and their daily driven task was to multiply their wealth. Their monthly task, for which they had gathered this day, was to enhance the environment in which they could further prosper and to expand the notion among the masses that individual wealth was socially good and its uninhibited pursuit the noblest social purpose. Nothing sinister or cynical drove them, because they believed in their cause – that commerce is the well from which all water is drawn, as Poore might have put it to their consternation. But most of them felt their progress had been unnecessarily slowing. Richard sat down at the head of the table and mumbled greetings without looking up, and the conviction of the others – that he was working too autocratically and almost by rote – was confirmed. After a minute, Jason Dodding stood up and annoyed himself for a moment by involuntarily clearing his throat in a theatrical, nervous way before picking up a piece of paper and starting to speak.

The shifting of feet beneath the table and the portentous silence suddenly grabbed Richard's attention. Something, he realised, was up. 'After talking to a number of our institutional shareholders and among my board colleagues,' Dodding said, glancing around the table without looking at anyone and certainly evading Richard's nailing stare. 'I've decided to nominate Eric McLeod as our new chair and executive director.'

'What?' shouted Richard.

'And I'd like to second that,' said Tony Smallboys, leaning forward over the table on folded arms.

Richard abruptly stood up. 'What the hell's going on here? I'm the chairman and I don't accept the motion.'

McLeod eased himself to his feet, walked a few steps behind the other chairs, slid an A4 page in front of Richard and, as he stepped back to his own place, announced that he was to become the new chairman, that he had the numbers on the board and would those who supported the change raise their right hands. Richard was still standing as all but two of the hands went up, making the obvious result seven-to-three against him. He knew his unaccustomed silence in the face of attack surprised them, but he also knew that if he hit back he would pull from McLeod all the things the usurper would like to say but couldn't without seeming even more gratuitously cruel than his colleagues had the stomach for.

McLeod knew then he'd win unchallenged. What he'd done was cumbersome and unnecessarily nasty. He could have approached Richard beforehand and told him he was outnumbered and that the two institutional shareholders wanted him out, but he was a whippy, ambitious young man who enjoyed both a fight and humiliating his opponents. He and Richard both knew that Richard could refuse the motion, walk out and attempt to recover his support. But they both knew something else too, they knew about a skeleton in Richard's filing-cabinet. McLeod spoke quickly, fidgeting with the watch on his left wrist, a barely perceptible twitch at the left corner of his mouth as his gaze swept past Richard's face and on around the table. But he was not afraid, just excited, his body pumping. He was twenty years younger than Richard, whose service to the company he now extolled in the polite formal phrases that smother rather than explain reality and that in this instance were insultingly insincere.

'This company would never have survived the bursting of the 1980s bubble had it not been for Richard Nevington,' he said. 'We all know that…'

Richard was scrutinising the paper and saw the declaration that the institutional shareholders backed McLeod.

'…and respect him for having brought the company through and for the consolidation and steady expansion that has left us asset-strong and cash-rich. In fact, it's because some of us feel we're too cash-rich that we've made this move, Richard…'

Richard had been staring at the shiny, yellow, oval tabletop where it curved in towards him but looked up again at the mention of his name and held McLeod's eyes. McLeod had large, round nostrils that seemed to flare as he spoke and, pulling his head back and dilating his eyes, he looked like he was taking a bead with a double-barrelled gun. Richard found himself watching with clinical dispassion as the cold anger that had suffused his body as he read the figures ebbed. He now looked at McLeod with contempt. As the younger man pulled his head back again, he puffed out his chest and rocked forward onto the balls of his feet as though challenging gravity to hold him down, and Richard was horrified to find in this performance a rendition of himself a decade ago. Kelly Johnnes had told him once about having dinner with McLeod and how he had simpered and then whimpered, almost sobbed, as he told her how lonely he was and how his estranged wife had a coldness in her heart that even his enduring love and reassurance couldn't inflame. And as he whimpered he took her hand and filled her with disgust. Well, he wasn't whimpering now. He read Richard's body signals accurately and, emboldened, continued in the muddled but safe clichés: 'We will value your continued presence on the board, Richard, because of your immense experience in this industry, but we believe the time has come for a new executive chair, for new blood to strike out with renewed energy into a marketplace that's bursting with opportunities for those prepared to take considered risks. We have the money and have already isolated some of those opportunities, opportunities you certainly know of but have avoided with the caution that has served this company so well in past business environments. Admirable caution. But we believe this is the time to move…'

Richard slowly stood up. It was galling that at the time of his gathering contempt for people like McLeod he should become his victim, and at the very time of life when his defences should have been shored up by experience. He dropped his papers into his briefcase and walked from the room, his contrived nonchalance faltering as he caught his shin on the table leg. 'Fuck!' he said just above his breath, loud enough for those nearest him to hear and smile in their small triumphs. The big triumph belonged to McLeod.

All he'd wanted to do was to get away from the McLeods, from himself, from the whole ambience of his working life. He was in a funk. He thought of his fine moments as he sat hunched on the miserable bed, of the raiment of respect he had worn among his peers, and wondered when he had first begun to sense the futility, even the absurdity, of the tribal uniformity of business, of the suits and tasselled moccasins, and airline captain's bags hanging open, and the four-wheel drives and the collegiate talk of all the enterprise culture cronies. Eric McLeod was in his mind, an insistent image of a pontificating prick. He'd grown, if that's the right word, thought Richard, from a serious, clever but pleasant lawyer who had embraced the business culture and its rituals with enthusiasm into a travesty of a barrister, a television barrister in a period drama. The Moët confused Richard and his image of McLeod was in a frock coat, grasping his lapel with his right hand like something out of Trollope. Richard found the absurdity comforting.

Richard's change had been no epiphany. He sensed it went back to his holiday in Queensland with his parents two years before. He hardly knew his father, unless what seemed the thin frontage of his personality was all there was to know. The old man had always been there, reading and gardening and hedging his bets on any beliefs with his calming moderation. On that holiday he had been morally forced to take because his father needed his physical help after a hernia operation, he had been constantly exasperated by his parents' enjoyment of everyday things they made exceptional. Was it that subconsciously he knew his father was happier than Richard could ever hope to be? 'Life's lonely, mate,' he'd said to his son over the years, 'and you can't fill the void with nothing but sensations.'

The bedside phone rang. And rang. He ignored it.

Richard's parents had been dairy farmers on the Kaipara for thirty-two years of hand-crusting work they had shared and enjoyed. When they retired, they bought a house in the suburbs and miniaturised their lives with a vegetable garden for him and a flower garden for her to which they arose early each morning with

contentment in their lot and each other. When they started life with
nothing, security and stability were their joint aim. She had made a
million scones, both delicious and symbolic of her time, and he had
milked cows and pushed hoes and wanted nothing more. To
Richard they were as aliens – wanting nothing more than they had,
wanting to be nice to people and for people to be nice back. Their
happiness seemed to grow as they aged, and each seemed able to
regenerate the other when sickness or misfortune fell. Richard tried
to think of them as a case to be examined sociologically. Were they
just a happy, coincidental confluence of personalities, an equation
that equalled contentment? Or was there an unfulfilled yearning
somewhere in there bottled up and poisoning their insides? They
had very little money, and he sensed this was because they needed
very little and did not push for wealth beyond their needs. Their
condition had exasperated Richard. Drive and domination were
ends in themselves and had lifted the human race from the dull
metronomic lives of peasants and the higher animals. How could he
be their son?

His mother breathed more freely in her garden, was looser
limbed, released from what Richard thought of as the monotony
of time. She knelt on her large green knee-pad as lodged there as
a taproot. He could not understand it. What seemed to content
her would be for him intolerable diurnal drudgery. He had learnt
that years ago the committed mentally ill were kept in the
country, allowed out during the day in what was believed to be
the therapeutic freedom of the countryside, and locked up at
night. It probably had much to do with the belief during the
industrial revolution that towns were bad and the country good,
and something to do with the first European immigrants' need for
space. But it was revealed now for the myth it was, and Richard
would have sneered at the whole concept had it not been for the
ease of manner and mind his mother slipped into when in the
presence of her plants. She knew the common names of every
variety of every plant in her garden, but it seemed such useless
information, the fruit of an idle hobby. She picked a bunch of
flowers whenever she went visiting, and he remembered how she

caressed them into posies in green ruffled paper like Elizabethan collars, turning them, because of her love for them, into gifts beyond value. Nothing was beyond value to Richard. He had always dismissed her calm as insensitivity, the dexterity of her hands in garden and kitchen as an inevitable consequence of tedious practice. And yet she had this marvellous stillness at her centre.

Kelly had all the right moods, he thought as he sat hunched up against the two thin pillows at the head of the bed, well into the second bottle. She was brisk and smiling at work, languorous and attentive at dinner and, on that one occasion, wanton after night fell. When he danced with her the first time, she slipped fluidly against him and her black dress swirled around his thighs as they turned. She was slim and athletic and walked as she danced, with the same grace and energy. But most of all he was mesmerised by that same stillness that was at the centre of his mother.

'Sleep with me,' he said as they danced.

She smiled slightly without looking at him and said nothing.

'Tonight.'

She looked at him but still said nothing.

'I'm in room 758 and no price is too high.' God, why did he say that?

Was that a faint nod she gave as she smiled and still said nothing?

She didn't arrive, so he phoned the desk, got her room and phone number, and called. No reply. He dressed and went to the room and knocked. He was certain she was there so he knocked and knocked again, but it was 11.45 and he could not make much noise. He went back to his room.

Here he was, a model statistic, a representative modern man, married with one of each, then divorced, and then trying to like his kids half as much as they grew up as he'd loved them when they were very young. His children were the only two people he'd ever loved profoundly or at all in his life. Now they loved him solely for the money he could give them. He remembered the Oscar Wilde remark that children began by loving their parents, then judged them, and sometimes forgave them. He sensed no forgiveness. And as for their mother, she'd had an affair with ferret-face, the media maggot, when he lived next door to them in Karori, and here was the bugger next door to him again in a scungy motel, no doubt making someone miserable with his camera. What joy he'd get out of finding Richard skulking here.

Did he love Kelly? If love poetry or the big songs with their grand, swelling passion were near the truth, he'd never loved a woman in his life. He felt good with her, comfortable, at ease, but he was also obsessed with being, well, up against her, touching her. He wished her well and admired her poise without a trace of envy. If that was love, he was in it.

There was a loud rap on the door, and his arms and legs involuntarily jerked so hard he spilt some wine on his trousers again. And then he froze. Another, louder knock. He carefully, silently stood up, brushed himself down, tucked his shirt in his trousers and crept to the window beside the door. The woman who had checked him in stood there frowning and jiggling keys in her hand. If he didn't answer she'd come in. He opened the door a fraction and said, 'Yes?'

'Oh, Mr Lewis, a lady called on the phone and said she'd been trying to call you on your cellphone for a couple of hours and there was no reply. Kelly Johnnes.'

'Thanksh, I'll call her.' He heard himself say 'Thanksh' as he was confused for a second when she called him Lewis, and he realised the Moët had taken its toll and that she probably thought he was a lush paralysing himself in the privacy of his own motel room.

'Are you okay? When I saw the lights weren't on and I hadn't seen you all day I wondered if you were okay.'

'I dropped off. I'm sorry.' He enunciated carefully but not too carefully.

'No worries,' she said, her eyes searching past him into the room through the narrow slit he left her. 'Can I give you the number?'

'I'm sure I've got it in my diary.'

'Save you looking it up,' she said, thrusting a piece of paper at him. 'I thought you said your partner would be joining you this afternoon.'

'Well, yes, she's been held up. Thanks for thish,' Richard said holding up the paper.

'You want dinner?'

'Probably not.'

'We have room service.'

'Ah, well I might. I might just do that. What time?'

'Till nine.'

'Thanks. How long is the gentleman next door staying? Not that it's any of my business.'

She had suspicious, busybody's eyes and Richard began to feel uncomfortable. He'd descended in just a week from lofty confidence to a snivelling wreck.

'Perhaps you could ask him,' she said in a moralising tone that meant, 'I'm very discreet, and, yes, it's none of your business.' And there she stood, showing no sign of moving.

'No, no, no. It's none of my business. It's just that his car's parked very close to mine, but I can get in from the passenger's side. No problem. Thanks Mrs…ah…'

'Claridge. But nobody calls me that. Just Betty.'

'Well, thanks for the message, Betty. I'll call her now.' And he nodded, smiling as he slowly closed the door.


It was the coup of the business year. He'd written a brief resignation as executive chairman, noted that he had enough shares to retain his directorship and fled. That was last Friday. He went back into his office on Sunday and found the personal files on his share trading had gone. He had been trading Central Property shares under two names, one of them Kelly Johnnes. He had used it at the height of his infatuation. He bought and sold at times he knew would make him handsome profits. Worse, he had borrowed money from the company whenever he had to hold the shares long enough to have to pay. More from convenience than need. Not too many shares at a time but enough to make a steady profit. This wasn't a criminal offence in New Zealand, as it was in many Western countries, but it would be seriously embarrassing, as McLeod knew.

He guessed that, to spare the company some embarrassment, the board wouldn't blow the whistle on him; and they'd probably done some insider trading themselves. But he guessed they would all know and the CEOs of the institutional shareholders would have been discreetly told to back up his replacement. He wondered how long ago his files had been taken. His future hung on whether someone in the know would be unable to contain such rich gossip or whether someone disliked him enough to want to strangle his business career.

But what mattered most to him was whether Kelly would ever learn the details of how he had implicated her. He wanted to tell her and wondered if he should offer her some of the money he had earned as a result of using her name. No, probably not. It's just a name. Moët, he thought, despondent now, was just a bloody name too. He paid for the name on the bottle, an illusory distinction of flavour. Illusory to him anyway. His father used to laugh and say that his palate cut out at about twenty-five bucks and Richard was wasting money on him from there up. Maybe his father was right and a blind testing would find most people were working on pretension and it was just another leg-opener, except the legs were longer, younger and better dressed than gin could manage.

'Why haven't you had your phone on?' snapped Kelly when he got through. 'It's what… after half-past-eight and I've been sitting here waiting to hear from you for…'

'I don't want to talk to anyone. Well, except you. The media's been hounding me since the beginning of the week. I've been calling you and the bloody phone's been engaged or not answered. Anyway, I'm here now. Will you come over?'

'To the motel?'

'Yes, but you must park your car down the road a little way and walk in through the exit and don't knock. I'll be waiting.'

'Richard, I'm not skulking around a motel at nine o'clock at night.'

'Skulking? Who says you have to skulk? I just don't want you to be seen. You 'member ferret-face Simpson, the guy who…who…'

'The television reporter who ran off with your wife?' she said, and then after a pause, 'Are you drunk?'

'He didn't *run off* with her, he seduced her and left her.'

'No, Richard, he seduced her and you left her. Have you been drinking?'

'He's in the unit next to mine. Can you believe that I've come to this little dump you were brought up in t'…t'… get away from the godforsaken bloody media an' meet you and I find the…'

'What's he doing there?'

'I don't know. The bloody… Maybe he's looking for me. Why else?'

'Richard, I think paranoia has set in at last, and I'm not coming to the motel, and that's that. I'll meet you somewhere else.'

'I can't get outta here. I'm trapped by ferret-face.'

'Well, I'll tell you this: I'll be in the White Hart bar in half-an-hour. If you turn left out of the motel, and take the second on the left into High Street, and come right along to the end by the water tower, you'll see the White Hart on the corner.'

'Oh God, all right then, I'll have a try.'

Fifteen minutes later, Clarry Claridge, Betty's husband, was standing on the deck having a quiet cigarette, banned as he was from smoking inside, when he saw the door of unit eleven open and Lewis come slowly out, bending almost double as he opened the back door on the driver's side of his Mercedes, fumbling with the keys. He slid something onto the seat, gently closed the door, slid himself into the driver's seat and very slowly drove away, crouched over the wheel, with his lights off. Clarry bustled down to the unit and found two empty bottles of Moët on the floor beside the crumpled bed in the abandoned unit. He reached for the phone.

Richard left the car lights off to make his getaway and then forgot to put them on as he drove down Waipahu Street. He thought High Street was a sort of confidence course for drivers, a paved road that snaked from one parking bay to another. He was going about ten kilometres an hour, cursing at any traffic engineer who would be so stupid to build a street that curved past parking bays with cars having barely enough room to pass, when he came to an intersection, kept going to the right instead of stopping or turning left and clipped the back of a passing car on which he saw written 'POLICE'.

'Would you step out of the car please, sir,' said the police officer after waving his breathalyser in through the door. 'As a newt,' he called, laughing, to his colleague who walked away to answer the radio that was crackling from the car. The officers had two small satisfactions in this. They could not be blamed in any way for the accident and there was always the piquancy of catching a guy in a ritzy car.

The colleague looked at the car and the plates, put down the radio and said: 'He's done a runner from Morrieson's Motel.'

'God, eh? Got a Mercedes, leather luggage in the back and he does a runner from a ninety-dollar-a-night motel.'

'That's how the rich get rich in the first place – they don't spend anything. Okay, mate, we're off to the station.'

About nine-forty-five, Kelly Johnnes had had enough of being stared at and drooled over in her chic black dress and swing-back shoes among the track suits and jeans. She picked up her purse and drove disconsolately back to the farm.

# Little Things

Deborah stepped into unit nine. She placed her suitcase beside the double bed, careful not to disturb the towels that fanned open like birds' tails. In the bathroom there were unused soaps and the toilet was covered with a sash of paper ribbon for her protection. On the polished kitchen bench sat a new dishcloth, a new brush; the black cord was coiled around the electric jug. At first glance it was possible to believe nobody had ever stayed here. For a moment Deborah stood in the centre of the room, unwilling to touch anything, as if she, too, should leave no sign of her presence. And then, gradually, she began to see little things. There was a tiny tear in the net curtains, a scratch on the coffee table. A long brown hair clung to the duvet cover; a cigarette burn punctured the carpet; the remote control for the television was rubbed wordless around the on button.

Although she had never visited the town, she could close her eyes and visualise its exact layout. She had studied maps of the area for many months now and the streets were in her head, as real as veins. Through the window she could see the stone water tower, exactly where it should be. Everything was in the right place, she told herself. Everything was under control. Her eyes shifted to the top of the tower and she squinted against the glare. The stone rose from the ground like the trunk of a great tree. She had never pictured the town in three dimensions, she realised. The tower had been a dot on a map for her, and she had not imagined – had not let herself imagine – what could grow from a dot.

Deborah opened her suitcase and began making the unit look like home. She laid her pyjamas on the pillow and placed her toothbrush in a glass. She hung her blazer in the wardrobe – wire hangers only, unfortunately – and removed her shoes from their special canvas bag. She folded her underwear away in a drawer, ignoring the bright red bible left there for lonely travellers. Deborah had stopped going to church years ago.

'Here we are,' said a voice at the door. Betty Claridge bustled into the unit and placed a jug of milk in the fridge. 'Just sing out if you need any more, won't you?'

'Thank you,' said Deborah.

'I like my coffee without milk these days, actually, but Clarry just screws up his nose at that.'

'Does he,' said Deborah, hanging up her warm, just-in-case trousers.

'I cut back to skim milk first of all, so it wasn't too much of a shock to the system,' said Betty. 'And then I got rid of the sugar, and the butter on the toast.' She slapped herself on the hips. 'You've got to battle the genes somehow, don't you?'

'I suppose you do.' Deborah picked invisible lint from her clothes in the wardrobe.

'Well,' said Betty, addressing her back. 'The housekeeper will be in around ten tomorrow to make up your room, all right? And if you're wanting sightseeing brochures, we've got a whole stack in the office.'

'Thank you,' said Deborah. 'I know my way around.'

'Oh,' said Betty. 'Do you have family here?'

'I'm familiar with the area.'

Betty nodded, waited.

'Thank you again for the milk,' said Deborah, and continued unpacking.


By three o'clock the water tower was casting a long shadow over the town. Deborah paid the two-dollar fee at the tourist information office and received a ticket torn from a roll, as if she had entered a contest.

'You're lucky you're getting in today,' said the man. 'The tower's closed tomorrow and Sunday for inspection. They've had some worries about the masonry at the top.'

'I see,' said Deborah. 'It's quite secure, though, isn't it? I'll be quite safe?'

'You'll be fine, love,' he said. 'Just don't lean over the rail. You'll see the notices.' She began to climb the spiralling steps, squeezing over to the narrow side about halfway up so a Japanese couple could pass. Her heels hung over the edge of the steps and she grasped at the smooth walls for balance. She was too big for the space, she thought; only a child's little feet would fit the cramped tread. She waited for a moment, listened, and when she was certain she could hear no more footsteps descending she began to climb again. She found it easier not to look ahead, but she knew she was reaching the top when she felt a breeze on her face. She glanced up then and saw the sky approaching, and she emerged from the tower blinking at the town spread out at her feet.

She turned slowly, taking in the view, ticking off the landmarks she had memorised. CAUTION, said a sign, DO NOT LEAN OVER EDGE. Beyond the town the fields stretched away, as wide as an ocean, and beyond them the mountain rose to the sky. It made everything small. The lower slopes were dark, the colour of freshly turned soil, and a cap of snow covered the peak as symmetrically as if it had been drawn by a child. Here would be a healthy place to grow up, thought Deborah. Cows dotted the countryside, their udders heavy. She remembered asking her mother once why cows made milk if they didn't have any babies to drink it.

'They're separated,' her mother had said. 'As soon as the calves are born, they're taken away. The mothers make a terrible noise, but after the first day or so they forget.'

Deborah located the school: a collection of yellow prefabs, like blocks of butter and cheese. She looked at her watch. At three-twenty children began to pour into the grounds, running and leaping towards the weekend, jostling for space although there was plenty, or dawdling in twos and threes, little red and grey dots. At the gate the school bus waited to round them up and take them home to their mothers, and as they dispersed, the teachers emerged one by one and made their way to their cars. Deborah watched the men. She wasn't sure what she was looking for. Even the word 'man' sounded wrong.

Thirty years ago, she was waiting to start university. School had finished forever, Christmas had come and gone, and the February days were long and hot. She had banished from her mind the memory of the end-of-term party, where she had drunk vodka and gone for a drive with her best friend's brother. When she did try to recall exactly what had happened in his car, she could not remember. Her old uniform hung at the back of her wardrobe, already too small for her, and although the Auckland air was as thick as cream, she wore heavy clothes that hid her shape.

'Why do you insist on bundling yourself up like that?' said her mother. 'You look like one of those Russian dolls.'

'Shall I shake her?' said her father. 'See if she rattles?'

It was her mother's idea to have lunch on Rangitoto. 'A picnic on a volcano,' she said. 'Doesn't that sound like fun, Deborah? A nice family outing, before you start university and don't have time for me and Dad.'

The scoria track was hot and sharp beneath Deborah's shoes. She listened to her father explaining the difference between dormant and extinct.

'Think of a bulb,' he said.

'A light bulb?'

'No, Norma, not a light bulb. Once a light bulb is dead there's nothing to do but dispose of it. No, I mean a spring bulb.'

'Ah. Tulips and daffodils and things.'

'Yes. That sort of bulb might…'

'Orchids?' said Deborah's mother.

'No,' said her father, 'not orchids. They're non-bulbous. Now, as you know, a spring bulb might look dead, but at the end of winter it bursts into flower.'

'My jonquils never did,' said her mother.

Deborah let them chatter on. Although the climb to the top was gentle, she needed to conserve her breath; she had things to say. The shadeless track spiralled around and around the volcano like the curl of a shell, cutting through the scrub, and each time they passed the same landmarks in the distant city Deborah had to remind herself that they were making progress, that little by little they were climbing.

At the top her mother took charge of the landscape, selecting a spot to place the blanket, unpacking sandwiches, tidily arranging plates and mugs and the thermos. When they were all seated on the scratchy blanket, inside their room with no walls, and when the hot tea had been poured and drunk and the sandwiches consumed and the thermos dregs shaken empty, Deborah told them she was pregnant.

'Ma'am?' said a voice. 'Excuse me, Ma'am? We close at four.' The man from the tourist information office was touching her on the shoulder. 'I thought there was still one up here. I keep count of our visitors. I keep a careful record of how many go up and how many come down. We wouldn't want you stranded up here all night, would we?'

'I'm sorry, I must have lost track,' said Deborah.

'It happened once, you know. Lisa Blowse was working for us and she didn't keep count – she's a solo mother – and a Swede spent the night up here. He was very reasonable about it, thank goodness. Would have been a different story if he'd been German or American.'

Deborah followed the man down the winding staircase, and when they emerged at the bottom the tower's shadow had grown even longer, tunnelling across the town.

'You silly girl,' said her mother, snatching up the plates and cups and dropping them into the knapsack. Dirty cutlery clattered between the jumble of bright plastic. 'I've a good mind to leave you here.'

Her father spoke to the harbour. 'What a mess,' he said. 'What a disaster.'

'She has no idea of the pain involved,' said her mother.

'Of course she hasn't,' said her father.

'I'm going to adopt the baby out,' said Deborah, and there was a moment of utter stillness when even the sea stopped moving, and then her parents were at her side, plucking at her arms, her hair, pecking at her like gulls.

'Oh no no, we can't do that,' they said. 'Babies are a gift from God. We don't give away gifts.'

'You gave away the piglet salt-and-pepper set,' said Deborah.

'That was a gift from Aunty Yvonne, not God,' said her mother.

Her father screwed up his nose. 'And the salt came out the pig's snout,' he said.

'We'll raise it,' said her mother, her eyes on Deborah's stomach. 'I've always wanted a boy. I wonder if it's a boy?'

'It's nothing yet,' said Deborah. 'It's a dot.'


Later that day, her mother came to her room and said, 'We've decided to turn my sewing room into a nursery.' And, day by day, her excitement about the baby grew. Whenever Deborah mentioned adoption, she ignored her. 'Shall I be Nana or Grandma?' she said. 'Shall I be Granny or Gran?' She knitted tiny garments, holding them up to the dog for size. 'We'll need something nice for him to wear home from hospital,' she said. She crocheted a bonnet, her hook pulling at the fine white wool, making knot after knot. Every now and then she paused and told Deborah about the wonderful life they would have, how fortunate she was to have parents who loved and accepted her despite her failings. 'Yes, you are a very lucky girl,' she said. 'This would have been the extent of your options a few years ago.' And she brandished her crochet hook – an elongated question mark.

Deborah tried to picture what the baby would look like, but she kept seeing the Jack Russell in a matinée jacket. Later, when the child was born, she just had time to check that he did not have a hairy face, a wet snout, paws where his pink hands should be. And then he was taken away.

She listened to a record by The Seekers over and over the day she returned from hospital. She closed the wooden lid on her parents' radiogram and thought about the black disc spinning inside it like a flat planet, and sometimes she imagined herself climbing in there too, just stretching out full-length inside the polished box and shutting the lid. Every now and then her mother came into the lounge to ask where she and her husband had gone wrong, and whether Deborah was happy with herself now, and whether she, Norma, had been a bad mother.

They were told the name of the town where the child would be raised. It was six hours' drive from Auckland but for years it loomed in the house, as close as illness. Whenever it came up in the news, her father would clear his throat and begin talking loudly about the weather, and her mother would sit silently, ignoring his artless forecasts.

'It's just a place,' Deborah said once as her father boomed over a television report about the town. Local farmers discussed a downturn in the dairy industry, their faces grim, their heads shaking. 'It's just a word. It doesn't mean anything.'

'Whatever are you talking about, Deborah?' her mother said brightly. She picked up the dog and held him on her lap, her knuckles turning white as he squirmed to get away. 'What a good boy,' she said. 'Yes you are! Do you know, I think I'm going to make you a nice stripy jumper for winter. I've got lots of scraps of wool.'

Deborah didn't think about the baby. She got on with her life. She went to university, had boyfriends, was careful. She found it easy to meet new people, but none of the boys she brought home was quite right for her. Her mother would welcome them in, insist they sit in the most comfortable chair, serve them the choicest cut of meat, the largest and most perfect slice of cake. She would ask about their studies, murmur with interest at their comments on politics, music and other things she didn't understand. Only after they had gone would she express an opinion.

'His shirt was a bit funny, wasn't it, Roy?' she would smile. 'A bit frayed around the cuffs.' It would only ever be a little comment, and sometimes she would wait a few days before letting it slip, but it always came. 'Does he play rugby dear? No? It's just that his nose looked slightly crooked.' Or his voice would be squeaky, or his hair on the greasy side, or his father a problem drinker. And the next time Deborah saw the boy in question, all she could focus on were his flaws, even though she'd never noticed them before, and even though, as her mother said, they were little things that didn't matter a bit and it was what was inside that counted.


Deborah strolled down High Street and listened to the young people chatting and laughing in the cafés. Cars crept along the road, slowing at the judder bars like horses unwilling to jump. Eggs filled the shop windows: there were painted eggs and caramel eggs, eggs pierced by needles and emptied of their contents, eggs with surprises inside, eggs wrapped in foil and eggs in cellophane bags, soft marshmallow eggs and hollow eggs. Deborah didn't care for sweet things, but at the mini-mart – 'Everything you need under one roof' – she stopped and selected one large egg in a cardboard box with a rocket-ship on it. The gold-wrapped chocolate bulged from a hole in the rocket's belly, and through a window an astronaut waved as he headed for the milky moon.

It wasn't much of a gift, she knew. She thought of the things she had wanted to buy over the years, the things she had picked up and held and stroked in shops when she was by herself, and then put down again: first pairs of shoes, wooden trucks, cricket bats, computer games.

'Oh, and one of these,' she said at the counter, choosing a postcard from a stand.

As she emerged from the shop a young man approached her and asked for directions. She smiled at him.

'You're not far away at all,' she said, as if she were a local. And she told him where he should turn right, and where left and left again, and how long he would need to get there.

Strangely, when she began to make her way to the house, she took several wrong turns. She checked and re-checked the address on the letter, even though she knew it off by heart. She walked up and down the wide residential streets, past beds of roses, fishing gnomes, wooden butterflies settled on weatherboards, stone cats chasing stone birds. She took note of the name of each street, becoming less and less convinced of the accuracy of her mental map. Perhaps she was lost. Perhaps she had given wrong directions to the young man on High Street, and now he was lost as well. She thought of the Swedish tourist who had spent the night on top of the water tower. She wondered at what point he had stopped calling for help; at what point he had made a bed for himself from a jacket, a backpack, tried to pretend the stone encircling him was home.

And then she saw the car; one she recognised from the school. It was parked in the driveway of an ordinary house, and she looked at the number on the letterbox and saw that it matched the number on her letter, and she walked back to the end of the street and saw that the street name also matched. And she knocked on the front door.

'You must be Deborah,' said the young woman. 'Come in. Mark's just through here.'

Deborah shook hands with him, admired the garish living room, the cat, the weather. He said that it was unseasonably warm this year, that Bootsie was almost twelve but still acted like a kitten, and that his wife was in charge of the décor as he himself was colour-blind.

'It's just as well he wanted to be a teacher, and not a pilot,' said his wife. 'My cousin's colour-blind, and the air force turned him away. He was devastated.'

'I hope it hasn't been difficult for you, Mark,' said Deborah.

He shook his head. 'It's nothing. I never even think about it.'

Deborah opened her bag. 'I brought you some chocolate,' she said, placing the astronaut egg on the coffee table and wishing she had chosen differently. But his wife said thank you, and that milk chocolate was Mark's favourite, and Mark said yes, it was.

They gave her a present too; or rather, they returned it to her: a crocheted bonnet he had worn on his way home from hospital.

'My mother kept it for me, because you made it,' said Mark. 'We thought you might like to have it now, as a souvenir.'

'Thank you,' said Deborah. She smoothed the tiny bonnet on her lap, the white wool glowing like a waxing moon, and thought of her mother's busy crochet hook flashing as she made plans for the baby.

'I can't believe he was ever that little,' said his wife. 'Do you still crochet?'

'Not these days,' said Deborah. 'I've almost forgotten how.'


She declined a ride back to the motel. 'I have an errand to do on the way,' she said.

'No problem,' said Mark. 'I don't mind waiting in the car.'

She asked him to stop at the High Street post box. 'Won't be a moment,' she said, and took the postcard from her bag. She wrote her message standing on the footpath, then addressed it to her parents. The picture showed various local sights: the water tower, some farmland, the oddly symmetrical mountain. Emblazoned across the middle, as big as a swear word, was the town's name. She smiled and dropped it through the slot, then went back to the car where Mark was waiting.

He saw her to the door of unit nine and kissed her on the cheek. 'Next time you'll have to stay with us,' he said. A curtain twitched in the office window.

Deborah unfanned one of the bath towels, opened a new cake of soap and shut herself in the shower. His hair was starting to recede, she thought. He could lose a little weight. He used tea bags, not loose tea. There were some heavy metal CDs sitting on his stereo. She had seen an ashtray. Little things, things that didn't matter. His wife was lovely. He liked animals. He was a careful driver. He had laugh lines round his eyes.

As she lay in her unfamiliar bed that night, Deborah listened to the hum of the fridge and fingered the soft bonnet under her pillow. She would see her parents on Sunday evening and she would have dinner with them the way she did every Sunday; and, like every other Sunday since 1970, she would not mention Mark. She would compliment her mother on the bacon-and-egg pie or the corned beef, and they might watch the BBC drama on television. And everything would be the same as it always was, except that her card would be on its way to their letterbox.

It was Palm Sunday that week, Deborah realised as she was falling asleep. Her mother would give her a little green twig collected especially for her at Mass and would remind her that it symbolised joy. It wouldn't be from a real palm, but from the evergreen trees at the back of the church. It would hold its colour for a few weeks and then it would turn brown, but Deborah would keep it anyway.

# Saturday March 27, 1999

# Family Unit

Life changed at the Mokau River. Tribal boundaries as much as geography and local customs. 'History so often altered tack at rivers,' she said. Bernice Irwin spoke as the forest-green Volvo was obliged to slow down behind a stock truck with viscous calf shit dribbling from beneath its back palings. At the same moment she glimpsed the big stone embedded in concrete behind stumpy pillars and painted chains. 'That's the Tainui anchor stone.' Declared, rather than said it. This was her territory, history, after all. Such details were hers to announce.

'What's Tainui?' Simon asked.

'The outfit behind the worst rugby league team in the history of the game,' his father said. 'I thought that stone was tied round the entire back line but I've got it wrong. Someone must have hocked it off to help pay for the corporate box.'

'Do you have to, Tom?' Bernice said. Not even anger in her voice, simply a weariness that he boiled over so easily.

A girl spoke from the back seat. Louise was fifteen. Her voice was confident, mildly dismissive of those she spoke to. This surely was her right now that she had found God. Her best friend had taken her three months ago to the Assembly of God. She had been inundated with warmth and a spreading shimmer that her father, watching the mudflats from the veranda above Cox's Creek, described to his wife as tidal. 'It will go out as quickly as it came in.' For the moment, faith was on the flood.

Louise said, 'We ignore history at our peril, Simon.'

Her eleven-year-old brother had come to swearing at much the same time as her own conversion. He loved its disruptive power.

'God,' he said, 'friggen wanker,' not bothering even to raise his voice.

'Mum!' Louise shouted. 'Don't you even care he talks like that!'

'Don't show off, Simon,' Bernice said.

'Only the second commandment,' Louise said. 'Not that God's word matters, does it? Not if it's Simon.'

The car lurched as it took the long bridge across the river.

'I meant the Warriors,' Simon defended. 'The whole world knows they're wankers.'

'For Christ's sake,' Tom said, 'how do you expect me to drive with this zoo?'

'That's the second time,' Louise said. 'In thirty seconds!'

'Twenty,' Simon said. 'Can't even count.'

'I told you not to show off,' Bernice said. She turned and leaned across and her hand slapped down at her son's white skinny thigh. She clipped him harder than she intended. But Simon rallied and shoved his sister hard on her chest. Thought she was so cool, didn't she, just because she had tits. As if the rest of the world had never seen them before. 'Slag,' he told her.

Bernice's hand slapped on him again. The stone in her engagement ring flashed like a drop of falling water.

'Leave him, can't you!' Tom said to her. His own voice now louder than he liked to hear it. And saying it again. 'Christ!'

Louise said quietly, 'That's it. That's it then, Dad.' She scrabbled at the lock of her door and had no doubt, at least for several seconds, that she would simply rather get out. She didn't care how fast they were going, she would not ride with blasphemy.

'Louise!' As Bernice turned yet again she glimpsed the smear of moving roadway as the back door opened. Tom braked as the car left the bridge and swung in towards the grass verge. There was a moment of what later Bernice called 'cluttered' silence, the car lurching onto uneven ground and rocking to a halt. No one spoke. Even Louise knew not to push her luck and invoke the Lord. The car had turned half circle and the family, at the beginning of their weekend away, looked at the dull brown stretch of river. Simon snivelled and leaned his head on the back of his mother's seat. Bernice's hand stroked his hair. Tom looked in the rear vision mirror at his daughter's pretty, frightened face. 'You all right?' he said. 'Louise?'

'Yes, Dad,' she told him.

He turned the car back onto the road. 'Then if no one minds,' he said, 'we'll push on to Morrieson's, shall we?'


The motelier glanced at the form his guest had just filled in. Tom held out his hand for the key with its black plastic tag and embossed number eight.

'T?' the nuggetty man put to him. As if there was no holding out *here*, believe you me.

Tom already dreaded the thought of it, the two days in what looked like a state house with a tip about itself, the red brick hoop of units around its patch of grass, its trampoline, its pint-sized pool two adults could scarcely splash in at the same time. Bernice had picked the place out of a brochure. 'Matrimony,' that's what she had said, serious-jokey in a way that irritated him. 'Matrimony needs the odd brush up, don't you agree?', which meant she had phoned 300 kilometres away, booked the motel, informed the children, and then told him. The enormity of it came in on him now, as he saw the owner of the place eyeing him with what, he supposed, was supposed to pass muster as shrewdness. To think all this was actually planned, four bloody hours in a vehicle with a wife who thought premeditated flirting with her own husband was a cure for middle age. Four hours with a foul-mouthed child whose intellectual horizon was to sit at a computer downloading songs off MP3 and an adolescent driven by God knows what to sing hymns, non-stop as good as, between Pokeno and Te Kuiti. Until he could not take another verse and bellowed out to the same tune as she herself was singing, 'What a friend we have in hormones.' Even Simon, the little turncoat, had shouted at him, 'Shut up, Dad.' While Louise, milking the drama of it, said in the mild voice the Master may have used when reprimanding Peter for cutting off a non-believer's ear, 'It's better if you don't go on like that. It only shows how *small* you are.' Certainly he was in no mood now for chat with this chirpy bugger whose finger prodded at the form lying between them on the counter. 'T?', asking it again.

'Tom,' Tom said.

'Clarry,' the other man told him. He rubbed a thick forearm with his opened hand. It sounded like sandpaper. Tom was aware that his own hands were office-soft.

'Tell you what,' the amiable Clarry said. 'I know what it's like driving with a carload of kids on a warm afternoon. Drop the good lady off and you'll find the bar within crawling distance.'

'Thanks,' Tom said. This was only Taranaki but it made him think of their honeymoon in New Caledonia. Even when he had thought of something to say to the locals he was unable to say it.

Clarry took his guest's courtesy for acceptance. He looked across his shoulder through the office window. He saw his wife crossing to unit eight with a carton of milk and said, lowering his voice simply for the effect of it, 'Pity Laura's not on this arvo. That would've been another reason to quench the thirst.' He winked, conspirators together. 'Two good reasons, matter of fact.' Then, because he may have come on a touch too familiar, Clarry looked past Tom to the sleek dark car where the family waited. 'Nice to drive, like the ads say?'

'I'll know one day,' Tom said. 'When I don't have to think about something else.'

Clarry clicked his tongue, which Tom guessed was dialect for 'You needn't tell me about that one, son'.

Tom closed the car door, switched on the ignition, and placed the key to the unit in his wife's opened palm. 'Number eight,' he said.

'You were long enough in there,' Bernice said. 'These two are at it again.'

'If she'd just lay off saying the Bible at me,' Simon complained.

'See?' Bernice said.

'Yes, love,' Tom said. He eased the car round the drive towards the far unit. Clarry stood at the top of the steps, taking in the car's purring movement. He raised one thumb and jerked it slightly.

'I will bet you,' Tom said, 'any money you can think of, Simon, that that man just said "Nice one".'

'I don't even know what you're on about,' Simon said. And Tom did not know either that Clarry turned back into the office with the frowzled cat he'd have had put down years back if it hadn't been for the wife, and said, 'Aucklanders. You can smell them a mile off.'


Bernice said, 'You two bring in whatever's in the boot, OK?' and slid back the unit door along its metal grooves. There was the faintly acrid smell of a newly cleaned carpet, before she took in the sky blue duvet on the double bed, and the matching settee that was another bed in disguise, waiting to be found out. There was a television so much smaller than the one at home that she anticipated Simon's whine of complaint. The pale lemon walls were broken by the big square of a Rita Angus print, fishing boats flat and toy-like on a sea as blue as the divan. The carpet, thank heavens, was a neutral grey, what Bernice sometimes called 'family shading' because Tom's rellies, collectively, had much the same effect – inoffensive, colourless. As she stepped towards the kitchen area, the generous figure of the proprietor's wife rose from where she had placed the complimentary milk in the colour co-ordinated lemon fridge. The woman turned and startled. Both women shrieked together.

'Betty!' Bernice cried. 'It's Betty Benton!'

'Bernice! Someone pinch me will they!'

The women threw themselves together with the force of twenty years gone by without clapping eyes on each other. Tom heard the racket as he unloaded the boot and handed carry-bags, a chilly-bin, a carton of walking shoes to his reluctant children. He stepped to the door, tugging back the lightweight curtain so forcefully he heard the rip above his head as the material went limp in his hand. He saw his wife's arm around a dumpy woman's waist, while the stranger's hand, like a busy white crab, brushed over his wife's shoulders and along her cheek. Bernice beamed across at him. 'Training Coll,' she called out to him, 'can you imagine that? We even flatted together in Glenmore Street.'

'Flatted!' the other woman said. 'Slummed it, don't you mean?'

Tom strained to show interest. 'You must be Linda?' he said.

The women shrieked again, their arms flailing, swimmers in distress. 'Linda Donovan!' Betty said. 'You'd need to bundle six of her together to make one of me.'

Tom thought, unkindly, how could a woman get such a kick out of looking like that, then joking about it? It was Joan of Arc lighting her own faggots.

'Betty,' Bernice repeated. 'Betty who would have been our bridesmaid, Tom, if she hadn't been leering it up in Sydney.'

'Less said about that lot the better,' Betty said, her eyes big and rolling towards the office and a presumably unenlightened spouse.

'Clarry's wife?' Tom guessed.

'Got it in one.' Betty smiled back at him. He thought what a bastard he must be to see his wife enjoying herself so much while he resented everything about it. He tried to look jolly even as he realised that he had never used that word in his life about anything. *Jolly* for Christ's sake! He'd no more use it than Bernice would say 'leering it up', and yet that had happened too. He disliked everything about what was going on.

A moment later they all — Bernice, Tom, Betty, the kids — looked towards the tall shape who eased back the white sagging curtain and stood outlined against the afternoon sky. He was like a stick figure. He wore nothing but black, with two startlingly pale bands of naked flesh in the inches between the sleeves of his T-shirt and the top of the long mittens that stretched to above his elbows. There was a small silver skull on a black cord around his throat. His jeans tapered down to leather boots, where the skull motif was echoed in metal buckles. His hair was a dark stubble above a face preternaturally white. A nose stud glittered for a moment as his head turned and he took them in, then attended only to Louise. Very slowly his tongue emerged between his black lips, until another metal stud, the size of a ballbearing, popped into view. He looked at Louise with what he believed was a transfixing beam. 'Boris,' he said, his voice husky, irresistible. He then hitched at the rim of one of the high mittens so the bands of exposed pale flesh matched as exactly as bangles.

Tom was the only one who reacted. Almost as quietly as the Goth, he said, 'I'd get that pathetic arse out of here son before I boot your ring through that black gob of yours.' He was amazed at his own vehemence. Never in his life had he spoken so rudely to anyone. Was this part of the stress, he wondered, that Bernice insisted was getting him down? The stick figure backed out and slid into the afternoon. Betty shrieked yet again, tapping at Bernice's arm. 'Celeste Boddy's youngest, would you believe that?'

'Celeste here too!' Bernice said, her voice higher, more girlish, than her family had ever heard it.

'Brilliant, apparently,' Betty confirmed. 'Pop band of his own. Drums like an angel.' She went on to say how Celeste had married into *old* Canterbury money although her husband apparently had let a sheep station turn to custard so to speak and had no definable interests beyond breeding birds.

'Birds?' Bernice said. There was too much coming in – wasn't that the phrase her psychologist friend used about stress, about not quite being on top of the information swill that was modern life? 'He what?'

'There's a convention in town this weekend,' Betty said. 'Bird fanciers of the world unite,' which set the women off again, swathed in killing nostalgia.

Louise looked with dubious contempt at her mother and her mother's friend. She opened the small print Bible she carried with her most places and found the Song of Solomon, which she had never heard mentioned at the Assembly of God but decided she didn't half mind reading as her very own discovery. She had thought the stud on the tongue something special too. 'You always ruin things, Dad,' she said. 'Do you mean to do it, or is it just you can't help it?'

Tom sighed, jangled the change in his trouser pocket, and turned from the unit. He leaned against the door jamb, looking out at the car park. Two men stood at the back of a four-wheel drive, lifting with almost exaggerated care a large box from the vehicle onto the ground. When it turned side on he saw the wire mesh and realised it was a cage of cockatoos. There was a quick panicking flutter of wings as the cage tilted and then settled on the ground. He could feel for the birds. For some reason not apparent to him a quote from Stage II English more than twenty years before came into his mind. 'Most men,' – wasn't that how it went? – 'live lives of quiet desperation.' He couldn't remember who said it.

'What are you saying?' Simon asked him.

'Muttering,' Tom said, 'that's all.' He was surprised that the boy edged in against him, leaning on him as he used to do until a year or so ago when the idea of affection towards his parents turned overnight to anathema. But he pressed against him now and his father was grateful for it. He touched his son's rough tangled hair and said, 'All right there are we, cobber?'

Simon looked up at him. He said, 'That was wicked what you said to him, Dad. Telling that dick piss off like that.'


Tom walked around the town. The tall concrete water tower seemed to loom over him at every turn. But he could see why his wife liked the place, and he hoped the long drive, the couple of idle days, would do them good. The town was compact and neat. It was laid out. It didn't come by chance. (He thought of Huntly, Levin, the towns of his own childhood, which he loathed in memory.) This was pastureland and immaculate paddocks that became a town for a few hundred yards, then again turned back into pasture and paddocks, after the interruption of asphalt and clumped commercial buildings and ordered streets. He walked along a side road, past Cudby's Family Funeral Home and a

125

second-hand shop with high, old-fashioned hospital bed-ends stacked along one wall.

Tom pondered, in a vague way, how he quite liked the idea of order until it took him over and then he hated it. Well, grew bored with it anyway. Bernice, on the other hand, loved it more than anything in the world. Which is why she made lists of tasks for the family to do and attached them to the front of the fridge with magnetic sunflowers; why she told you her schoolteacher tidbits as you drove through the country, because that put the past in order as well. Sometimes when they visited friends he yearned for the mess he glimpsed through half-closed bedroom doors or saw on kitchen shelves where neatness had quite broken down. Yet the thought of Bernice not there to do it, not ordering the sun and the moon, as he put it when they argued together, was inconceivable. That was looking into the gulf. He now sat at a pavement table in the neatly cobbled main street and thought of his panic last year when she was sick. Then thought, thank God I don't need to think of that. Not any longer. A basket of geraniums bloomed above his head. He smiled at the friendly girl who told him it was cappuccino or nothing, when he asked for a latte. As he waited he watched the groups at the other tables. Bernice's being ill had brought home to him what mattered and what didn't. And her back teaching again and as good as cleared by her specialist, and yet this gloom, so often, even now when there was no need for it. Here he was within spitting distance of a partnership in the firm, and both the kids were certainly brighter than he had been at school, even if Louise drove him up the wall at the moment and Simon had a tongue like the inside of a sewer.

'There we are,' the girl said, putting the coffee in front of him. The cinnamon froth had spilled over the side and ran in streaks towards the pool at the bottom of the saucer. 'That's perfect,' Tom told her. The girl moved back and the geraniums swayed their bright red clots as her shoulder nudged against them. He felt a touch sorry for himself, drinking coffee alone like this. Because Bernice, when he had asked if she had fancied a walk, said she would read her novel for a bit, did he mind? 'Remember I was brought up round here,' she said. 'Stratford, anyway. I don't *need* to see it.'

'It was your idea,' he reminded her.

'To come here,' she said. 'Not to have to gawp at it.'


She would have the unit to herself for an hour or so at least. It was odd, she supposed, how she liked motels, yet she was hardly ever in one, was she? Tom was so convinced the family bach where he spent his own boyhood was everyone else's idea of a perfect holiday as well. She disliked the sea, in fact, although that wasn't something she let on even to Louise. This was as close as you could expect to get to bliss, she supposed, after a certain age – or was that too sardonic? A room that wasn't your own, dishes you didn't have to do, simply a story to slip into when no one else was around. Those car trips too – she wondered why they gave her such pleasure, especially since her illness, simply sitting there, thinking of nothing in particular, watching hills rise and recede, the coastline running its scribble on and on? Safety and distance and hints of infinity, so many things rubbing together and yet no compulsion, no desire much even, to untangle them, to sort things out. Simply to think, this is all happening, I am the centre of all this.

How she loved it, for instance, even this afternoon, when they first saw the mountain. She had seen it almost every day for the first twelve years of her life, before the Power Board shifted her father south. She had liked those nights when her father and a group of men in oilskins and heavy boots stood in the kitchen and drank whisky from small thick glasses and said they'd start the search again at dawn. She would lie in bed, while the wind shook the house like the dice box when they played Ludo, and watch the skinny strips of light beneath her bedroom door and hear her father's boots clunk on the floor in the next room. Two or three times a year someone would be lost on the mountain. Most times they were found, and her mother would say how an experience like that aged them. Young men looked middle-aged if they'd been up there for days, 'battling the elements'. Her mother always said that. And once or twice the lost were not found until they were dead, and there was an English woman called Phoebe who was never found at all. Bernice had thought of her this afternoon. Still somewhere up there, she supposed, as she had supposed when she was a girl and tried to imagine it, Phoebe, whose name made her think of fluffy pale hair, lying against the ugly scoria, the English coins from her dropped purse sprinkled around her. Even now, that's how Bernice visualised the bones that were never seen, the sixpences and shillings that would tell you, the minute you picked them up, where the bones had come from. 'Your heart goes out,' her mother had said, when she unrolled the paper from New Plymouth and the young blonde woman looked straight at them. 'Your heart goes out to her parents, God help them.'

Bernice let the novel lie open on her chest. Even those pictures, she thought, even motel bedroom pictures she quite liked for a night or two. Lion Rock rested on the sea like a chunk of blancmange on a plate. And another picture that up close said 'View from Fanthams Peak', showing a swirl of competing greens across a shoulder of ash. They were art class stuff, but she liked them. Someone had taken the trouble. It was real paint; you could tell if you licked your finger and prodded them. It was one mind, one gift, however limited, taking life in on its own terms, then trying to put it down for someone else to look at. 'There,' the pictures said, 'this is real because it is mine.' Yet she'd have hated them at home.

'Minimalist,' she had said to Tom when she bought them their joint Christmas present. 'It soothes, doesn't it?' 'So does aspirin,' Tom had said. They laughed together and knew they would never see most things the same way. And he made love to her on the sofa beneath the exquisite black picture she had looked at over his shoulder while he lost his breath, and 'yes,' she had said to him quietly, 'yes,' and held him against her. They would never be closer than that, although this was something Tom failed to understand. It was never enough, wherever he was. At work. With the children. With her, especially. What more could she give him, what else was there for her to declare? And yet his feeling, she knew, that she was somehow holding back. As if there were something to her beyond his knowing, beyond what she gave. Life isn't like that. If only she could make him see. He looked at life as that painter there tried to look at a view: there were demarcations and blocks, this part so different to that, and over it all there was *placing* things, there was control. But it couldn't be like that. You walked through the dapple of so many competing things. It was the flow of them, not the pattern, that made this day real and the next quite as real again. And it was so hard to put into words. You said what you knew, the way the poetry she taught to the bursary girls said as much as it could, but then there was the point when it could say no more – the flow kept on, but you were here. That's all you could say.

'Mum?'

Bernice turned to Simon, who stood at the bedroom door. What on earth was the boy carrying? She raised herself on her elbow, and her book clattered to the floor. 'I was completely out to it,' she said. 'Sorry, love.' Then, taking in the solemn moon face level there against her son's, 'Who on earth have you got there?'

'Charlie,' Simon said. 'Charlie belongs to Lisa.' He jerked his arm so that the child's weight was more easily managed. He laughed. 'See him?' How long was it since she had heard him laugh like that, in sheer good humour, the surly foul-mouthed yobbo that so distressed his father quite discarded.

'And who is Lisa?' Bernice said.

'She's in the kitchen,' Simon told her. 'She's cool.' A word that could not carry a fraction of what was in the boy's mind as he said it.

The woman had turned from bending at the stove as he looked in at her from the corridor behind the dining room. She wore a green dress that went almost to her feet and as she stood up, he could not believe how lovely the long fall of her hair looked as she flicked it back; and her arms, which were this colour like honey, rose and scooped great handfuls of her hair and settled it behind her head. As she turned from the stove the front of her dress had fallen forward and there was nothing underneath, only Them, big as grapefruit. He felt his face flare as though someone held a torch beneath it, because she'd seen him looking; but she just held his eye and smiled at him. She did not even ask him who he was or what he was doing there, looking down her dress. Instead she said to him, as though she'd been talking to him already and was carrying on from there, 'Twelve people in for dinner tonight, the chef's late and now the stove's on the blink.'

A baby in a high chair behind the kitchen table clattered a plastic plate onto the tiled floor. 'Don't you start,' she told the baby, smiling still, not raising her voice in the least. Simon bent to take up the rolling plate that ran towards him like a hoop. His fingers scrabbled the dab of mashed whatever it was from off the floor and flicked it at the edge of the plate.

'You could get Clarry if you like,' the woman told him. When she talked to him her eyes were right on his, holding him as if she'd set him there until she decided to let him go. He looked back because he knew she wouldn't mind. And he still said nothing, glazed with an enchantment he had no idea of defining because he had never known such a thing before. She told him, 'That old guy with hair like a dunny brush? Reckon you can find him?'

'Reckon,' Simon told her. He found the man she wanted, who was tightening the canvas on the trampoline.

'Only children up to ten,' the man said, when he saw the boy beside him. 'Can't have you big jokers bouncing on it.'

Clarry was unaware how he withered in the boy's contempt. 'She wants you,' Simon said.

Clarry seemed amused. 'She's the cat's mother,' he said, 'haven't you ever heard that?'

Simon – taking in the bristled hair, the fat nose, the grin where one tooth was such a different colour from the others – thought, you dopey old dork. But for *her* sake he said politely, 'The lady in the kitchen. She wants you right away.'

Stubble head winked at Simon and said, 'The trouble with ladies, that, take my word for it.' He slapped one hand against the edge of the trampoline and hooted. Simon thought, have I missed a joke or something? And why wasn't shitface here jumping when she asked for him? 'The stove,' he said. 'It's on the blink.'

'That's news is it?' Clarry said. He seemed amused all over again.

Back in the big kitchen the baby was bawling and smashing a spoon against the tray of its highchair. The lady, who was lovelier than anyone Simon had ever seen, looked as though she might cry. Her hair had fallen forward again and covered half her face. Clarry grunted and crouched and looked into the oven – like some old perv looking in a window, Simon thought. He pulled at a lever at the bottom of the oven and pressed a switch beside the dials. There was a 'pop' where the gas jet sprang up and the old joker's face turned blue in the light. He said to Lisa, as he grunted again and stood up, 'I'll send Betty across to help out. That bird mob can be a handful.'

'Quiet, Charlton,' Lisa said. Simon hated to think how upset she was, how frazzled, as his grandmother would say when someone got bothered like this. Then he thought of something brilliant. It was like those drawings in comics where 'Wham!' is written in big letters and there's a splashy flash over everything. He saw Lisa bending over near the highchair to pick up the child's furiously thrown spoon. Her dress fell forward again. Even more than before. He said, 'I could take him for a walk if you like. I wouldn't scare him.'

'Oh, would you now?' Lisa said. She hoisted the child from its wooden cage, rubbing his face with a hanky she wore in the puffy top of her sleeve, before she handed him across. 'He loves being with men,' she said. Simon felt the pelting in his chest. Then the most extraordinary thing happened. After he had taken the boy, who had stopped his racket just like that, Lisa said, 'Oh, you don't know how sweet you are doing this!' and kissed the top of Simon's head. He would look after the baby for a year if she wanted him to. Then she said, 'Talk nicely to him and he'll be good as gold.' Talk nicely, is that all it took? He'd show her what talking nicely was.

'So I'm taking care of him,' he told his mother when she looked up. He'd never seen her so surprised. Or Dad, if it came to that, who came into the unit behind him. 'It's five o'clock,' Dad said, 'I've walked round for two hours and there's nothing else to see.'

'I reckon I'll take him for a walk by myself,' Simon said. 'I've got his pushchair out here.' Charlie, delighted at hearing his favourite word, jigged on Simon's arm and tugged at his hair. Simon laughed and grabbed the fat jerking wrist. 'Come off it,' he said. 'You'd better behave or you'll know about it.'

'My God,' Bernice said, when Simon had left the unit and the wheels of the pushchair crunched on the metal path outside the window. 'Are there miracles, Tom, or are there?'

'There's worse than miracles,' her husband said. He had seen one at the last corner as he walked back from the main street. High up, where you'd expect visions to take place, he had spotted the concrete tower and Louise standing on its platform, her arm flung out to whatever it was she saw. Beside her, thin and black as a tarred broom, stood the Goth he had ordered from his sight. Tom was appalled and puzzled. He experienced, as he did quite often these days, the sense that certainties wobbled, that the ground tremored beneath him. His fastidious God–bothering daughter against the skyline with *that*!

'The young like being together,' Bernice reminded him. 'No one's choosy much at that age.' She put her hand across her husband's. 'It's not the end of the world.' Which even Tom might have conceded had he heard his daughter say, her hand flung towards Mount Taranaki, 'I lift up my eyes to the Lord, the Lord who giveth joy to my youth.' Or seen the emaciated young man, who had booted in the door at the back of the tower for them to get in, lean towards her and ask, 'How come you talk like that? Are your family foreign?'

Louise said, 'It's God talking. I'm simply passing it on.'

'He's more of a dude than I thought,' Boris said. And she started, half chanting them for him, verses she recently had learned.

'Can't you hear that with a decent backing?' her new friend said. He told her to keep going, this jasmine stuff, this flesh like lilies gig, it knocked the shit out of Marilyn Manson. But she stopped when she was half way through a section she really liked, and looked at him. 'Show me,' she said. 'Show me your tongue, will you?'

He let it emerge slowly, like something that had not seen daylight for a long time. The stud was even bigger than she expected. It looked so bright and silvery and mean. Without asking him even she raised her hand and one finger outstretched like in the famous ceiling, almost touched its glittering hardness.

'It licks like you wouldn't believe,' he said.

'Shhh!' she told him. Their hands were now very close together on the concrete ledge. She turned from him and said in a voice that made him think she was talking to someone else, but knew he would get a buzz off it as well, 'My love, my dove, my beautiful one.'


And so life in Taranaki seemed to have taken on a fresh glow for the family. It may even have bathed it in a beam that lasted into the next day, had it not been for dinner that evening in the motel's pastel dining room, whose pink table napkins had been folded into upright semicircular fans by Simon after he'd returned Charlie to his mother. 'You could do something else to help me,' she had said.

Boris the Goth sat at the next table to the Irwins, with a mother who leaned across and joked with Bernice because she too had been at Training Coll, would you believe it? They reminisced about Jack Shallcrass and Jack Lasenby, with whom Celeste had been in love and never dared let on. 'And so I married into Birdsville and Jack wrote upsetting books about teenagers.' She meant that she had married a man whose passion was breeding cage birds, whose study in upper Wadestown would tinkle in an earthquake as the rows of medals swayed on their velvet pads and the trophies jiggled on their shelves. She was waiting for him now. 'The rage he gets in when he doesn't win, mind!' Then the restaurant doors swung back and a dozen enthusiasts, that moment back from the Mokoia Hall where the bird convention met, poured in to take seats at their tables. 'Drinks all round!' Celeste's husband called out. His name was Cliff Macdonald. Elated at having cleaned up for the third successive year in several categories – the Timnek African Grey, the Green Winged Macaw – Cliff now stood behind his wife's chair, his hands on her shoulders. He grinned at the next table as he was introduced, and told Bruce – which was Boris's real name – to shift his uneducated chuff and bring in the bottles from the boot. When the event occurred.

A tall man at the doorway balanced in front of him a cage almost too large for him to manoeuvre. In its semi-darkness there was an agitation of wings and shrill avine cries. The milling bird people, still finding their tables, paused in their exuberant chatting. Tom heard one of them, a woman in heels so high he expected her to lurch at any moment, say behind him, as if to herself, 'Oh no. Not this.' This being, he supposed, what the tall man with a thin sliver of spit glittering across his chin now did. He dropped the cage to the floor and with a wide exaggerated sweep brought his hand round to the catch on the front, and tugged the hook free from its staple. As the man called out, 'You and your birds, Macdonald!' three cockatoos swooped into the dining room. The creatures zoomed across the tables. A sauce bottle twirled and smashed to the floor. One of the birds rose to perch on a curtain rod above the diners, another clawed at the shoulder of a Japanese tourist.

'Sprung,' Bernice's friend announced with enormous coolness as she looked at her husband. The woman in the high heels pushed through the confusion to the tall man behind the grounded cage. She raised one foot behind her, reached back to remove its shoe, then used it to beat the man whose chest she barely reached. He made no effort to stop her, even when the heel ripped open his neat striped shirt. There was a look of great fulfilment about him.

Simon leaped from his chair, beside himself with the shambles. He shoved at his sister's shoulder, telling her to look, couldn't she, Holy Ghosts all over the fucken show! But Louise was caught in a different drama. She could not believe it and yet there it was, a few feet in front of her. Boris who had lied for her sake about his name now slipped a stiletto from the side of his boot. The blade was not much wider than a nail nor longer than the kind of hatpin you could buy at the Victoria Market. One of the birds, perhaps recognising Macdonald, swooped above the next table then whirred, braking, its wings spread wide, balanced in mid-air. A half second in which the black-mittened arm shot forward. The stiletto flowed with a quick slick of light and there the bird was, impaled, briefly shrieking, then dead, a white heavy rag at the end of the Goth's upraised arm. He tilted the blade so the bird slid onto the pink cloth in front of his father. 'That's from mum,' he said.

'Jee-zuz!' Simon said. Before one woman shrieked and Bernice's friend Celeste from Training Coll, who had been in love but never spoken out, stood up and walked between the tables. Poised and unfussed, she stopped in front of the woman with one shoe who now sat sobbing on a chair just inside the door. She stopped and said to her, so the entire room heard in the now extraordinary hush, 'It's not Macdonald's cock I give a damn about. It's his rotten taste in birds.' Her son walked out behind her, the silence ringing with exhilaration. Then Clarry clapped his hands and said, a touch absurdly, 'Dinner will now proceed as normal.' Already, the efficient Betty was wrapping newspaper round the dead bird that lay, oddly serene, in Cliff Macdonald's lap. There was the sense of order restored. The Japanese addressed their steaks as though such events were local custom.


'That was one choice thing last night,' Simon said. No one had spoken for a hundred kilometres, until the change of tempo as the tyres left the normal highway for the long Mokau Bridge. The brown placid expanse of the river lay to the right of the car, while over there to the left, Tom imagined the turmoil of the river water meeting with the sea.

Lisa had given Simon a photo of herself and Charlton, and told him it was a long time since she'd met anyone so helpful. 'You'd be perfect,' she had told him, 'if you didn't swear.' He'd helped her again in the kitchen that morning, while his parents stayed in bed longer than he'd ever known them to – were they sick or something? Louise was at church with her new friend. Simon heard Clarry snorting and telling Lisa's mother how that rooster with the god-awful missus had asked him at seven o' bloody clock where the police station was, would you believe it, he needed to report two missing cockatoos? Simon told the others about it now and the family laughed together.

Then, 'Thoreau,' Tom said suddenly.

'What about him?' Bernice was patting Simon's hand where it lay on the back of her seat.

'I couldn't think of his name. Yesterday. "Most men live, etcetera". You must know the quote?'

'Most women too,' she said. Tom's fingers spanned just above his wife's knee, as he moved his hand across from the wheel. And risking a joke that might not come off, he half turned his head to ask Louise, 'What's happened to the Bible there? We haven't heard a quote since the motel.'

'He asked me for it,' Louise said. 'You can't say no to someone who asks for the Word.' And taking in the cosiness between her parents and Simon sucking up to them, she said, 'No one minds if I get my nipple pierced? No one minds that, do they?' She shoved a hand between her parents' heads and opened her fist. A silver stud, the size of a ball bearing, lay on her opened palm.

Tom surprised himself by quoting what he had read in bed last night, in the Gideon from the bedside drawer. 'Thy breasts are as the fruit of Lebanon, as globes of alabaster.'

The car had taken the diversion out of Awakino and was entering the rugged narrowness of the gorge before Simon said, so quietly the others hardly heard him, 'That's right, Dad. That's exactly what they're like.'

# Spring with the Sumerbottoms

I'm here because of Elvis Presley. The guy has a long reach, not just beyond the grave, but from the other side of the world. Here, in this small town hemmed in by dairy cows, is the Elvis Presley Memorial Record Room, reputed to have the most extensive collection in Australasia.

My editor told me to get up here and do a feature for the weekend leisure and arts section. She knows I don't much care for Presley; that adds to her enthusiasm. So I'm at Morrieson's Motel, which is just off the main street. I'm in unit two and listening to the owner, Clarry, go on about the Memorial Room.

Clarry's a retired dairy farmer, of course: perhaps that's why he doesn't want to put down my regulation pottle of milk for unit two and leave me to unpack. Clarry tells me the Elvis Presley Room is private and do I realise that? That I'll need to make arrangements to visit and so on.

I've been to this town once before, nearly twenty years ago. Maybe even before Elvis Presley came. In my first university year at Massey I lived in a hostel, dutifully following the advice of the school counsellor. The theory is that students become friends with a wide range of peers and maintain contact with them throughout the rest of their time, even if subsequent years are spent in flats or boarding houses. Presumably that prevents them from becoming emotionally isolated, or bonding too closely with inappropriate folk.

When I left the hostel after one year, I took considerable care to avoid a good many of the people I'd met there, and in some of them I noticed a similar disposition towards myself. A colony of late adolescents is a restrictive introduction to adult life. That careers counsellor, however, who was also a collector of Antarctic memorabilia, was indirectly the reason I met Andrew Sumerbottom and his family. Andrew's room was in a different block, with a better view to the campus, but he was doing a couple of the same units, and was one of the few guys with a reasonable game of tennis. He had a strong baseline game with few unforced errors and a heavy serve, but he wasn't comfortable at the net.

He was blond, cheerful, slightly overweight, and apparently took no offence at the fun made of his absurd name – sun bum, spring arse, winter top. Within the hostel he had a reputation for clownish amiability that passed as popularity, but few of us, I think, progressed from being acquaintances to being friends. His good humour deflected those enquiries intended for a heartfelt response. Games and rituals he liked – activities of agreed and predictable routine. I noticed in his room books on career success and personal development, but he said it was just stuff that had been there when he moved in. He had a gorilla suit, which was famous in the hostel, and even his regular clothes were better than those of most of us. In the winter I noticed that his coat was special. It had a blue lining, and suede lips on the pockets. Ready cash was always a problem though, as it was for almost all of us.

In the spring, before exams but after lectures had finished, he invited me to go home with him to Taranaki for a weekend. We had been working late in the library, and he gave the invitation awkwardly as we walked back to the hostel. We both knew it was something rather different in that time of tennis, shared tutorials and casual company. Maybe with the end of the year in sight he felt able to open up a bit.

Mrs Sumerbottom came in to collect us on the Friday afternoon. 'Call me Miranda,' she said. I imagine the invitation was less natural informality and more the wish to avoid being called Mrs Sumerbottom. Miranda was blonde like her son, but underweight in comparison. She was attractive in a slightly desiccated way, and had a tremulous intensity that hurried her words and caused her blonde bob to quiver. 'Such a delight to meet you at last,' she said. Her wrists were showing from her Country Road shirt and the tendons on the underside stood out parallel and pale beneath the skin like brittle spaghetti. 'I never get accustomed to the city traffic,' she said, as Andrew and I put our bags into the ageing Toyota. Miranda sat forward and very upright to drive, her unobtrusive chest almost brushing the wheel, as if that way she could gain a fractional advantage to deal with emergencies. The gear lever she treated as if it were electrified, her hand making apprehensive sorties towards it, then giving the stick a sudden wrench and releasing it as she felt the shock. 'Now tell me all about yourself, Hugh.' My name was pronounced with positive emphasis, maybe so she could the better remember it, and she swivelled her head in a quick flash so that she could make eye contact. Then, before I could begin to reply, there was just the back of the trembling, blonde bob again.

The Sumerbottoms lived here, in this dairy town. Mr Sumerbottom used to have a thriving dental practice in Wellington, but someone in the hostel told me that there'd been some professional misconduct, largely hushed up, and the family had come down in the world in both economic and demographic terms. If that was true, then the house they'd bought was appropriate. It was one of the few grand older homes, and it stood near the edge of the township on a section that must have been over an acre. Full grown oaks, pines and sycamores shaded the rough lawn, and the gravel paths almost claimed back by the weeds. The trees crowded the two-storeyed weatherboard house, even on that section, so that it was almost always in shadow. It was a property that had a sense of past gentility and future potential, both of which must have appealed to the Sumerbottoms, but there were the failings of the present also. The last paint job had been a cheap one, and the high guttering left rust trails down the weatherboards. One of the small stone lions that guarded the front steps had lost a paw, several of the hall leadlights were damaged, and the furniture was a menagerie of styles.

'We're taking things one at a time,' Miranda said as she gave me the tour. 'You need to live in a place a while to know what's best for it. We're almost sure the flooring is kauri.'

I followed her up the worn carpet of the stairway to the room where I was to sleep. It had a small, black iron fireplace blocked with a flap of breakfast food carton. 'You'll love the birdsong,' said Miranda, 'but we found that they sometimes come down the chimneys for some reason.' It was an ugly, small room with bare boards that may have been kauri for all I knew. One light hung from a fabric-coated cord, and the bed had Flintstone transfers on the headboard. 'Such a marvellous vista,' she said, and so it was: a powerful oak to one side and on the other a view over a scatter of houses towards Mount Taranaki.

One patch in the wilderness of the lawn had been roughly mown, and on it was a new trampoline, its bright, commercial colours at odds with all about it. Miranda told me they'd bought it for the children of home-stay guests. That was how the Sumerbottoms planned to make a go of it all: an elegant, patrician home-stay property for wealthy people from the cities. At that small window of an upstairs room, I realised that my view was not at all what Miranda looked upon. She saw the complete and ideal restoration, and allowed hopeful deceit to blind her to the truth that she didn't have the money to achieve it. She bought a new patio awning, a gate sign with heraldic device, rimu kitchen furniture from a restaurant foreclosure, a cheap red and green trampoline, while all the time beneath such cosmetics the antiquated plumbing system boomed in malfunction, the slate tiles cracked and slid, the massive tree roots heaved up the brick wall at the front gate. I didn't have the heart to ask her how many families they'd had to stay. I excused myself from her fixed optimism and went to find Andrew.

The Sumerbottoms had a daughter much younger than Andrew. Diedre would have been no more than eleven or twelve, and she came home from school with the same vulnerable eagerness of her mother. She took a shine to me and wanted us to play swingball together. 'Don't go bothering Hugh,' her mother told her indulgently, and so Diedre and I stood in the long grass not far from the trampoline and used purple plastic bats to keep the yellow ball going.

'Andy never plays with me,' she said directly, and Andrew, sitting on the veranda steps, gave a smile clumsy with embarrassment as I acted out my role as guest. Diedre had a pony tail, and as she jumped and twisted to hit the ball, her pale hair, her thin arms and legs, were caught in the dapples of late afternoon sun through the confining trees. 'Play properly, play properly,' she shouted if I seemed to be holding back at all. I hardly knew her, most likely we'd never meet again, nor recognise each other if we did, for she was growing quickly and her gender allowed an escape from the name of Sumerbottom. I wondered how much longer she would retain her easy, unquestioning affection.

Mr Sumerbottom returned in the stillness of late afternoon, bouncing his small car over the roots at the entrance, and apologised, after meeting me, for holding up the meal. 'Another session with the accountant. Jesus,' he told Miranda, and to Andrew and me, 'Wait till you have to deal with GST and all that carry on.' He was well-dressed, well-groomed and he flapped his hands in front of him as if warding off a flurry of financial paperwork. He tried an easy smile, but it twitched at the corners, and Miranda's head trembled. 'Anyway, anyway,' he said, 'What have you people been up to?' and he left to wash before the meal. Mr Sumerbottom was darker than the rest of the family, but just as lean as his wife and daughter. I wondered where Andrew got his round face, his heavy arms and legs. Mr Sumerbottom moved and talked in bursts and had times of almost dummy-like passivity in between.

We had tea in the big kitchen with the attractive foreclosed furniture and fine, old, blue and white porcelain tiles above the sink. Only a few were badly damaged. The meal was of that variety to which I became accustomed, but not reconciled, during my time there: largely uncooked, cold and vegetable – potato salad, bean sprouts, salsa, bread, pasta and nuts, couscous, tomatoes, rocket and lettuce. True, there was the smell of salmon, but the pale, fragmentary substance of it was elusive amongst the greenery. Andrew's addiction to burgers during the academic year and the gracile frames of the rest of the family were sufficiently explained.

Unlike his wife, Mr Sumerbottom wasn't sensitive about the family surname, and never volunteered a Christian one. Without prompting he told me that the origin was the old English word, summer, meaning a large, horizontal beam used in construction.

'So there you are then,' he said, as if satisfying my query. 'We're builders from way back, from Warwickshire in fact. And we certainly need to be builders in this house.' He leant over the table towards Diedre and began to sing, 'We're builders, builders, builders. We're builders, builders, builders.' After each repetition his voice went up an octave. 'We're builders, builders, builders.' Diedre began to sing too, and Mr Sumerbottom then made conducting motions to the rest of us as a sign to join in. Miranda took it up immediately, and then Andrew and myself. 'We're builders, builders, builders.'

So we sat amidst the salads, and sang the extempore Sumerbottom genealogy. Diedre enjoyed it immensely, Miranda was seized with febrile gaiety, and Mr Sumerbottom seemed delighted with his improvisation and broke off several times to cast his head back and give a machine gun laugh. His dark, soft hair was thrown back from his forehead when he did so. But then he was suddenly still and silent while the rest of us were left chanting. I didn't look at Andrew.

He and I helped with the washing up, and then walked down to the pub. After a term drinking in the same city bars full of students, I found it strange that Andrew and I were such a youthful minority among the regulars there. The locals looked up as we came in, and were baffled to find they didn't know us, as people are in very small places. We took our beer on to the veranda and sat in the dusk facing a Wrightsons store across the road. A window full of gumboots, drench and slick parkas. Andrew said nothing about his family. We talked about varsity and the hostel, with all the more freedom because the year there was almost over. Both of us, it turned out, had decided to go flatting for our second year.

Andrew was hoping to go in with some ex private school girls, he said. The parents of one of them had bought a house close to Massey to rent out. My own plans weren't so promising: two guys from the same rugby team who said a room would be coming up in their flat, which was a jerry-built addition to an old dump in Pitt Street.

The bar was just starting to fill up when Andrew and I left.

We walked back to the Sumerbottoms' section and warily made our way through the extra darkness of the trees to the house. There was just one outside bulb, on an arched bracket above the front steps, and its buttery glow had little penetration. The stone lion with missing paw matched its twin in an Assyrian pose, and Miranda's thick, Trade Aid door mat was jaundiced in the artificial light.

The Sumerbottoms weren't downstairs. 'I should say goodnight to your folks,' I told Andrew, but he said it was okay because they'd be watching television in their room. So I said goodnight to him at least, a courtesy we never bothered with in the hostel, and went up to my room with the Flintstone transfers and the narrow black fireplace blocked with cardboard to keep the birds out.

On my bed was a matching towel and flannel set. The flannel was folded in a way that made it stand up as a small pyramid on the towel, and the pale blue of the set was repeated in an individual round soap no bigger than an egg yolk. I imagined Miranda's absorption as she searched the shops for such trivial but achievable perfection, while all the time the borer had the old house by the throat and the guttering rusted out. And in an airing cupboard somewhere, she would have a dozen matching powder blue sets awaiting the rich people she dreamed of as guests.

I took the towel along the top hallway to the bathroom, and when I turned on the upright, chrome taps a cacophony of snorts and hiccups began far away in the plumbing. The eventual flow and temperature were in inverse proportion to the noise that heralded them. The lavatory was on a lead sheet base, which was cool enough even then to make me wonder how it would be on the feet in winter, but the cistern was new and its gilt handle gleamed.

Later, as I lay with Barney Rubble and Bam Bam on the single bed and watched the tip of a fir tree against the sky, I wondered who had built the place, and how many families had been part of its glory days and then slow decline. I saw the first proud owners carting water to the oaks and sycamores, which now were higher than the house, and the workmen rolling out a resplendent fleur-de-lis carpet strip down the kauri hall and crimping the sides with brass. Old houses retain something of the lives within them even when the people are dead or gone: smells most of all. Home-made quince jelly and apricot jam, damp gaberdines and galoshes at the hall stand, a reek of mortality from the room where the old lady is dying. Sweat and tobacco and mutton fat and yellow laundry soap as hard as cracked cheese. The favoured perfumes; the lavender sachets, talcs, and potpourri jars. By the favourite possie in the sunroom may linger the living smell of the black Labrador buried long ago beneath the macrocarpa. White roses in the front room, and the fragrance of happiness floating in with childish laughter. Why should everything of experience be lost just because people don't remember any more?

The next morning there was nothing cooked for breakfast of course; I'd twigged to that. Halves of grapefruit, muesli, yogurt, juice, croissants, and toast in a chrome rack with a ring to carry it. A fine show on the crisp table-cloth, and I saw Miranda look back from the bench in innocent appreciation of her own artistry. Everything in her life was seen as if it were a magazine layout, and judged that way.

Miranda had development plans for the day, and we were the workers she had in mind. She had begun the creation of a patio outside the sunroom door. There was a large heap of used bricks crushing a yellowed rhododendron, and a few tentative lines of bricks were set in the lawn immediately beside the steps. She had at first carefully removed all the old mortar, but then become more impatient. Andrew and I took out turfs and levelled an area, laid some bedding sand, and chose bricks to put down. Mr Sumerbottom made a show of assistance, mucking round with pegs and string to mark out the final boundaries, but well before eleven he went off with his golf-clubs, and a wave as he bounced down the drive. 'It's so important that he has a complete change of pace from the pressure of his weekday surgery,' Miranda told us. 'People don't realise the level of accountability in the professions these days at all.' She had new gardening gloves to protect her hands and carried bricks one at a time. 'When the trees are topped,' she said, 'this will be one of the warmest spots on the section, and it could be set up for barbecues, maybe Devonshire Teas.' Andrew and I could see that there weren't nearly enough bricks to reach the string with which Mr Sumerbottom had sketched his wife's ambition, and we didn't grieve. The patio of used bricks would become yet another of those stalled improvements that were apparent everywhere in the place: the wainscoting half stripped beneath the stairs; the pink primer on the worst of the window frames; the new garden plot by the road gate, which had become a riot of twitch, the laundry tubs lying on the floor and the pipes to which they'd been connected plugged with corks. After a month or two the weathered string would be broken, and the sand pile scratched out by cats and dogs, while Miranda searched the small ads, if she remembered, for more bricks.

Diedre had a friend to play, to show that she had equal rights of hospitality within the family no doubt. The friend was a solid, freckled girl, all smiles, heavy brows, the complexion of an unripe strawberry, and just a year or two from the devastating realisation that she was plain. At our healthy lunch, when all the bricks had been placed, both girls were happy and talkative, and there was just one early moment, when the friend surveyed the table, that her face allowed a fleeting but poignant bewilderment at all the glistening greenery, pale vegetable flesh and vinaigrette.

Andrew and I planned to play tennis at the high school courts in the afternoon, but the Telfers arrived soon after the meal. A massive, four-wheel drive gleaming in dark blue and towing a jet boat. Mr Telfer came part way up the rough drive and then realised that he wouldn't be able to turn because of the trees, so he just switched off there. He and his wife came smiling towards the veranda, sure of a welcome although they had given no warning of a visit. Wealth and affability are conducive to social ease, and besides they had been close neighbours when the Sumerbottoms lived in Island Bay. Mr Telfer wore a red, linen shirt, pale trousers and a half smile, as if a successful joke still lingered in his mind. Mrs Telfer was taller than her husband, more stylish but less handsome, and careless of her arms and legs so that they always seemed to be reaching, flexing, crossing – blocking the passage of other people. 'Miranda, how wonderful,' she said, and claimed her with a long, silvered arm. 'We thought we'd drop in on the off chance,' he said. 'We're going to do some boating for a day or two.'

Andrew got a beer for Mr Telfer, who sat smiling on the step next to a lion and showed both interest and knowledge concerning university courses. He was a member of the vice-chancellor's industry advisory panel at Vic, though he said modestly that he couldn't figure why they wanted him.

Miranda took Mrs Telfer on her tour of the house and grounds, and we heard their voices advancing and retreating as the two women wandered through the rooms and then over the large section. Diedre and her friend followed for a time, attracted by the novelty of Mrs Telfer's extravagant arms and legs, but then they tired of the long stops during which Miranda outlined her plans, and went to watch television. 'Of course,' Miranda would say, 'there's just so much to be done, and you can't get the tradespeople you want at a drop of the hat out here. I'm determined not to rush it. I want to do it just the once and do it right. I've had a really good landscape person recommended, who used to write regularly for *Contemporary* magazine.'

Mrs Telfer was entirely diplomatic and encouraging in what I heard of her replies. She marvelled at the trees, patting the great trunks as she would have the old Labrador – 'Money can't buy a hundred years of growth,' she said. She agreed with Miranda's hunch about the floorboards, one foot roving and tapping to check resonance – 'It must surely be the period of kauri flooring.' Yet when they came back to the veranda, when she held a glass of chardonnay and after she had contained herself to some extent within a basket chair, there was about her just a touch of condescension that friendship couldn't repress. To see friends reduced in circumstance arouses sympathy, but also a small human satisfaction, celebration almost, that for the moment it isn't us.

I liked the Telfers. They were intelligent and conscious of the feelings of those about them; they knew that their own lives were of less interest to others than to themselves. They were accustomed to success and so believed, even with a touch of cynicism, in the benevolence of the world. And best of all, there was still tolerance and humour between them after years of marriage.

When Mr Telfer stood up to leave there was a stain of lichen, or bird shit, from the steps on the seat of his cream trousers, and Miranda was full of apology. She was about to rub it with her small, folded handkerchief when she realised that was too intimate and drew back. 'Don't worry about it,' he said mildly.

'He's just a complete grub,' said his wife.

We all walked with the visitors to the car and continued alongside it as Mr Telfer backed slowly to the entrance, not an easy job with the crowding trees and a boat trailer behind.

Mrs Telfer gestured with one sinuous arm out of the window, and carried on the conversation with Miranda, while Andrew and I made up a sort of chorus of fatuous goodwill. Even Diedre and her substantial friend had appeared, their interest in the Telfers renewed by their departure.

As the Telfers drove away in a panoply of expensive machinery, they would commiserate with the Sumerbottoms, voice their apprehensions concerning the ambitions Miranda had for the property, speculate as to the soundness of the marriage beset by stress, shake their heads at the lapse that had cost Mr Sumerbottom his professional reputation and savings, and then, refreshed, press on to their boating recreation.

Miranda was stirred to even more activity and brightness by the visit. Her eyes glittered, and her laugh became more frequent and more brittle. She disappeared upstairs briefly and came back wearing a silk top. 'I should have had it on earlier,' she said. 'Wasn't it just a lovely surprise to see them. You were very friendly with Chris in Wellington, weren't you Andrew.'

'He was okay.'

'Chris was only a year older than Andrew,' Miranda told me. 'He's doing medicine at Otago now.'

'He was okay,' said Andrew.

'They had a covered swimming pool,' said Diedre. She used the information to awe her friend, who nodded and smiled with the acquiescence children often show when away from their own territory.

The Telfers took something of the afternoon's gloss with them: the sky clouded, the tabby vomited on the trampoline when the two girls tried to make it bounce, and when we inspected our work on the brick patio, there was less done than we'd remembered and the surface was clearly uneven. Miranda responded by throwing herself into preparations for tea and making Andrew scrape the front steps, which had soiled Mr Telfer's trousers. 'It's too late now, Mum,' he said. 'And anyway the birds perch on the overhang there. It won't do any good.' But he did it all the same.

Miranda made an asparagus and blue cheese quiche, and chilled a bottle of Marlborough Sav Blanc. We held off until half past six, but then ate without Mr Sumerbottom. Even I knew it was a good quiche and I told her so, but that was one small thing against the day's tide of circumstance.

Andrew and I had brought swot books with us, and for an hour or so after the meal we made some effort to prepare ourselves for the coming exams. Diedre, bereft of her friend who had given up the wait for tea, completed her homework with greater success and then wanted me to play swing-ball. She and I were playing in the half-dark when Mr Sumerbottom came home. He dragged his golf bag from the back seat and waved in answer to Diedre's calls. For a moment it seemed that he would walk over to us, but then he waved again and, tilted against the weight of his clubs, went inside.

I let Diedre win the last game, not difficult after the yellow ball caught me a blow on the left eye in the dusk. She looked up at the first of the stars. 'Yes,' she said fervently, 'I am the champion.' When she went inside, after giving me an innocent, friendly hug, I walked through the trees to the road gate and on towards the town for a few minutes. Quiet, dark farmland was behind me and the strung lights ahead. I'd been with the Sumerbottoms for less than two full days and already the family disconcerted me with its vulnerability. My own people were wary, humorously pessimistic, and kept a shield of emotional reticence against the vicissitudes of life.

At that turning time before full darkness, there was complete stillness in the world. Few cars came down the road that led to the main street; no people looked in the windows of the few closed shops ahead of me; no music sounded from the houses, whose lights were yellow lamps. The trees and shrubs were dark masses as steady as the buildings, and all the birds had gone to roost. The town at night was swamped by the fragrances of all that countryside around it: pine windbreaks, hay sheds, turned soil, the cloying drift of dairy effluent. At the pubs there would have been some leisurely talk and movement, fried food, but I didn't walk that far, instead turning at a transport yard and walking back to the Sumerbottoms. Long before I reached the place I could see the dark towers of its trees, higher than any others around.

As I came through those trees onto the dark, uneven drive I saw that the Sumerbottoms were inspecting our morning's work on the brick patio. The side door was open, and Miranda and Mr Sumerbottom outlined there in the spilling light. 'Oh well, it's a start,' he said, and I stopped to listen and ran my fingers through the soft leaves of a sycamore.

'We need to get a lot more demolition bricks,' Miranda said.

'We need to get out of this place,' Mr Sumerbottom said with sudden bitterness. 'I'd like to ditch the whole idea of a fancy bed and breakfast and go back to Wellington. I can hardly believe that we've ended up like this. How's it happened?'

Miranda didn't say anything for a while, maybe she was deciding whether she wanted to get into all that. She came out on to the freshly laid bricks. She looked directly back at him. 'The Wellington life's gone now,' she said. 'I realised that again when the Telfers were here this afternoon. All that's gone.' There was no accusation in her tone, just finality.

'You know, after golf today I stayed on drinking and talking, and I knew I should have been getting back here for tea, and I didn't want to. Not you, of course, but this house and all the stuff to be done. And no bugger comes here anyway, despite the advertising. We'll go bankrupt soon, I just know it.'

'We're only getting underway though.'

'And I don't even like most of the guys at golf here, yet I could've sat with them all night. We're in a tail spin. I see us going bankrupt.'

'Home-stay tourism is what everybody recommended. It's a boom thing, but you have to give it time to take off.' Miranda went back into the doorway, and stood close to him. Her stance, her voice, her lifted face were all part of a positive attitude that she didn't dare let go.

'We're coming down in the world, that's it. After all this time I'm working for somebody else,' said Mr Sumerbottom. Maybe the drinks in the golf club allowed him to release his regrets and fears. 'I know, Jesus, you don't have to tell me why it's all happened. But it's hard isn't it, coming down in the world.'

'It must, must work out though,' she said. Her voice was lower than before, yet it had greater intensity. It barely carried through the night to where I stood beneath the sycamore.

'No, but we are. We're down-sizing on everything, including our opinions of ourselves.'

Miranda closed the door then, and although I could still see them through the glass, I couldn't hear any more. They were both slender, nimble, and at that distance could have been two much younger people starting out together – but they weren't, of course. I waited amongst the night trees a while longer before going up between the lions to the front door. I didn't want the Sumerbottoms to suspect they had been overheard.

I wanted the next day to be there already. I wanted Miranda to have dropped us off at Massey and to be driving away like a jack-in-the-box at the wheel of the Corona. I didn't want to be an observer of the family any more. Some people are born sport for the fates. I could pick a future for them. Andrew would press on under the guise of amiable laughing stock, innocent Diedre would have something terrible befall her in the park on the way back from music lessons, Mr Sumerbottom must suffer increasing humiliation because of his own weakness. Miranda, worst of all, would pit her bright desperation against the odds in an anguish that is more than pain, that becomes a bewilderment of suffering.

Maybe all that and more has happened. Just an hour ago I looked for the Sumerbottoms' place and found six squat town houses on its site. 'Do you remember a family called Sumerbottom?' I ask Clarry. He laughs, then realises I'm not joking. 'Years ago,' I say, 'they had that great big tiled place in Powys street, but it's been replaced by town houses now.'

'It was the homestead of the Wattlington estate,' says Clarry, still holding the milk that is rightfully mine, 'but I don't ever remember any Sumerbottoms having anything to do with it. There's no local family called that.'

So Elvis Presley lives on here, from beyond the grave and the other side of the world, but I seem to be the only one who remembers the Sumerbottoms.

# The Best Man

The Volkswagen flew across the plain, or so it seemed to Bron, sitting in the passenger seat with Daniel, her best man, behind her, leaning with his elbows as if to urge the car on, and Roland crouched over the steering wheel, his lanky frame doubled up. Roland had an absolute certainty for the first race, but they had left New Plymouth late. Now the racecourse was in sight, its white gate and ticket box, white-coated officials, and spectator stand, which sat in isolated splendour in the green fields.

'I'll put our bets on,' Roland said, uncoiling himself and racing off. 'See you in the stands.'

'Is it too late for the birdcage?' Bron asked. She prided herself on knowing a few words of anything she was expected to take an interest in.

'I expect so,' replied Daniel. 'Roland's cutting it fine.'

They climbed up into the stand together, feeling conspicuous but trying to look nonchalant. Bron wished she had brought dark glasses. Daniel had his binoculars slung over his shoulder. There were an amazing number of hats and suits, white shirts and ties.

'Who would have expected such formality,' she said to Daniel as they climbed to the top row, but she doubted he heard. Neither of them was very fit and there was a low ache in Bron's stomach.

Roland joined them, panting and looking downcast.

'What's up?' Daniel asked as he squeezed himself in beside them.

'Scratched, can you believe it? An absolute utter cert and then withdrawn at the last minute. The best tip I've had in ages. Strained fetlock or something, I suppose. Bloody animal.'

'You did bet on something?' Bron enquired, pressing her hand to her side. It seemed to hurt when she took a breath. She had handed over ten dollars of her housekeeping money unwillingly, but it was nothing compared to the hundreds Roland was willing to bet.

'So who did you put it on?' Bron asked.

'Trompe l'oeil,' Roland replied with a sheepish grin. 'Doesn't it mean deceive the eye?'

'And where is this illusion?' asked Daniel, for the last stragglers were now in the starting gates.

'I can see my ten dollars vanishing,' groaned Bron.

'Magenta tunic with white spots, white sleeves,' read Daniel from the form guide. 'Two wins, one fourth, finished strongly'. Perhaps there was a chance.

Then there was a whirl of colours, a pounding of hooves, a flashing and waving of whips – jockeys swore a lot, Bron knew. An agitated block of air moved and was past, and the calm air resumed. Trompe l'oeil was somewhere in the front bunch as they went around the bend.

'Not bad,' said Roland, looking through his binoculars. His face had a set tense look, a bit like a greyhound. 'Come on, you beauty,' he shouted. 'Let her go.'

There was a collective exhalation of breath after the horses crossed the line and the results were announced over the public address system. Trompe l'oeil had come second.

Roland's mood was practically restored. 'You'll get your housekeeping money back,' he said to Bron. 'And a bit over.'

But when it was time to collect their bets Bron stayed behind. 'Invest it for me,' she said to Roland. She couldn't even be tempted down to the birdcage.


By the sixth race Bron could no longer conceal how she was feeling. A stabbing pain in her side caught her breath like a stitch, her stomach felt as taut as a drum. She had eaten a sandwich at lunchtime and drunk a few mouthfuls of Lemon and Paeroa. Half an hour later the pain increased. Daniel, who had been best man at Bron and Simon's wedding and her friend before that, suggested a visit to the emergency doctor before they left town.

'Can you take me now and come back for Roland,' Bron asked, in a voice so faint Daniel had to bend over to catch her words.

'Are you sure you can make it to the car? There's probably a doctor on duty here.'

But the thought of a loud voice over the public address system asking a doctor to come forward was more than Bron could bear. Instead she took Daniel's arm and he supported her down the steps. Perhaps they imagine I am a woman who has lost all her money, Bron thought, pressing her hand against her side to prevent jarring.

They drove around for a long time before they found the emergency doctor.

'Hospital at once. It looks like an acute appendix. I'll phone and say you are coming.'

'What will you and Roland do?' Bron asked, stretched out as flat as she could on the back seat.

'We'll stay,' Daniel replied. 'Find a motel and wait for you.'

When Daniel got back to the racecourse, the last race was over and the sun was sinking. The ground was covered with betting tickets, pie wrappers and hot dog sticks. He didn't need to be a homing dog to know he'd find Roland in the public bar. He was standing next to a curvaceous blonde with a lived-in face. Roland always went for older women, Daniel reflected, as he approached.

'How's Bron?' Roland asked, raising his head from his glass.

'In the hospital. They're keeping her in overnight.'

'The poor thing,' the woman, who hadn't been introduced, began, and Daniel realised he'd have to explain. His last sighting of Bron had been a prone form in a hospital gown being trundled along a glacial corridor by a hospital porter. 'She'll sleep,' the porter had assured him. Just before the injection took hold Bron gripped his hand and apologised about messing up her outing.

'I've told Laura the story,' Roland interrupted. 'Condensed, of course. Laura Blowse. Meet Daniel Straub.'

They shook hands over near-empty glasses, and Daniel went for refills. On impulse he brought back three whisky chasers.

'Good man,' said Roland. 'Laura here's not just a pretty face. She's made a suggestion regarding accommodation. Morrieson's Motel. She's even phoned ahead to winkle out the last unit. She's used her influence and got us into numero seven.'

Laura Blowse was as good as her word. A stocky man with a weather-beaten face greeted them at reception and, when they had signed the register, handed over a key and a carton of milk.

'Can we take it for Sunday as well?' Daniel asked. 'One of our party is in hospital. We don't know when she'll be released yet.'

'I'm so sorry.' A woman had appeared in the office door.

'I'm Betty and this is Clarry. In case he hasn't introduced himself. If there is anything we can do to help.'

'Came on at the races,' Roland said. 'Sixth race. Speedy Gonzales. One I collected on.'

Then, seeing Daniel's face, he pulled a handful of notes out of his pocket and put them on the counter. 'Speedy's contribution.'

'Wife?' said Betty, looking at Daniel.

'No. I was her best man. Missed out, I'm afraid. I'm keeping an eye on things while her husband's away. This was meant to be a treat.'

'At least she topped up the housekeeping,' smirked Roland.

In the silence that followed Clarry counted and wrote a receipt for the banknotes and Betty tidied some brochures on the desk.

'Number seven is one of our units with separate bedrooms,' she said, holding Daniel's gaze. 'So if your bride...friend...needs to rest.'

'Thank you,' was all Daniel could manage. He left Roland to park the Volkswagen and set off to locate number seven.

'Perhaps after that little fiasco I'll take the bridal suite,' Daniel said when Roland showed up.

'What fiasco? I didn't notice anything.'

'You wouldn't. All you can think about is races and pubs.'

'It's hardly my fault if *my* day hasn't been ruined.'

'And mine *has*. Bron's crook in hospital, I can't contact Simon without her say so, and I've been made to look like a eunuch in front of a couple of country bumpkins. They're probably nutting it out right this minute. The country's probably full of best men wandering about in search of brides who've got away.'

'Take the double bed, see if I care. I've got a date with Laura. We're going dancing.'

'That old pullet!'

'Not that old,' Roland replied. 'I'll pass over the insult. Never underestimate the restful quality of a mature woman.'

Daniel phoned the hospital and was told Bron was resting comfortably.

'Have there been any more symptoms?' he asked.

'May I ask if you are the next of kin?'

'In a manner of speaking.'

'What does that mean?'

'Her husband's overseas. I was best man at her wedding.'

'Well, you can rest easy. Doctor will be around to see her in the morning.'

'When can I visit?'

'Just avoid meal times.'

The phone was put down and Daniel wandered around inspecting the motel. His room with the double bed would at least thwart Roland and Laura. The thought of Roland's lanky frame curled up in the single bed made Daniel smile. Then he reflected that if Laura was hot to trot, she undoubtedly had a bed of her own. He sat on his double bed and tested the springs. He opened the kitchen cupboards and looked at the carefully rationed plates, the kettle with its cord tightly twined and tucked through at the end, the fish slice and the electric frypan. He couldn't imagine disturbing any of them. Then he sat at the kitchen table and read the brochure: 'Morrieson's Motel, conveniently located close to High Street, possesses its own intimate licensed restaurant.' Picking up the key with its cumbersome tag, Daniel went in search of culinary delights.


The restaurant was incongruously decorated with swords and horse-brasses; each table had a lamp and a tiny vase of fresh flowers. Daniel was correct in surmising whatever main he chose would come with a generous helping of chips. Still, the chips were golden and well-drained and his fillet steak with a smear of French mustard exactly what he needed. Hadn't he read that Marie Curie, near collapse on rice or lentils cooked on a gas ring, had been revived by steak and chips? As he ate, Daniel tried to put his problems aside. He imagined he was an animal, a cow perhaps – they had passed a huge black and white concrete cow outside something called 'Dairylands', but Bron had been too ill by then for him to pay attention. Besides cows had four stomachs: an indigestible thought had four chances of being broken down.

'Would you like to see the dessert menu?' A young woman was bending over the table, and Daniel realised he was miles away.

'Apple pie, chocolate mousse not made with real chocolate, cheeseboard,' Daniel quoted as though he and not the waitress were holding the menu. 'Am I correct?'

'Deep dish apple pie, that sounds better. But you're right about the chocolate mousse. It's mainly from a packet.' Then she put her hand over her mouth as if the words had slipped out. 'Sometimes there's rhubarb crumble.'

'I think I'll take a walk,' said Daniel.


Roland, with Laura Blowse beside him, was speeding through the night towards a country hall, where one of the local bands was playing.

'It's just a matter of time before they're discovered,' Laura told him.

'Sometimes things are at their best in the early stages,' Roland suggested. 'Take The Clash for instance. Or Sting. Fame thins them out somehow.'

'Then you're in for a treat,' Laura replied, peering through the car window at dark fields where dark shapes huddled.

'It's the same with women,' Roland went on, guessing she would not be offended.

'Or men,' Laura replied, as if she were reviewing a great catalogue. 'Before you have to wash their socks and cook their meals.'

There's nothing like a mature woman, Roland thought, not for the first time. They know how to seize the moment. *Carpe diem*, he said to himself and wondered where he'd heard it. Then he remembered: *Dead Poets' Society*. He felt like a poet tonight.


Daniel, walking past lighted houses and drawn curtains, caught a lungful of clematis blossom and wondered why, like the sound of a stream or rainwater in a culvert, it came on the senses suddenly. One moment there was nothing: silence or clear air and then this eruption. Was it a certain distance travelled? Five steps beyond the bush and you get assailed by scent? Someone should write a learned paper. It was too late to phone the hospital again, he thought, as he turned down Waipahu Street, though probably a different nurse would be on duty. 'Best man…,' they might say, might be saying already. 'Did you hear about the guy wanting to see this patient and saying he was the best man? A likely story.'

Daniel came to unit seven and inserted the key. Then he stood at the kitchen bench while the jug boiled. He tore open a sachet of coffee – 'Faggs,' it read – and made himself a drink. He sat staring out through the dark window for a long time, nursing the coffee as if it were a chalice. He knew Bron had been mistaken two years ago when she married Simon.


It was 3am when Daniel woke in the double bed. He had slept restlessly – too much food too late in the evening on a tense stomach. He half-rolled out of bed and went to get a glass of water. The second bedroom – two pristine single beds, like husband and wife tombs – was empty. So much for caring for your friend's wife or sharing the best man's responsibilities, he thought bitterly. But Roland was just one of a group of loose friends who surrounded Simon, attracted by his charm and energy. Daniel suspected Bron might by now have seen another side of this charm; certainly Simon travelled a great deal. 'It's a pact,' Bron had explained to him once in the days when he regularly visited for Sunday supper. 'We both want time apart, to grow.'

'To grow what?' Daniel wondered, as he dashed cold water on his face. His mouth tasted foul, and there was something sordid about sleeping in your underclothes. Just in case there is a message from the hospital in the night, he'd reasoned, before he turned in. In case someone knocks on the door. He poked his head out between the drapes before he turned in. A full moon with trailings of cloud rode above the town.

'Well, what do you make of that young man in unit seven?' Betty Claridge asked Clarry, after he had made the second of his nightly visits to the bathroom. He was always alert for a while before sinking back into sleep. But Clarry made nothing more than a non-committal grunt. He knew Betty would have been working on the young man's analysis since she first sighted him at reception.

'You don't think it's an abortion?' she asked musingly, looking up at the ceiling. 'I wonder why he had to mention being the best man. It's not something men usually set much store by, I should have thought. Not like a stag do.'

When Clarry didn't respond, Betty reached a hand over the side of the bed and fished up an extra pillow in a frilled pillowslip. This she eased under the flat pillow she always slept on. Then she folded her arms under her head and lay back to think for as long as sleep withheld itself. Illicit love affairs, fathers with 'nieces', curtain rings on third fingers, were nothing in the motel business; Betty prided herself on being able to sniff out every permutation. Yet something about the young man eluded her. Had he got his friend's wife pregnant and stopped in a country town for a termination? Yet terminations were rarely carried out at the hospital and not without a great deal of consultation. There was something sorrowful about the young man. Perhaps he was indecisive and the woman had made the decision. But why, in that case, were they at the races? Of course the other man, the tall one whom Betty liked less, had a good deal of money on him. But somehow the story would not knit together. Then, just before sleep came, she had a brainwave. She knew Sister Gillies at the hospital. She would phone her in the morning.

Pressed in the back seat of the Volkswagen, Laura Blowse felt like a ship in a bottle before someone pulls the cotton and the tiny sails and masts stand erect. One leg and a foot beyond, which hung in space, was draped over the seat in front. Roland was crouched on his knees in the space where feet normally went. Laura's back, pressed tightly against the side window, ached. She reached out a hand and pulled at Roland's hair.

'There's not enough room,' she whispered, and her voice came in odd pants.

'Just hang on, Laura love. I've done this before.'

'I bet you have. But I prefer a double bed.'

Then, somehow, he got himself in position and there suddenly seemed to be more room. A little more air entered the steamed up car. Laura's elbow had forced open a back window flap.

The band, the beer, the dancing had sent the little hall rocking. Laura mentioned cousins, and she certainly seemed to know everyone. Roland was never sure if it was someone's twenty-first or a golden wedding anniversary or both combined. There were even a few babies asleep in carry cots in the supper room. Soon Laura and Roland were jiving in the centre of the floor, feeling each other out, improvising and coming together, relieved that they sensed each other's pattern.

'Do you often do this?' Roland asked, when the band took a breather and they edged their way to the bar.

'As often as any talent shows up,' Laura replied. 'I love to dance. Always have.'

They sat out the next couple. Then the band started on 'Spanish Eyes' and Roland held out his hand. Laura transformed her face into a sexy pout; she arched her back and jutted her hip as if layer upon layer of frills cascaded to the floor. As they swooped past a table covered in white paper Roland plucked a plastic rose from a vase and held it between his teeth.

Bron woke in the semi-dark ward and wondered where she was. The screens around her bed were pulled apart, and a nurse thrust a thermometer into her mouth. Gingerly she put a hand down to touch her side and felt no pain.

'Have I been operated on?' she asked the nurse.

'Not as far as I know. I've just come on.'

She flipped the notes at the end of the bed.

'No. No operation. I think you're just under observation. I expect the doctor will make a decision when he does his rounds.'

'What day is it?' Bron asked.

'Sunday.

Bron lay back on her pillows and closed her eyes. She knew better than to try to think things through. Thinking drives people mad, her father used to say. He was scornful of her mother's hankering after detail as if life were assembled like a five-thousand-piece jigsaw puzzle. He had tried to impress on Bron the notion of not seeing the wood for the trees. Into her mind came the thick trunk of an oak tree, then its spreading majestic crown. She raised herself into the air – it felt like standing on her toes – and imagined oak after oak, meadow after meadow, running down to a cliff edge and the sea. Whatever was going to happen would happen.

But she knew what was going to happen. Dawn would come and a nurse would bring the mobile phone and she would speak to Daniel.

Lisa Blowse was not concerned when her mother did not come home. She got up, made her bed, and gave Charlton his Weetbix, toast fingers with marmite, and a glass of milk. Then she sat him at a small table she had bought at Baby Swap and gave him a large blank drawing book and a handful of crayons. Later she might take him to the park. The seesaw was his favourite, but unless a child of approximately equal weight was around Lisa had to lower and raise the vacant end with her hand.

As she washed the dishes Lisa thought of the young man in the restaurant who had cleverly guessed the desserts. She would like to have surprised him with something exotic, like baklava or crème caramel. Lisa spent a lot of time reading cookery books. At least he hadn't chosen the chocolate mousse – chocolate instant pudding with a tablespoon of rum added and chocolate chips dissolved in boiling water to improve the colour. What if a real chef should visit? But then she consoled herself that that was unlikely. No chef with a Michelin star was going to visit Morrieson's.

Daniel showered and shaved before phoning the hospital at 7am. 'Resting comfortably,' was the reply. No other information was forthcoming. In the background there was a crashing noise, as if someone had dropped a bedpan.

Betty Claridge, in a pink tracksuit with a bandeau holding back her hair, beckoned to him as he walked past the office.

'Is it true your wife is in hospital?' she began.

'Not my wife,' Daniel explained patiently. He felt as if he were taking a lie-detector test. He could feel the blue eyes boring into his skull. 'Bron is the wife of my best friend. He's overseas at the moment. Business. I just keep an eye on Bron while he's away.'

'I believe you were the best man,' Betty said. 'Was it your friend who said that?'

Another minute and she might comment on the missing Volkswagen.

'I'm just off to the hospital now,' Daniel said. 'We may need the motel another night. I'll let you know when I get back.'

'Do that,' said Betty.

The minute he was out of sight she picked up the phone and called Sister Gillies.

'Appendix,' Margaret Gillies boomed down the phone. 'Kept her in overnight. Mr Forbes-Hamilton won't operate unless it's practically bursting.'

'I'm relieved to hear it,' said Betty Claridge. 'I thought it might be something else.'

'Meaning what?'

'A termination.'

'Whatever gave you that idea?'

'I suppose it was the best man.'

'Sorry. I didn't catch what you said.'

'Don't worry. I'll be in touch. And thanks for the info.'


Daniel walked down High Street debating whether to look for a coffee shop, but he walked straight on until the town petered out and he was in suburban streets. The sound of someone playing the piano drifted through an open window: it sounded like 'Für Elise'. He imagined he heard a voice say, 'More expression.' The hospital, low and squat, was set in carefully manicured grounds. A few saplings were enclosed in sacking. He gave his name to the woman at reception and walked through to the ward. Bron was propped up with pillows; there was colour in her cheeks.

'Daniel,' she said. And then, 'The pain's gone, vanished.'

'Are you sure?' Daniel asked, pulling up a chair. 'Are they certain it won't return?'

'No certainty in this world,' Bron replied, but the look she gave him was gentle. 'They say I can be discharged later this morning.'

'Then I'll wait. I'll go for a walk and I'll come back. We'll keep the motel for the night and push off in the morning.'

'The motel?'

'Morrieson's. I think it's named after a writer. A bit of a ratbag.'

He wouldn't mention Roland and the missing Volkswagen.


Betty Claridge, carrying a bouquet of late roses, sped along the corridor. Nothing made her feel so alive as a mission. She felt herself powerfully drawn to the young couple, seeing them as thwarted lovers. Perhaps the absent husband, surely a cad, would never return; perhaps the young man would reclaim his bride. It made her think of Clarry, patiently waiting in the wings while she dated another. And of course she must offer hospitality and a complimentary meal. If the young woman wished she could use the Claridges' spare room, where the bed was far superior to any in the motels.

Bron looked up in surprise as a woman in pink approached her bed.

'Betty,' the woman said. 'Betty Claridge. You won't know me, dear. That nice young man is staying at my motel. Morrieson's.'

'Yes,' Bron said. 'He told me. We intended to leave after the races. Funny, that seems so long ago…'

'And the young man who seemed so worried about you?'

'I expect he's walking around the grounds. I'm being discharged after the doctor comes.'

'My car awaits you,' Betty said. 'And I've put some soft pillows and a rug on the back seat.'


'Will you tell Simon?' Daniel had asked, resting his hand over Bron's as it lay on the sheet. She let her fingers splay to let his between.

'No, I don't think so. Perhaps it can be an anecdote sometime in the future. One that will probably pass over his head. He may not even hear it, being so concentrated on himself.'

'So you know that?' Daniel asked. 'I always thought you weren't aware.'

'I think I always had an inkling. It's what made him attractive to me. Certainty and selfishness are probably very close.'

'Poor Bron,' Daniel said, and squeezed her fingers.

'It's not a matter for pity,' she replied, looking stern. 'It's given me some of the things I most desire. Privacy for one. My own identity. Without having to rise to the challenge I mightn't…'

'Good for the character,' Daniel said bitterly. 'I never thought you married for charity.'

'It's not like that,' Bron said gently. 'If it's any consolation, you have a more special place.'

'It's not a consolation,' Daniel said, looking fixedly at the mechanism that raised and lowered the bed. 'Sometimes I wonder what our lives would have been like.'

'You will meet someone less foolish,' Bron decreed. 'And I will attempt to love her. There'll probably be grinding of teeth.'

'I think I'll go for a another walk in the garden,' Daniel said. 'Tear the heads off a few flowers, kick a cat or two…'

'Come here,' said Bron and she held Daniel's face in her hands and kissed him in the infuriatingly equal continental manner.


Back at Morrieson's Motel, Laura and Roland made love in the double bed. Then they showered together, and Laura changed the sheets. Neither mentioned a further meeting, though Roland did note the date of the next race day.

'I might take the car down to the car wash,' he said. 'For the return journey.'

'Good idea,' Laura agreed.

She kissed him lightly on the mouth, turned to check the unit was shipshape, and left the key on the inside of the door. As the Volkswagen pulled out onto Waipahu Street, Betty's Volvo drew up outside the office.

'A grumbling appendix,' the young tired house surgeon had said to Bron on Sunday morning. 'It's settled down now but it's likely to be temporary. Eventually it'll have to come out.'

'Something to look forward to,' Bron said, and the young man looked at her, puzzled.

'You might not have an attack again for a long time. It might even die down…'

'I'll keep an eye on it,' Bron promised.

When he had departed, she swung her legs over the side of the bed, felt her side again with the flat of her palm, and started to dress. Then, in a confusion of Daniel's arm supporting her, roses, and the chattering Betty, she had been taken to the mythical Morrieson's Motel and into the parlour behind the motel office. Betty fussed about making tea and offering arrowroot biscuits. 'Won't you stay another night?' she asked. 'As my guest. Would you like a complimentary meal tonight or perhaps room service? I can arrange something from the restaurant.'

But Bron wanted to go home.

'It's a very nice motel,' she said to Betty. 'Perhaps I could walk around and have a look before we go.'

Daniel had excused himself and gone in search of Roland.

'So you do turn up,' he said.

'I could say the same of you.'

'Do you think Bron will manage in the back of the Volkswagen?'

'I won't speed, if that's what you're implying.'

'You'd better not.'

'Will you settle up at the office or shall I?'

'Leave it to me,' said Daniel. It was becoming a refrain.

In the chintzy office Betty Claridge had taken Bron's hand. 'He's a good young man,' she said, looking into Bron's eyes. 'The first choice is not always the best. I found that out with Clarry.'

'He is my best man,' Bron said.

Then Clarry's head appeared in the doorway.

The Volkswagen turned out of Waipahu Street into High. Bron sat in a nest of pillows donated by Betty. 'Just return them any time you're passing through.'

'The next race meeting,' Roland offered. 'I'll drop by then.'

I bet you will, Daniel thought. He turned to look at Bron in the back. She looked pale but starting to be interested again, like a child beginning a convalescence,

'Okay?' he asked.

'Okay,' she answered.

# Spineless

Charlotte didn't answer his question, which he considered had been innocuous enough. Instead she rammed a CD into the player and turned it up loud. He'd hoped she'd meet him half-way in the communication stakes; neither of them had said a word since they'd left the shiny foyer of the Lodge, since they'd got back in the car and driven though the Lodge grounds, which had peeled away from their departing car as smoothly as expensive skin away from the surgeon's knife, though entirely the wrong colour.

He stole a glance at his wife's profile, chiselled, new. She'd told no one she was going to do it; just arrived home one day from a business trip that wasn't a business trip. It had been a subtle job – apart from the reshaping of her nose. The lines around her eyes were diminished and her scowl line, which she'd had since her early twenties, had risen like yeasty dough to lie level with the plains of her forehead. Bryce had thought she looked different, but it was one of his female teaching colleagues who'd filled him in on all the details, going entirely on her own observations. Perhaps women have a better eye for that kind of thing, Bryce thought.

Charlotte's hair swung away from her shoulder, a blonded, perfumed swathe, obscuring her face. He knew exactly the expression it wore as it gazed at the passing paddocks: the eyes wounded, and below the vivid slash of lipstick, the square jaw set. In the rear-vision mirror he checked the glowing, rectangular vision of his son, still asleep in his carseat though his eyelids flickered now at the first onslaught from the brass section. Berlioz, Charlotte's favourite.

'Turn it down a bit, Char.'

'I like it loud.'

'You'll wake up Liam…'

'…who isn't supposed to even *be* here. You stuffed up. Again.'

'Char…'

'Classic. No nanny. And now no Lodge.'

'This motel is supposed to be good. A cut above the average. The woman at the Lodge said…'

'If you knew how much I looked forward to this. A facial. A wallow in the spa. A massage… Christ, look at this place. What a dump!' She turned her head to lay her critical gaze on the passing Waipahu Street.

'It'll be all right,' Bryce soothed. He patted Charlotte's thigh. Immediately the offending hand was plucked up and thrown back.

'Don't pat me! You're not my fucking grandmother!'

Replaced on the steering-wheel his palm retained some of the sensation of her silky frock, a cool, grey synthetic more suited to the boardroom than a weekend in a country town. More suited to a gin and tonic at the bar in the Lodge. Liam gave a little moan and eyes peeled open, bleary, lambent, impossibly blue. Bryce met them in the mirror.

'Gidday, mate. Woken up?'

'Where is this shit-hole?' Charlotte asked through clenched teeth, 'If he chucks up again before we get there you can drive me to the airport and I'll fly home in peace.'

'I don't think they have an airport.'

'Do you think they have a baby-sitting service?' she asked, mimicking his tone exactly.

'We'll ask…ah bugger!' He'd overshot it, only just catching the sign at the corner of his eye – 'Morrieson's Motel'. He executed a U-turn, Charlotte clinging exaggeratedly to the grip above the passenger door.

'All this way,' Charlotte was saying, 'Just to stay here!'

Like a good many of the newer houses they'd passed so far, the motel was red brick and low to the ground. Central in the circular lawn squatted a trampoline and to one side a rusty single swing hung emptily on its skew-wiff frame. His heart sinking – and he knew it would no doubt sink more as the afternoon progressed – Bryce took the car up the drive and drew it to a halt in a covered carport. A small sign dangled: 'Office'.

'You stay here.' He unbuckled his belt, 'I'll see if they have anything.'

'They have.' Long suffering finger-tips rose to her temples.

'How do you know?' He allowed himself a certain terseness, though he'd promised himself – and Charlotte and Sandy in their last counselling session – that on this weekend there'd be none of that. None of his terseness, snappiness, refusals to engage. None of the attributes of his increasingly ragged personality that drove his wife wild. And no patting.

Charlotte jabbed over her shoulder. 'The sign. It says "Vacancies".'

On cue Berlioz gave out a loud crash of cymbals and drums, and Bryce got out of the car.

'There's trouble in the camp there,' said Betty, on her return after she'd booked them in, 'Mark my words.'

Clarry, sitting at the table with the sport section of the newspaper spread over the accounts – accounts that moments before Betty had been attending to – only grunted.

'You should have seen Mrs,' Betty went on, 'Must've sucked a lemon all the way from Wellington.' She bent over the table, gathered up the paper and shoved it at her husband, 'Anyone else comes, you do it. Shift.' Betty heaved herself back into her chair, took up her pen and resumed her correspondence with the IRD; the end of the financial year was just around the corner.

'How many of them?' Clarry seated himself in his Laziboy and reopened his paper. 'Di'ja check?'

'Three counting a little one. That's how I saw the wife – when I checked the car. They're not the type to sneak extras in anyway.'

She switched on her calculator. 'Provisional tax. Sweet Jesus. Make us a coffee will you love? It's after three o'clock.'

Liam stood outside the unit, his cuddly in one hand and Pokemon in the other. It was warm on the little porch in the late summer, late afternoon sun. He squinted up at his father, who was going in and out carrying bags. Two for Mummy, and one each for Dad and himself. Mummy was angry about something again. Even though the music had been so loud in the car, coming from right behind his carseat, and he hadn't been able to hear her exact words, he could tell. Now she was lying flopped on the big bed inside and if he turned his head slightly he could see her through the connecting door, just her feet, which twitched slightly just like Fluffy's tail used to twitch, when they had Fluffy. But he wouldn't think about that now because it made him cry – the screeching of brakes on the road outside their house, the stranger who'd come to the door with the limp little body – Liam blinked away his tears and caught at his father's hand on his return journey.

'How ya going, Tiger?' Bryce picked the little boy up and caught a whiff of the child's earlier car-sickness. 'Into the bath with you!' he announced, 'If they have a bath.'

There was only a shower, and because showers terrified Liam – the upside down nozzle pointing right at him, the cold, cramped, echoing walls, the water stinging him like hard rain (at crèche Linda and Sue called them out of the rain with the first spits) – he screamed throughout. He tried not to – he tried to be a good boy – he always did. 'Su-ue!' he yelled, even though he knew she wasn't there.

On the bed Charlotte embarked on a relaxation exercise. She took a deep breath, which she sent with all the force of her concentration to her toes. Exhaling peace and contentment she took another breath, sending this one to her ankles. Another to her shins, her knees and so on to her thighs, in and out, each departing breath leaving the part of anatomy she had focused on soft, tingling, relaxed.

It wasn't working. She flung up off the bed and passed into the main room of the unit, with the kitchenette and television cabinet in matching dark, wood-grained laminate, and opened the little refrigerator. No minibar. She should have known. And nothing in her suitcase. Tipping her head back she closed her eyes to the ceiling, a conglomerate of cream, fibrous squares, and tried to picture a hotel from one of the business trips she'd made this year. The Park Lane in London. The Four Seasons in Chicago. Golden Star in Hong Kong... A singular coolness, a sense of peace, spread from the image that arrived in her mind, which was not a particular room but a generic one: puffy, floral bedspread; a lamp above an easychair; the window draped in sheeny white. An empty, quiet room, and herself on the beige carpet in stockinged feet, her shoes kicked off at the door. She saw herself half fill a glass with ice, empty a small clear bottle into it and top it up with tonic. Clean and dry the gin slicked her tongue in three quick gulps...

The shower halted, the echoing yells ceased and at the door to the bathroom stood Liam wrapped in a towel, his hair dripping. Behind him appeared her husband, who smiled at her – that careful, guilty, tender smile she so despised. Her PA had begun to smile like that too, until she'd put a stop to it.

'Sorry,' said Bryce, and as the word slipped from between his lips he knew what his wife was thinking and that she was right. He was spineless. His spine even felt soft, except for at his lower back where it twinged from holding a wet, slippery, protesting three-year-old under the shower. It must be different for young fathers, he thought. Forty-eight-year-old spines don't bend as easily.

'You don't need to carry on like that, Liam.' Charlotte dropped her gaze, unaltered, to her son. 'You're a big boy now.'

The child's eyes widened and he rushed for her, the towel dropping to the carpet, a white rift in the wild orange pattern. She felt his wet head collide with her thighs, his wet arms lock around her knees.

Bryce gave her no time; he never did. He removed Liam, wrapped him firmly in his towel and carried him into the second bedroom. Couldn't he see she had been about to attend to the boy, wrap him, sort through his things and pick out a little outfit? It was hopeless. Her handbag was on the sofa. From it she took her Filofax, found the date of their next counselling session and wrote 'Giving me time with L' as a discussion point, even though she considered that as she and Bryce were about to enter a period of flux, other matters might take priority on the day.

A girl, Sheilah, organised by the motel, came to baby-sit. Bryce had made a dash to the dairy so that Liam could have baked beans for dinner just the way he liked them: mashed with a fork to an orange paste. Daddy Beans, Bryce called them. When Sheilah came in Liam hardly batted an eyelid.

'He's dealing with his abandonment issues,' Bryce said to Charlotte as they closed the door after them, 'That's good, isn't it?'

Above the restaurant table, hung on a chain, was a drooping fake fuchsia, whose once pink and red blooms had faded to an orange as homogenous as Liam's beans. One tendril, silvered with dust, hung between Charlotte and Bryce and swayed slightly in the current set up by the air-conditioning. Bryce grasped a bottle of Rawson's Retreat, for which they'd paid two-and-a-half times the Wellington price, and refilled her glass.

'Okay?' he asked softly, patting her hand. 'Sheilah's got a son of her own, so we don't have to worry.'

Charlotte sipped at the wine, licked it away from her teeth. She had been miles away, going over her Friday morning meeting with the regional manager from Sydney. He wasn't short on praise for the restructuring; Charlotte the Knife, he'd called her in the first five minutes. Lovely, cheeky Aussie charm, she'd thought, even before he'd made his proposition…

Bryce was still patting. Would he never learn? She yanked his hand away, and there was the waitress in her red and white gingham apron. Charlotte hadn't looked at the menu.

'The fish, whatever it is. So long as it isn't shark. And for godsake don't batter it.'

'It all is,' said the waitress.

'What?'

'Pardon,' said Bryce under his breath. He looked at the waitress with pity. People looked at her PA like that.

'Battered,' said the girl. 'It comes like that.'

'You can always peel it off, Char,' said Bryce helpfully. She would have protested, but he was too quick for her. Again. 'The steak,' he was saying. 'Medium rare.'

'You need to tell them rare in a place like this,' Charlotte told him after the girl had gone. 'It'll be like leather.' Which is how he actually prefers it, she added to herself, not being a true carnivore. When they'd met he was a vegetarian, but she'd persuaded him that a regular intake of red meat would increase his aggression, his manliness.

He called the girl back.

'The salad instead,' he said, in a moment of rebellion, 'and tomato soup. With bread.'

'The soup will be tinned,' said Charlotte, loudly.

'Actually,' said the girl, fearless, 'It isn't. The chef makes it himself.'

'From tins,' persisted Charlotte, her glass rising to her lips, and the girl made off for a second time, more quickly than she had the first.

The restaurant was filling slowly. At the next table a young couple sat down. Locals, by the look of them, thought Bryce. The man had his best checked shirt on, his hair slicked back from his red brow. The girl was plump and soft, head to foot in pink cotton knit. A new engagement ring flashed on her finger as they held hands over the table, the man's hand calloused, work-stained. He looked at her with a kind of wonder, as if he couldn't believe his luck. Soon they would marry and then he would carry her back to his farm, or flat above a mechanics workshop, or whatever...

'What are you thinking about?'

Bryce started. She hadn't asked him that for years. In the early days that question was always on her lips, as though she held his momentary silences as a personal affront. Nearly twenty years ago she had trained on him the full force of her considerable attention and smoked him out, working firstly on her own and then in partnership with a series of therapists. The question struck him now with a sweet, old-fashioned nostalgia like a song from their courting, such as it was. It spoke of naïve curiosity, a mid-twentieth century lack of jargonism. He held out his hand, palm up, and wriggled his fingers. Reluctantly, sighing, Charlotte gave him hers to hold.

'I'm sor…,' he began.

'Don't!' She would have pulled away but he held on firmly.

'But I am. I didn't know I had to confirm the Lodge booking. They didn't tell me that when I rang…'

Charlotte shrugged, as if it was quite extraordinary that he didn't know, as if everybody knew.

'And the nanny – well, okay, I didn't try hard enough. You're right. That's the truth. I think I secretly wanted Liam to come with us.'

Charlotte rested her fingertip on the point of her knife and depressed it so the handle see-sawed on the table cloth.

'We can still make our decision, can't we?' Bryce said softly. He considered his intonation, hoped it wasn't pleading, or wheedling. 'It shouldn't affect that.' That was better. Firm. As if he'd just swallowed a sirloin steak, whole.

'I've already made the decision,' said Charlotte. He could see she was wrestling with herself, forcing herself to be kind. He met her eyes.

'The deal we made with Sandy was…'

'Sandy's got nothing to do with it …'

'…was that we would make the decision together this weekend. And I've been thinking,' he rushed on, leaning towards her, 'I can take leave for a year, maybe two. So the next one won't have to go into daycare so early. Remember how sick Liam got that first winter, poor little guy. We can survive on your income – more than survive. I'll stay home and look after…' But Charlotte was shaking her head.

'You see, Bryce,' she spoke slowly, deliberately, 'It's not your decision. You're not the one who has to spend hours at the fertility specialist being pumped up with hormones and poked and prodded and all the rest. To say nothing of what happens when the bloody thing decides to be born. Or not, as the case may be.'

'But I…'

'And as for living off my income, I don't really think that's a good idea. It's better the way it is, split down the middle, absolutely. It's hard enough for your ego as it is, earning half of what I do.' She paused for a moment, calculating. 'Less than half.'

The waitress brought the soup and bread. She put it down in front of Bryce, dark and rich. A handful of fresh basil had been scattered over it.

'Now there's a surprise!' Charlotte was smiling, gesturing at the soup, 'Who'd've thought they knew about basil in Morrieson's? Oh come on, Bryce.' He was staring at her, an ugly red flush spreading up his neck from his black T-shirt. 'Darling…'

Darling? Bryce almost looked over his shoulder.

'Listen to me. I've got some exciting news.'

The smell of tomato soup was making him feel sick. He breathed through his mouth. The buzz of voices in the restaurant was suddenly loud, blurred. He could hear what the couple at the next table were saying more clearly than he could his wife. Something about cattle. He was a farmer, then.

'I've said yes.'

He heard that. 'What?'

'To Sydney. I'll commute. At first anyway, until I get daycare sorted. Then you can join us at the end of the year, if you like.'

'Us?'

'Liam and me.'

'You're not taking Liam!' he was shouting, banging the table. Around them the restaurant fell silent.

'If you must know,' Charlotte whispered, a sibilant hiss, 'I've already discussed this with Sandy and she says…'

'Fuck Sandy!' He stood up. 'And fuck you too!' On his way out he looked at no one, side-stepping the waitress, eyes on the door.

He wouldn't go back to the unit, he decided. Not right away. He'd walk for half an hour or so. Down the drive he went, past the trampoline on the lawn, its mat a shining oblong with the gleam of black water. It had been dark for an hour now, the sun sunk somewhere over the South Taranaki Bight. Perhaps he could stride out to the west, head for the beach. The day's warmth had completely faded; it was as cold now as it was in Wellington…bugger it! His jacket was still squared over the back of the chair in the restaurant. Charlotte would pick it up, maybe even use his visa card. Who paid for the last restaurant meal? he wondered, his feet pounding beneath him away from the bright lights of the High Street intersection towards the suburban end of Waipahu Street. Who the hell cares?

Around him the gardens were soft and dark, the scent of turned earth from the Saturday labours of the town's men and women was sweet in his nostrils. There was the perfume of freshly mown grass, stronger than usual from the showers earlier in the day. In the window of nearly every house a television flickered. In one living-room a man bent over his wife with a cup of tea, on a front porch a teenage boy sat smoking a cigarette – Bryce sniffed the air – or was it a joint? Why couldn't he have had a life like this? Bryce wondered. It didn't take much to satisfy him really, his appetite was easily made replete. A job, somewhere to live, a car that went, a few good mates, a wife and family. For some people that would be a hell of a lot, riches; for other people, like Charlotte, it wasn't nearly enough. It was one of Charlotte's current questions: What do you want, Bryce? What do you really *want*?

And finally he'd answered her. What I really want, Charlotte, is another child.

'Baby On Board' read a yellow card on one of the parked cars he passed. He slowed his pace, put his hands in his jeans pockets for warmth, and cast his mind ahead to the next corner. When he reached that, he'd turn left and around the block.

His jacket was neatly folded on the rubber doormat. He picked it up and unlocked the door. As his key slid in he heard the click of the remote and the ensuing silence of the television. Sheilah looked up and smiled.

'That was quick,' she said.

'Yes,' He put his hand into his pocket, pulled out a couple of twenties.

'Nice dinner?' asked the girl.

'Mmm.' He didn't want to get her talking.

'Oh, but that's too much,' said the girl now, 'I've only been here for an hour and a half.'

Is that all, thought Bryce. It felt like a lifetime ago he fed Liam his Daddy Beans. Liam in Sydney, on the other side of the Tasman. Never.

He opened the door.

'Oh,' she said, as if she had just remembered, 'Your wife left you that.' There was a folded piece of notepaper on the table, a page torn from Charlotte's Filofax.

'Thank you,' he nodded, closing the door after her.

He had almost reached the table when a terrible fear gripped him, a snap-freezing of the tissue around his heart. About-wheeling like a panicked bird he flew into Liam's room with soundless, rapid footsteps. It was dark, too dark; he couldn't see anything at all. He quelled the desire to snap on the light and stood quietly, breathing. Yes. There, almost at the same moment, he detected the soft fluttering breath of his child. His vision adjusted and he could see the faint glimmer of Liam's hair, the shining blonde of it on the pillow. He crossed to the bed, hot with relief, feeling his blood pump behind his eyes. What had he been thinking of, anyway? Charlotte would have gone for a drive, he should have checked to see if the car was there. That was the pattern at home when they had a row. He went walking, she went driving. He would go to bed and read his book until she came back.

He picked up the folded page, brushed his teeth and arranged his pillows, the book lying ready for when he had finished Charlotte's note. He felt strangely calm, as if a very important aspect of his fate had been taken care of by a powerful force of nature, something irrefutable. There was no logical explanation for this feeling, but it coursed through him nevertheless as he opened the paper to read in rapid scrawl: 'I asked at the office if someone was leaving for Wellington and someone was, right then, so I've got a ride home. Couldn't wait for you to explain. You need some time on your own to work out what you really want, and I hate this place. Better I go. You have a nice weekend with Liam. We'll sort it out when you get home. C.'

What are you thinking, Bryce? I'm thinking rapidly and clearly, thinks Bryce, so many years of intrusion making him aware of the style of his thinking as well as the content of it. I'm thinking how I once read an article in a magazine about separation, an article that stated that the partner who leaves has the least rights. He's thinking of how this would look to a family court judge, Charlotte banging off in the dark leaving Liam behind. He's thinking of how he has given most of the care, been the – what did they call it? – the primary caregiver. He's thinking of how in the morning he'll ring his lawyer and find out what the best course of action is. He's thinking how it's school holidays and he could drive with Liam to Auckland and stay with friends, spend a night at Taupo on the way. He's thinking that he will apply for custody.


Charlotte sits in the back seat of the car. Paddocks and towns and billboards flash by, amorphous in the dark. She feels her singularity, her almost virginal sense of being. She feels inviolate, clean; she's escaped the tumultuous welter of Bryce's needs. If only he gave her something to respect him for. But he doesn't, and there's no point in going over and over it. Even the getting of Liam was a hard-won procedure; it cost them thousands. But, she reminds herself, she has a duty to Bryce. She knew from the moment she met him that their partnership would be unequal, that he would be more a limpet than a support. It didn't bother her then and it wouldn't now. He was a sweet, gentle man and, as Sandy had said, several times now, he deserves cherishing. Charlotte resolves to do her best, to ease him through the changes.

# Sunday March 28, 1999

# Tact

He was sorrier for the car than for his wife. In four years of driving it had never let him down. There had been one flat tyre but the AA dealt with that, and once he'd left the lights on and flattened the battery (the AA again). There'd been a dented panel in the driver's door where a woman had reversed into him in the library carpark – small women in big wagons were a menace – but none of the mechanical troubles that had afflicted every other car he'd owned, from the second-hand Hillman in 1949 to the Rover he'd traded in for this, his Swedish car. There were sneers about Volvos – a tractor, a tank – and sometimes the name led to a sniggering joke; but look at it, square-browed, rock-solid, dignified, and drive it, feel how it held the road, feel how it cruised. He'd known the day he drove it home that he owned the car he deserved. And now it was complicit and he could not decide whether or not its dignity was impaired.

'How do you feel?' said his wife.

'I'm okay.'

'You should have let me drive.'

'No. I'm fine. I wish I hadn't eaten that scone though. It was all dough. Pardon. It didn't have any dates in it either.' He smiled at her. The small disappointments of life no longer threw him out of step. He passed them on to her because they seemed to give her pleasure. This motel was a disappointment too, with its cheap furniture and the even cheaper pictures on the walls. Was that supposed to be a Venetian canal – gondolas in Taranaki where there should be cows – and this the Parthenon, by God, as white as bones in a purple dawn? He would have liked some dignity, for himself, for Vera too, a little good taste. On the other hand, there was a fitness in returning to the second rate – or was it third? – and reminding himself of how he had started.

'You're tired,' she said. 'Lie down. Do you want your pills?'

'It isn't time.'

'You don't have to swallow them by the clock, Tom. It's how you feel.'

'I feel fine. I'll unpack.'

'No, let me.' She put his underclothes in a drawer, hung his shirts on those insulting hangers that let you steal only part of them, made you feel accused.

'This place was a cow paddock,' he said. 'A man called Findlay owned it. His brothers got killed in the first war and his son in the second.' He smiled. 'That's not bad,' meaning his memory. He had not thought of the Findlays for close on sixty years.

'Do you want to give me your jacket?' she said.

He took it off and stood in his shirtsleeves, watching her. She was a tidy woman, meticulous. He admired her efficiency even more than her prettiness – her kid-glove skin and creamy brow. Some of his friends praised her for looks and intelligence, others for her tact – she knew when to stop being intelligent. They imagined a happy life for the Greggs, which was accurate up to a point. They did not know how sensitive she was to inattention, how she put a distance between them that required planning and energy to close, and often more time than he was able to spend. They had whole days of estrangement but managed well – through habit he supposed, and fondness too – when they came together. Yet each time something was lost, until it had come to seem enough that he amused her.

'Do you want to have lunch here or in town?' she said.

'In town. Just a sandwich or a salad. We can have a look at the main street first.'

'Do you want to walk that far?'

There was tact: not 'can you?' but 'do you want to?' He could manage a stroll through the town. The slower pace might let recognitions occur. Names on shop windows; he'd made a bet with himself that there would be one at least. Wasn't it a sociological fact that there was a type of person who never got out of these one horse towns – the same house, same job, same daily walk – while others, like him, were gone as soon as they finished school and never came back? He smiled to himself – almost never – then smiled at his wife, thanking her.

'I'll take it slowly. But I might have a little snooze first.'

'Me too.' She took off her skirt and hung it on a chair, placed her shoes neatly side by side, then lay down with her arms crossed on her chest – as smooth and as mild as a madonna – and sank straight away into one of her magical five-minute naps. That switching off, absenting, had offended him once (it belittled him), but now, like everything about her, he admired it – cat-like and efficient, and somehow inviting, including him. He crossed his own hands. This was an extraordinary day, he had no pain and not an ounce of fear, no curiosity, nothing but interest; and Vera beside him, perfect in every way, and no need to be afraid that she would not cope…

He woke in half an hour and found her gone. There was no wrinkle or dent in her matching bed and the room was so empty that he cried, 'Vera.' A new cold element lapped around him, something that had flowed in while he slept and carried her away.

'Vera.'

He saw her shadow cross outside the windows. She opened the door and smiled at him. 'You're awake. I've been sitting out here in the sun.'

'I thought you were gone.'

'Silly boy. You were sleeping so nicely. I crept out.' She was busy at the table between the beds. 'Here,' – that ugly rattling – 'take this. Wait, I'll get some water. There now. Sit up a bit more.'

'I can do it.'

'I know you can. I went across to see the restaurant, it looks quite nice. We're booked in for dinner, is that all right? The owner's name is Claridge, does it ring a bell? He used to be a farmer and he thought he might remember the Greggs but he's not sure. I couldn't tell him exactly where your farm was, just out by the coast, is that right? Anyway, I sat in the sun. There's some lovely roses but no scent.'

Like date scones with no dates, he thought. And this was Vera in her rare chattering mode, denatured too. It was only in quietness that she became herself.

'I remember a Claridge at school.'

'It might be his father.'

'But don't tell him, okay? I don't want to talk.'

'It might be interesting. He's a friendly man.'

'Just let me get my wits back.' He was frightened of being dizzy when he stood up and of hearing his stomach run down the scale like a set of bells or make the oozing screech he must apologise for. On his feet, he took the old man side-step that kept him on balance, and knew that the main street was beyond him. He should have let her drive and saved his strength for all that practical stuff he still had to do. Perhaps he should be getting ready for it. He glanced at his watch. Five hours – which had the ring of days, of weeks, of years. How should he fill in the time? Sitting in the sun, she had said. The words had a simplicity that brought tears to his eyes.

'What's the matter, Tommy? Does it hurt?'

'No. No. I think I'll sit outside for a while. I can't…'

'What is it?'

'I can't manage a walk yet. We'll go in the car later on.'

'We don't have to go at all.'

'I'd like to see…' What? Old shops? Shop windows? Familiar names? But now what he wanted was 'sitting in the sun'. He craved the sun.

She carried out two chairs, set them side by side like her shoes, and they sat upright, comical looking he supposed, facing the opposite wing of the motel and the mountain climbing, not quite immaculate, behind. The Volvo rested in the carport. It had something of the beast about it, heavier and squatter than the stud-farm Jersey bull they'd stopped to admire outside Wanganui yesterday afternoon. Was that yesterday? He could not sort it out and it did not matter. The sun was warm on his hands. He rolled up his sleeves. Warm on his arms. But after a moment too hot on his head. Vera got up without being asked and fetched his hat from their unit. She put it on his head at a jaunty angle and he let a moment go by before setting it straight. He undid two buttons of his shirt. The warmth was – no other word for it – glorious. If he'd needed to worship anything it would have been the sun, no lesser god. Religion must have started there.

'The water tower,' he said. 'Isn't it…'

'Wonderfully ugly,' she agreed. 'Like a man in a mask.'

In a town without hills you needed a feature like that to mark your place, and here, of course, to make obeisance to the dog's-tooth mountain in the north. He had climbed the tower as a boy, seen the shops and houses crusted like a scab; had half-climbed the mountain as well and only by straining picked out the tower-spike in the cloth of farms rolling to the sea. Then he had left without a backward glance and not counted as coming home the painful Christmas visits to his parents, or the expedition – he had been expeditious – to help them shift when they sold the farm. They had gone north to Tauranga at first, then to Howick, away from him as though by choice, and he had visited them more willingly and not come back to this town until today. There had been nothing to bring him in all those years. But something now: the memory that had filled him like the climax to a symphony – only a week ago, was it? – illuminating him in every fibre, so that his fingers itched, so that his mind possessed again that instant in time when he had been thoughtless, accommodated, accommodating, standing on the clifftop with the sea in motion at his feet, hearing it boom. Why that moment? He had not known it was special. Could not remember when he had stood there – as an infant, a child, a boy? Now he could only remember remembering.

So, he had thought, stone-still in his bed, hearing his wife breathe, hearing all the years of his life breathe away, I'll go back there.

'Potty, if you ask me,' Laura said.

'Why?' Betty said.

'Coming all this way and then just plonking down on chairs. What's the point?'

'He used to live here,' Clarry said, coming in. 'Had a farm, at least his old man did. I don't remember any Greggs.'

'If he's ever milked a cow I'll eat my garters. You could blow him over breathing on him,' Laura said. 'I'm off.'

'He's a sick man,' Clarry said. 'You can tell by the colour of his skin. You going, Laura?'

'Check the clock. I'm on my own time. Number three had a you know what. You could charge them extra for disposing of things like that.'

'They're holding hands. I think that's nice,' Betty said.

'She's holding him up if you ask me,' Laura said.

They watched her walk across the lawn rolling her hips, light a cigarette at the gate and turn towards High Street.

'She always has to mention it,' Betty said.

'What?'

'What she finds.'

'Yeah, that's Laura. These two are booked for dinner.'

'And only one night,' Betty said, looking at the computer. 'They're not like tourists.'

'*I'm going to make a sentimental journey…*,' Clarry sang.

'Do you think so?'

'Last look at the old place is my guess.'

'That's sad. They didn't want lunch?'

'Going uptown.'

'What do you think he's got?'

'Dunno, I'm no doctor. He's used to bossing people, I'll tell you that. He snapped my head off when I tried to help him get his bags out of the boot.'

'If you're sick you don't want people butting in all the time.' She went out of the office, walking on the path – must remind Clarry to stop Laura taking shortcuts on the lawn – and along to number ten.

'Clarry was meant to ask you about the low fat milk. We've got full cream.'

'We prefer low fat,' said Mrs Gregg.

'And everything else is all right?'

'Yes, perfectly.'

'If there's anything you want…'

'We'll let you know. Thank you.'

'Fine,' Betty said, trying to match the woman's 'perfectly'. A little resentful, she added, 'Okey doke.'

The man gave a clacking laugh. His mouth was mottled gray, shining in the sun, and his eyes, under his hat brim, lizardy – seeing other people as merely something that moved, no more than that. Then, surprisingly, he said, 'It's a lovely day.'

'Yes, Taranaki weather.'

He laughed again, getting the joke. 'What are the roads like out to the coast? They were only shingle in my day.'

'Most of them are sealed now. Which way do you want to go?'

'Out past Manaia.'

'There's good roads there.'

'We might take a drive.'

'Your roses are lovely,' Mrs Gregg said.

'Yes,' Betty said, then drew back. The woman was not starting a new conversation; she was, by some social shift, sending her away. She felt herself blushing. 'Well,' she said, 'I'll be off. Duty calls.' She walked back to the office, confused. She was used to guests being strange but it usually didn't take her long to get a handle on them. These ones kept behind a wall even when they were acting friendly. Yet there was something nice about them, as if, keeping private, they smiled and said excuse us please and no offence. There was something sad too. The wife was holding his hand again, still in love with him, even though he was sick and twenty years older than her at least.

'Nosy-parkering,' Vera whispered.

'She's harmless. If you hadn't let that out about the farm…'

'I was passing the time, Tom. This sun's getting hot. Shall we find some lunch?'

She helped him stand, thinking it was all very well for him to refuse a stick but it turned her into his prop, didn't he see? Her own prop, the feeling that sustained her, was pity. Pity was strongest, although she felt anger too at his stupidity, and sadness that he had come to this: deceiving her, protecting her, pretending all the time, when honesty and talk were what she longed for. If he would put his hand out wanting her, not needing to be helped from his chair, how simple this journey would become, like walking together on a path by the sea, where they would tell each other where they were now.

She helped him put his jacket on.

'Shall I drive?'

'Yes. That way I can see out the window.'

She backed the car out carefully – this brute of a car – and went crunching gravel out to the road.

'Tell me when I need to stop.'

They turned into High Street, where she eased the car up and down over judder bars.

'These things weren't here,' he said.

'They weren't invented.' Any small town would have done, but she found herself willing him to find a shop, a name. Some country solicitor was likeliest – a son, or grandson now, called back home to carry the practice on. She kept her eye out for gold lettering, brass plates. Shoe shops, menswear shops would have come and gone, and grocers and butchers were gone forever.

'They've turned it into quite a nice town,' he said, surprised.

'Do you see anyone?'

'It's hardly likely. Anyway…'

He did not want to, she understood. No old school mate, no old flame to whom he might have to explain himself. She was the only person in his life. What he was after was a place that would lock on him, engage with him the way parts of engines clicked together or the way space stations docked. She believed he might rest then. She looked again, left and right, wanting to find a building, a window, a house down a side street, anything.

'It's bit too much like toytown, though,' he said.

'There's a lunch place. Shall I stop?'

She found two spaces and nosed into the front one – hated reversing this wretched car. They went into the coffee shop – Maybelle's, with a Maybelle woman mopping a table and a citified boy at the espresso machine. She would have liked a table out on the street; but Tom was never comfortable with people walking by, so she said, 'There's a courtyard. You go out. I'll bring it.'

She chose from the rather limp display, egg sandwiches for them both, a sultana pinwheel they could share, freshly squeezed orange juice in two glasses. The coffee machine startled her with an ugly clearing of its throat. There was nowhere in the world, she supposed, where you could get away from these things. Except in your own home. She had a sudden longing for it, so intense tears came into her eyes: the quiet house, the garden, the harbour at her feet. And here they were in this flat town, looking, desperate but oh so polite, for what? For what? And moving, by the minute, by the hour, towards the huge event they could not talk about. It was going to be, she realised, terrible – and they could not talk. Her hands began to shake, rattling the tray, and the boy, in his international haircut, squinted at her.

'You okay, lady?'

'Perfectly, thank you,' she said.

She went into the sunny yard and put the tray on the table Tom had chosen by an ornamental pond. Red fish with albino patches rose and sank in the green water. A cat slept at the foot of an iron wall that must pour heat on it like a radiator. Tom was watching it. He did not like cats, or any animals; but when challenged he claimed that he liked birds, and shags the best, because they wanted nothing, they asked for nothing. She supposed that he would make his usual cats-in-foodshops remark, but instead he said, 'We had one like that. It could be the twin.'

'The cat?' Smoky gray with a white chest. She put his drink and sandwich in front of him and sat down.

'Miss Twiddle.'

'Who?'

'I called her Miss Twiddle. From the *Katzenjammer Kids*.'

'What was that, a book?'

'A comic strip. There was Hans and Fritz and the Captain and the Inspector and Miss Twiddle. Not bad, eh?' He grinned at her painfully, then she saw tears gather in his eyes and slide down his cheeks.

'Oh Tom, Tommy, talk to me,' she said.

'Can't. No point.'

'Tom…'

'There's nothing to say.'

She heard her own breathing, fast and light, and wondered if she would hyperventilate. She put her mind to controlling it, and said, when she was calm again, 'Then eat your sandwich, Tom. Come on. And here, wipe your cheeks.' She offered her hankie but he took his own and dried himself.

'Stupid oaf,' he said.

'No you're not.'

'Getting worked up about a cat.'

He gave a small sigh and she saw, amazed, that he was satisfied. Was this all it took? The memory of a comic strip? Could they stop driving through the main street now?

He bit his sandwich, made a face, opened it. 'No parsley.'

'Eat the pinwheel then.'

'I don't think I want anything.'

'Drink your drink.'

She ate her own sandwich (surprisingly tasty, it had celery salt) then broke pieces off the pinwheel, nibbling sultanas like a monkey. He waited politely.

'Where to now?' she said, dabbing her mouth with a paper napkin.

'Anywhere. Just drive around. Up towards the mountain if you like.'

'Don't you want to try and find your house?'

'I'll do that later.'

She drove into the country, taking any roads, made a loop through farms and bush, then headed back towards the dairy factory and the tower that looked as if it should crack and fall. They went down the main street again, through safety bays and over judder bars. Tom did not look left or right.

At the motel he said, 'I think I'll have a rest now.'

'All right.'

'What will you do?'

'Sit in the sun. I'll read my book.'

'Take your shade.' He opened her drawer and took it out. 'I don't want you hurting your eyes.'

'Thank you, Tom,' accepting the sun visor, putting it on. It was as near as he could get to saying sorry – and saying, perhaps, I love you, Vera.


He woke and sat up carefully. Parts of him were as brittle as kindling wood, threatening to snap if he moved too fast. He eased around and put his feet on the floor. The body was a machine and when it grew obsolete... He tried to smile. It was made of working parts, just as property law was working parts, perfectly adjusted, oiled and tuned. He was glad he'd spent his life in the law, and glad his body had worked so well for so long; but on the edge of panic that his mind might wobble and turn him away from the path he'd chosen now.

'Vera,' he called, too furry in his throat for her to hear. She was outside reading. Books were her consolation, her nourishment. She became world traveller, scientist, artist, philosopher. She was a people-collector; he never knew where she might turn, who she might admire this week, or worship, love, the next. It was James

Murray at the moment – she must be getting near the end – the man who compiled the dictionary. He could read twenty-five languages, she said. He had two tons of paper slips with words on them filed in his shed. Her cheeks grew pink, her eyes were alive, when she introduced him. Four million quotations, she cried.

Tom stood. He made his side-step. That amassing, that profusion, when all he wanted was paring down and no more than two or three words. He did not care how many languages…

'Vera.'

Still she did not come. He made his way through the bathroom, slid open the rumbling door, sat down. It had been his fear through his middle years that he would die on the lavatory, as men did now and then, in strange hotels, and he had formed the habit of searching the vinyl on each new floor for misshappen faces – was this the last person he would see? But it turned out that heart was not the thing killing him, he had no need to fear that smallest-room indignity. Nor would he have people fiddling at him with tubes and wiping with damp cloths. He was seeing to that, making a pre-emptive strike. He smiled at the pattern between his feet.

'Tom?' she called.

'In here.'

'Are you all right?'

'Yes,' he said, adding 'dammit' under his breath. Only in the last few days had she taken this step too far.

'You were sleeping like a lamb,' she said, when he came out.

'What's Mr Murray up to now?'

'Oh –' she made a nervous laugh – 'nothing much. Tom, there's a lovely colour on the mountain. Come and look.'

'I've seen it before.'

'Yes,' she said, 'yes,' and sat on her bed. The heavy book slid to the floor. He was afraid she would cry.

He touched her hair, then lifted the sun visor from her brow. He did not want to see her wearing it; would have preferred her dressed up now in one of the flowered silk dresses that brought out her own silkiness, accentuating with their long sleeves the sparrow quickness of her hands.

'How many books do you think you've read in your life?'

'Oh thousands, thousands.'

'And how many do you remember?'

'What a ridiculous question, Tom. You remember tiny bits and pieces of everything you do. I might have only one word from each book.'

'And not know you've got it?'

'Yes. And one thing from each day I've lived.'

And not know that either, he thought. Only two things were real for him: the moving endless sea and Vera sitting on the bed. She was the sum of every day they'd shared. It surprised him how sensuous his knowledge of her was, he had never been much alert to that; nor – he felt it like shame – had he been sensual. The thought of how little they had lived in that way disturbed him – how much there was to apologise for and he had no time. Time only for a word or two.

'Will you stay in our house, Vera?'

'Yes, I will.'

'Always stay?'

'There's nowhere else I want to go. Tom…'

He saw her try hard, try to say it.

'…I think we should go back. I think tomorrow morning we should go.'

He smiled as a way of thanking her. 'Maybe. Maybe.' Then turned and put the sun visor on the table. He heard her pick up her book.

'That sleep has freshened me,' he said.

'I'm glad. Is there any pain?'

'I feel like a boy. I could score tries.'

She laughed with a clicking sound, like knitting needles. 'Oh Tom, I wish I'd seen you then. Scoring tries.'

'I didn't much. All I got in was the second fifteen.' He felt a malicious pride in what he had done – money, professional success, a beautiful wife – alongside those one or two failed first-fifteeners met by chance on Lambton Quay – beery men, potbellied, in shiny suits.

'It's strange. There's a balance,' he said.

'Not always.'

'In my life. I believe in…' But there was nothing, in the end, but necessary steps, holding on to sufficient knowledge for that. He felt her receding and he said, 'I think I'll take the car for a while. Do you mind if I go by myself.'

'No, Tom. If that's what you want.'

'I'll drive out and have a look… I shouldn't be too long.'

'Take your hat.'

He touched her lightly on the head.

Driving away, he looked in the rear-vision mirror and saw her standing at the door with one hand raised.

Tom Gregg could not find a cliff. He could not find the place where he had stood as a boy. It was a disappointment at first, but as he went down a sandy path made by children's feet his mind began to fill with contentment at the ordinary way things turned out. He walked to the water, watched it wash up the beach and shrink away and could not connect it with that other sea. That other was equally real, even though this one wet his feet.

He turned and saw the Volvo low-slung in a hollow, where no one at this hour was going to interrupt. He stepped away from the waves and walked up the beach, hearing his shoes squelch and smiling at the thought that he need not worry any more about catching cold.

When he reached the car he ran his hand on its smooth side. He thought of Vera. Who was she − bright and tactful, beautiful and sharp, soft-tongued, enigmatic, always at a distance yet always in this room or the next? Vera, who had travelled with him all through those years, as they learned how much they could be together and how much they must stay apart.

He would have liked to touch her hand again.

She went in to dinner by herself. The restaurant was less than half full. Several people had finished their meals and left − she had heard them pass by to their units – and others were starting on dessert. She nodded at the waitress.

'Gregg. I'm sorry I'm late.'

'No problem,' the girl said. 'I thought there were two?'

'My husband's gone for a drive. I'll start without him.'

She ordered fish, then called the waitress back and said she'd like a half bottle of riesling. 'My husband will probably want something different when he comes.'

There was, she thought, a fine edge between pretence and horror, and she did not know how long she could stay on this side or if, when she tipped over, she would in fact find horror there. Perhaps only sorrow, perhaps grief. She had known the former all her life, it might be described as her natural state, which she'd settled into finally and almost comfortably when she and Tom had learned that she could not have a child. She doubted though that she was capable of grief – was puzzled and sometimes contemptuous when people went on television after tragedies and talked about needing to go through 'the grieving process'. What was that?

'Oh,' she said, 'oh,' not knowing where the exclamation came from – some place away from all this turning of her mind about herself; somewhere still, where Tom had gone.

The woman from the office brought her wine.

'Are you all right?'

'Yes, I think so. Will you…'

'What is it? Can I help?'

'Will you sit with me for a minute?'

'Isn't your husband coming?'

'Oh yes, he will. He went for a drive. He's like that, all hours. He's one of those men who needs to be alone.'

The woman sat. She had an anxious look. 'Here,' she said, handing over Tom's serviette.

Vera had not known that she had cried. She dried her eyes. 'He's got a cancer,' she said. 'I suppose you could see how sick he is. There are secondaries…'

'I'm sorry,' the woman said.

'It's in remission. That's why we can make this trip.'

'Has he come back to see his farm? Where he grew up?'

'Oh that, yes. And the sea out there.' She almost mentioned the comic strip. 'He's got a place waiting at the hospice. But he hates the idea of not doing things for himself.'

'Yes,' the woman said, 'I can understand. Would you like my husband to go and look for him?'

'No. Oh no. I'm not worried. Tom would hate that.'

Her fish came. She ate it and drank a glass of wine, surprised at how she had babbled. I don't do that sort of thing, she thought. Yet there had been a need for words, for things to come into the open a little way.

She thought of him working in his shed, cutting with his prompt unfussy hands that length of tube he would tape to the exhaust pipe of the car and lead up to the window where he sat. She had no doubt the measurements were correct.

'Go away, Vera,' he had said, coming sharp at her, and she had turned away, closed the door behind her and stood in the garden, looking over the harbour, watching a ferry steam out, thinking, I knew, I knew – striking the phrase like a tinny-sounding gong. Driving out for groceries next day, she found the tubing, coiled and tied, hidden under sacks in the boot of the car.

The waitress took her plate away and brought the dessert menu.

'The sorbet, I think,' Vera said. 'And then, do you have some herbal teas? You do? Chamomile.'

So cold, the sorbet, and the sips of tea so hot. She wondered what she would do when there was nothing left – an empty cup, an empty bowl. Dark out there now, so cold and lonely. Oh Tom, she thought, I wish there had been some other way of loving you.

Carefully she lifted the cup and bowl away from her. She beckoned the office woman from the door. The woman's husband came too, both uncertain, bent a little at the waist, knowing something was wrong.

Vera dabbed her eyes with her serviette. She smiled at them apologetically. 'I'm worried now,' she said. 'Do you think someone could search? It's getting late. I think he's missing.'

# Home Town

I don't recognise the woman behind the reception desk. No reason why I should, of course; it's more than twenty years since I left. Still, it's a relief, in a mild sort of way.

'Call me Betty,' she says. 'Everyone does. It's more friendly that way, isn't it?'

'I don't know,' I say, not having views one way or the other and what the hell.

Betty gives me a sharp look, laughs, nods. She has hardly any neck and one of those large high-rise bosoms. Chin and chest may collide at any moment.

'And we won't charge you the single supplement,' she says, 'even though we're full up or nearly. It's hard enough on your own, isn't it, without paying more for it?'

'I like being on my own,' I say and kick myself. Betty has the sharp, winkle-picking eyes that often go with kindness. My business is Betty's business, no doubt about that.

'Well, it takes all sorts, doesn't it,' she coos, then snaps her head back and shouts, 'Clarree.'

Out comes Clarry and I nearly laugh in his face. Now I know I'm back in the home town, the small town, the town where it all started. Clarry has grey hair and a red face. He is all the fathers of all the kids in town, or nearly, and all the uncles, and all the old guys leaning over the rails at the sale yards or yarning at the bar of the Central Hotel or roaring at the footie and drinking beer on old sofas on back street verandas of a Sunday while they fix the kids' bikes. He puts out a hand the size and texture of a crocodile handbag. 'Call me Clarry,' he says.

'Thanks. I'm Jess.'

'If you'd just mind the desk, dear,' says Betty, 'I'll show Miss Fitzherbert her room.'

Clarry's ears prick like a heading dog's. 'Fitzherbert,' he says. 'That's a name that rings bells. No, no, Bett, I'll take the lady. Unit twelve, okay? Has it been cleaned yet? Milk in the fridge? Right then, dear, this way. Number twelve, exactly half your age, eh?'

Betty raises her eyes to the acoustic tiles.

I give a sick smile. Why fuss? The clunking come-on is just knee jerk stuff to Clarry.

'Fitzherbert,' he says again. 'What was y' dad's name?'

'Arthur.'

Clarry stops short, so suddenly I nearly bang into him. 'Big family, am I right?'

'Yes.'

I can hear Clarry's mind clickety clacking. Wasn't there something? Something odd? Different? He'll ask Bett. Bett should know. He gives an odd sort of leer. 'Long way out of town, were you?'

'No, just round the corner. Kowhai Street.'


Number fifteen to be precise, a rambling broken down old villa where Mum and Dad functioned on a mattress labelled Lullaby and then there was me. And continued to do so, at it like rabbits they were, till finally there were Timothy called Tunny, and Jocelyn who was a boy, and Henrietta called Honey, the twins Lucille and Lettice, then Jack and Polly, and Melissa the last.

We were a close family, in more ways than one, and we tended to pair off into even closer buddy systems: Tunny and Joss, Honey and me, the twins, then Jack and Polly. Melissa, being the baby, was adored by all.

I was lucky with Honey. She was four years younger than me and a hero worshipper by nature. She was my adoring junior, my confidant, my friend.

So there were nine of us. Three boys and six girls. Five now. Honey died last Thursday.

As Clarry remembered we were a big family — a twenty-five double barracouta loaves and fifteen pints a week family. And like the large families of fiction we were as happy as the day was long; an unruly, untrammelled, physical contact family. A tumble of pink limbs on dusty lawns changing in time to strength or grace depending on sex.

'The Fitzherberts,' Dad told us frequently, slipping a roll y' own into place, 'are a family of great antiquity descended from the ancient Celtic kings of the North. A noble race, a race of strong men and beautiful women, and don't you forget it.'

We sensed at the time that others in the town were not so impressed, though Mum went along with the saga, probably because she loved him. She loved us all, made a quick head count at meal times and more or less left it at that. She had, in a sense, signed off. Not from lack of loving, Jean Fitzherbert was made for loving, but there were too many of us for refinements.

She was large and huggable and her hair fell down and her feet hurt. Her greatest treat was to put them up and see what was in the paper. She lay on the raddled old sofa, occasionally shaking her head in concern for all the sorrows of the world. Her range was wide, from the local farmers who needed the rain to tearful rage at the plight of the starving homeless in Africa. And the babies, those huge-eyed silent babies. How could it be? How could it?


Aunty Pat next-door's concern began with us. It was through her that I found out, as we all did eventually, that the Fitzherberts were different.

I was about eleven I suppose, head down bottom up, balancing on the freezer in Carr's Dairy hunting for Large Economy Size Chicken Wings when I heard Aunty Pat in full cry to Mrs Carr.

'If you could see the place. But what can you expect from a couple of no-hopers with a pack like that? Running wild the lot of them. As for the names, they sound like some bloody curse.' Her voice dropped as she chanted, 'Jess and Tunny, Joss and Honey, Jacky, Polly and Mel. No wonder I worry about them. Especially the girls.'

Maybe it was the word 'curse', or possibly my goose-flesh chill came from the freezer, but I slid the lid back in panic and hurled the chicken wings at her, screaming, 'You've left out the twins, you old cow!'

Aunty Pat ducked and shook her fist, outraged as Donald Duck on steam. 'See what I mean?' she cried to Mrs Carr who was dusting down the Economy Pack from the other side of the counter where it had landed.

One of the ways we knew we were different was that we didn't give a damn. We were Fitzherberts, that race of beautiful women and strong men. The rampant hedge, the worn dusty grass, the Wyvern rusting on its rims and the endless washing flapping on the line were part of us, part of our difference and our pride.

Other kids loved coming to play at Kowhai Street. They walked about wide-eyed and never wanted to go home. There was always something happening, they said.


Clarry puts down my bag and unlocks unit twelve. 'Kowhai Street eh? I'd have thought you were way out in the ulu.'

I am getting bored with Clarry. I look at him, innocent and wide-eyed as a marigold. 'Why?'

Clarry has not been expecting this. He looks all come over, or as all come over as an already red-faced man can, and mumbles, 'Just kidding. Lots of kids, y' know. Nothing else to do. Long way from the pictures.'

I let him swing. 'Pictures?'

Clarry is saved by the bell. Hipping and thighing round the corner comes what my father would have called a sonsy lass. A blonde, a blonde within the meaning of the act, a bottle blonde with a roving eye stands in front of us with a pile of bed linen in her arms. She is a player, this lady.

'Excuse me,' she says coyly, flattening herself as best she can against the wall of the herring-gutted corridor.

'No, no, we're here now,' says Clarry backing into unit twelve and dropping my bag.

The blonde gives a coy hoot. 'Well, have fun.'

'No, no,' says Clarry redder than ever. 'This is Laura. Laura Blowse, our housekeeper. Blowsie by name but tight by nature.'

But Laura and I are not listening. She drops the linen with a shriek and we embrace, flinging our arms wide, screaming each other's names and jumping up and down with the wonder of meeting again after so long.

'How's Lisa? How's Kitty?' we yell, embracing once again. Laura glances over my shoulder, extracts herself for a moment. 'Why don't you just fuck off, Clarry,' she says kindly. 'Me and Jess have got some catching up to do.'

She shuts the door in his face and flops onto the double bed.

'Well,' she says, bouncing up and down on the heavy-duty orange and brown cover with frilled cushions to tone. 'Talk about long time no see. That's a time we won't forget, eh? Hang on a tick.' She leaps to her feet, disappears out the door and is back in a flash, clutching something wrapped in a brown towel. She does a sort of 'alley-oop' flourish with the towel, and there's a bottle of gin, three-quarters empty but never mind.

'They do this sometimes, the regulars,' she says. 'Commercials and that. The decent ones'll leave a drop or two for me. It's never worth taking home so I keep it in the back of the linen cupboard for a rainy day. Never touch it on duty, of course, but it's nice to know it's there. Bit early in the day, I s'pose, but this is a special occasion, and besides, I need a hair of the dog – made rather a night of it last night. Where's the glasses? Good on you. Water okay?'

'Yes, I say,' shivering suddenly as I remember it all clear as yesterday. Laura lifts her glass, a button pops on her sky blue uniform. 'Here's looking at ya, kid,' she drawls and takes a swig.

There is a knock on the door.

Laura whips the bottle beneath the towel and hides her glass. 'Shit.'

'I'll go.'

Clarry is standing there grinning like a pumpkin, clutching a half-carton of full-cream milk. He doesn't put his foot in the door, or not yet, but I wouldn't bet on it.

'Bett made a snafu,' he laughs. 'You haven't got any milk.'

'Thank you, Clarry,' I say and shut the door gently.

'Stickybeaks, the two of them,' says Laura. 'Tell me, did Steven leave her? Marry you?'

'No.'

'After all that. What a sod.'

'He couldn't. How could he? And who'd want him?'

'You,' she says enfolding me in her arms and hugging me yet again. I pull away, hating her easy sentimental stupidity. I sit up straight, tight-lipped and prickly, the Jessica Fitzherbert Laura has never known.

'What about Duggie?' I ask quickly.

'Naa. Best thing really. Duggie was never what you'd call husband material.' Laura's shoulders drop. She stares wistfully into her gin. She is suddenly no longer what the boys in the bar at the Central used to call 'A real blonde. Big. A real goer, know what I mean?'

She sniffs. 'And now Lisa's got a kid. Charlton, of all daft names. Lovely little kid, but he runs rings round her, got her on toast, I don't know how it'll end,' she says glaring at me.

She gives a little regrouping bounce. 'Tell me about Kitty.'

'She's a cabin attendant with Air New Zealand.'

'Terrible hats,' Laura sniffs again. 'Still, as long as she's happy. Boyfriend?'

'Yes. Called Steven.'

Laura shakes her head slowly. 'You wouldn't read about it. Have you sung her Duggie's Stephen song?'

'Off course not! What'd you think I am?'

'You used to laugh.'

'Never,' I snap. 'Never.'

Laura bursts into song:

> There was a maid in a mountain glen
> Seduced herself with a fountain pen
> The top came off and the ink ran wild
> And she gave birth to a blue-black child.
> And they called the bastard Stephen,
> They called the bastard Stephen,
> They called the bastard Stephen,
> Until his dying day.

'He had a lovely voice, Duggie,' she says.

And now we are laughing again, crying, clutching each other with the battered camaraderie of the bad girls, the real goers, the town bikes. I haven't laughed like this for over twenty years.

'Remember that thug of a staff nurse, Porky Morton?' she says.

'How could I forget?'

'How she kept us out of the way in that cubicle down the back? And gave us our meals last. Imagine. It's not even twenty-five years ago. The old cow'd be lynched now.'

We sit silent, considering Staff Nurse Morton and the stream of time. Nevertheless, Porky Morton taught me a lot. The first thing I learned was that there are some people, men and women – not many thank God, but some – who can be total shits. Not the ordinary casual bitching most of us achieve occasionally, but the genuine, one hundred percent, fully paid-up article. Cruel, ruthless and mean as cat shit. I had not known this before, not even through Steven. I thought the whole thing was my fault.

Porky also taught me the importance of power. Of winning. I would probably not have become the woman I am now, the entrepreneurial whiz kid, the tiger in the corporate tank, without Staff Nurse Morton.

'Why on earth did you stay here, Laura?' I ask.

'Where else would I go? And Mum came round pretty

quick. Dad took longer, but Lisa was a cute little kid. Still is, if only she'd get over this "finding herself" crap. Why did you leave?'

'Oh come on. How could we stay here, for God's sake?'

Laura's brow wrinkles. 'Yeah, I suppose not,' she says finally. 'What a bummer though. What a bummer.'

I laugh, what else could I do.

'Must go,' says Laura, 'I've got to finish off here and I promised to help Betty set up the tables next door at the Oddfellows this afternoon. We're catering for a big jazz and poetry do there tonight … Hey! Why don't you come along to it? Should be fun.'

'Thanks all the same, but I'm not in party mood. I'd rather have a quiet night with the telly.'

'Tell you what, then,' she says leaping to her feet. 'I'll just knock off the linen for the annex and check on the spa pool, then we'll have our lunch here. How about that?'

I would prefer somewhere away from the motel. Clarry will have been chatting up Betty for details, and my guess is she may have them. The name itself should be enough for Bett.

I pull myself together. Sit up straight. 'Okay. What's it like?'

'Not bad. I get mates' rates, and we can share a dessert and split the bill.'

'Don't be nuts,' I say as she swings out the door with the linen.

Her face reappears. 'I forgot. Lisa's on at lunch. You'll meet them both.'


I stare at Lisa who is thin and blonde and lovely and vulnerable. More than her mother or I were, much more, and that's saying something. Lisa has that aura, that imprint on her pale forehead that reads 'Take me'. She is a throwback, Lisa, a yesterday's girl. An unhappy-looking young woman at risk in a long black apron and jeans. I think of Kitty, who is streetwise and tough and funny, and am glad she is not here. It would not be fair. The comparison, I mean.

'Hi,' says Lisa. She makes a vague movement with her hand

towards a white-haired toddler chewing a red paper napkin. 'Come and say hullo to Gargie's lady, Charlton.'

Charlton grins and makes a flying dive at Gargie's ankles beneath the gingham tablecloth. The table rocks, Gargie yelps as the baby teeth hit home.

'Good day all,' cries Betty sweeping in from reception. She scoops Charlton into her arms. 'Come and play with Auntie Betty and the new vacuum cleaner, sweetie.'

Charlton beams. 'Vacoom,' he lisps and leans his head against his friend.

'Fancy you two girls knowing each other,' says Betty disengaging the cord of her glasses from Charlton's iron grip. 'Talk about a small world.'

Laura and I smile.

'Wherever did you meet up?'

'In the maternity ward,' says Laura.

'Oh,' says Betty.

I am not drawn to Betty and her intrusive kindness, her veiled smiles. I suspect that Betty's views on matrimony, patrimony and family life are those of a small town Mesozoic flying reptile. However, after the two gins I give her what she wants. Or some of it.

'Yes,' I smile, 'in the solos' cubicle, down the end at the back, with our little bastards.'

I have overdone it. I do not feel smart, liberated or up-you-Bett. I feel sick. I might bawl my head off. I should not have come.

Betty looks at me with startled unease.

'Vacoom, Bett,' demands Charlton. 'Vacoom.'

'Pardon me,' says Betty. They sweep out.

'Why did you bite her head off?' says Laura pouring the wine. 'She's a good sort, old Bett. And why have you come back anyway, after so long?'

'Honey died on Thursday. Her funeral's tomorrow.'

'Hell's fangs. What about him?'

'He'll be there. Of course.'

'Christ Almighty,' says Laura.

It was one of the twins, Lettice, who rang. On Thursday as I said, so Kitty and Steven, her boyfriend, were there as usual. Kitty calls Thursdays 'Mum's Night In'.

She leaps to answer the phone as usual. 'No, it's not. Hang on and I'll get her. You, Mum,' she says handing over the phone and returning to the lamb shanks.

'Was that Kitty?' says a muffled voice.

I flop onto the nearest chair, gasping. 'Which one are you?'

'Lettice. Was it her?'

'Yes.'

'She sounds exactly like you,' says the tearful voice.

'Letty, what on earth's happened!'

'Honey died this morning. Cancer.'

'*No*! Why didn't you tell me? Let me know?'

'What could you have done?'

I open my mouth to cry, 'Come and seen her,' and shut it again.

Nothing. Nothing at the time or ever again for my sister, my darling, my friend. The wife of the father of my child.

Letty and I are both weeping now. Kitty and Steven drop their forks and sit gaping. I never cry.

'I thought you should know,' says Letty.

'Yes, yes. Thank you.'

'Perhaps,' she says, 'later on, you might like to come over and see us all.'

'Why not now.'

'We talked about it,' mutters the voice. 'All of us, but we didn't think…not now, I mean… Stephen's devastated. He was marvellous while she was sick.'

'I'm *coming*,' I shout.

'Oh, honey.'

'Me or her?'

'You. Jess, are you sure? Well, I don't suppose we can stop you but…'

'I'm coming.'

'Okay,' she says, and gives me details. Eleven o'clock Monday morning, their local church, local cemetery, then back to the house.

There is no mention of Kitty. There are too many gaps. Too many and too late. Both Mum and Dad are dead. Mum sobbed for a week, moaning, 'How could you? How could you? And her first baby too.'

Dad went to the Central.

'Thank you, Letty,' I say. I put down the receiver and curl into a sodden heap. My honey bear is dead.

Kitty is squatting beside me. 'Has one of them died?'

'Yes, yes, yes.'

'Which one?'

'Honey.'

'Oh, Gawd.' She puts her arms round me and hugs. 'Poor old Mum,' she says. Which helps.

'Poor old Mum nothing,' I snap. 'What about her? She's dead.'

'Mum, you haven't seen her for more than twenty years.'

'How could I? How could she? I slept with my sister's husband,' I shout at my daughter's pop-eyed partner. 'When she was in the maternity home.'

'For God's sake don't let's start all this "Woe! Woe!" stuff again,' says Kitty. 'You've told me a thousand times. You were drunk and my father was a sod.'

'Not drunk enough.'

Kitty, like me, has a short fuse. 'Mum, it happened. It's over. It has been for twenty-three years. Besides, how do you think it makes me feel?' she cries, shaking her ragged head at me. 'Some sort of two-headed curse of the Clan Fitzherbert!' She shrugs her shoulders, stacks the plates and stalks into the kitchen. 'Coffee all round?' she calls.

Steven (no relation) and I sit staring at each other. He grins. 'She's fantastic, isn't she?'

'Yes,' I say. 'Yes, she is.'

# How to Bring Down a Government

By the time she clears Inglewood, Carmen knows she is going to be late for the church. Those road works in the Awakino Gorge, she'll say to her mother in her silk suit. I was first car in the queue, honest; that leering Maori guy with the stop sign held us up forty minutes. Forty minutes, would you believe!

Carmen believes it. She's not counting the last lengthy call she is ever going to make to Jason-baby, in the early hours of the morning, and the hour then spent howling; nobody breaks up with her. Nor the early-morning date with her personal trainer at the gym, and the time taken to find the sexy black number that was the only suitable thing to wear to a brother's wedding. She'd meant to check last night how far it was from Hamilton, but Jason had stuffed that up.

On her right the mountain looms – naked rock, only a little snow in the gullies, but clear, stark, and so *close*. Trust Hugo, she thinks, a perfect mountain, a perfect autumn day. Perfect black and white cows on perfectly flat, green paddocks. A perfect bride with pots of money and a farm in due course. Talk about falling on your feet! But then, he always has.

With Celine Dion making the car throb, she burns southward across the plains at 148 kilometres an hour, passing only slightly slower through a string of country towns. Miraculously, the cops are patrolling other roads on this day, and there's a football match on television. Carmen has never seen such boring flatness; but hey, can her new Golf go on these ruler-straight roads! She loves the adrenaline-rush decisions involved in overtaking – shall I? A bit tight? Risky! Why not? *No.* Yes! Amazing how little room you need, really. Only twice have on-coming cars flashed their lights at her and, losing their nerve, begun to swing towards the rough verge.

Fuckwit, she yells out the open car window, as loose stones from their tyres bounce off her windscreen. The mountain drops behind.

Nevertheless, she is going to be late for the church bit. With luck, by the time she's been to the motel and changed, and done her face, she might be able to go straight to the reception. Arrive as the bubbles burst, which, if these people have any class, will be Moët or Bolly. Never Lindauer, darling, or even Verde.

She changes the CD to Robbie Williams and takes a swig of Pump water. That thirty-something Maori had been quite a spunk in his orange safety vest and rainbow beanie. She'd propped her new *Wallpaper* against the steering wheel and slowly turned its luscious pages while waiting for the road-mending machines to move over and his lollipop to swivel round and say Go. She knew he was watching her. They all did.

Tonight, with the wedding over and Jason as history, and a certain jazz event to attend – something pompously calling itself the Taranaki Festival of the Arts – she expects this endless and extremely boring trip will prove its worth.


Lisa Blowse is minding her son and setting tables. She can think of lots more exciting things she would rather be doing at two-thirty on a sunny Sunday afternoon. Like, sunbathing – alone and undisturbed – at the town's small pool, pretending it was Fiji; or on the hard purplish-grey pebbles of the windy cove fifteen minutes' drive away, dreaming of Surfers' soft gold. Or settling down, undisturbed, with a Diet Coke and a packet of crisps to watch her pirated video of *The Ten Commandments*, of which she knows every line and has seen so many times she's lost count.

But lunch at Morrieson's Motel's small restaurant has limped to an end, and now here's Betty and Laura, neither of them young nor overly fit, carting extra tables and chairs into the former Oddfellows Hall two doors away, where they are catering for tonight's jazz and poetry evening. Into the small space, newly swept and its bareness softened with potted trees hired from the Garden Centre, they must squeeze in another ten tables to seat ninety and still properly accommodate the band.

Laura knows this last is important because she has had a drink in the Central with the vocalist, a scrumptious younger version of Nicholas Cage. She promised him, over a discreet bottle of Marlborough Oaked Chardonnay, to have the inauspicious venue properly set up. She tells Betty they want to do a sound check about 5.30pm.

Clarry, who normally does the lifting and fixing, is over in the office seeing to a girl who's just screeched up to the entrance in a black Golf and is now demanding that the mini-van carrying all the band's gear 'move on, for God's sake'.

So, for the motel's women, it's all hands to the pumps.

'Could kill that festival person,' Betty huffs. 'Told her, I *told* her it wasn't our fault that The House on the Plains was booked for a big wedding and it would have to be the Oddfellows. Eighty at a pinch. And then she rings up and tells me the band has said they want ten. Squeeze in a few extra tables, she says. Really! When you've got organisers sitting on their fannies sixty-four ks away in New Plymouth, who haven't the faintest...'

'Go on, Betty,' says Laura, as they steer the last table in through the side doors. 'Stop whinging. You *love* it. Your chance to get into cultural tourism.'

'What the hell's that?'

'The new buzz word for what this town could be all about.' A few nights earlier, Laura, after one or two gins and then that promising half a bottle of Chardonnay, had found herself watching some arts programme; some gent talking about the Taranaki township that could, if it so chose, re-invent itself as a literary shrine. There was a grave. There was a 'Morrieson's Café', featuring timber from RHM's family home demolished in a shocking act of vandalism in 1992, and even a 'Morrieson's Motel'.

'We got a mention on TV the other night.'

'We did?' says Betty, thrilled. 'Which channel? Charlton-sweetie, put the salt and peppers back, good *boy*.'

'Some bloke in a suit talking about Ronald Hugh…'

'Not him again,' says Betty, torn between her desire to know how her beloved motel fitted into cultural tourism and her dislike for the books, the life and the local reputation of the eccentric writer after whom her motel was named. She and Clarry had tried to read at least two of his novels, but had given up, shocked and appalled. They'd faced a huge crisis of conscience when, worn out by farming, they decided to come into town in the early nineties and buy this motel, whose builder had gone bankrupt in the '87 crash.

The location, only a few minutes' walk from the High Street, was terrific, and the place itself nearly new, pleasantly understated red brick not masquerading as Spanish, Tuscan or Tudor. The price was a bargain, rock bottom. The unfortunate name was a real problem, but they shrewdly noted that although he was not mentioned even once in the town's 1981 centennial history, RHM's posthumous reputation seemed to be improving as time went on. With respect for the dead and pragmatism in about equal parts, they decided to retain it.

This was proving a good move. To guests asking about the legendary RHM, Clarry and Betty had a patter of polite generalities. No, he hadn't built this motel, the poor man died in 1972, alone, poor, neglected, just like Mozart, and yes, of course they were enormously proud of the three films written by him.

And of course it was *shocking*, the strength of feeling in the town only a few years before leading to a petition signed by 1300 people (though not by them – someone would inevitably pick up a name like Claridge – how could they?) and the subsequent triumphant demolition of RHM's family home, right where the KFC now stood. A prophet, they murmured, without honour... They handed over a Xerox copy of his entry in the *Oxford Companion to New Zealand Literature*, and sent guests off to the chain bookshop, where it could be confidently anticipated that the assistant behind the counter would never have heard of him or his books. They heard that some made it to Morrieson's Café, to drink their lattes under images from his films and framed blown-up copies of reviews from English and Australian literary journals; only the most rigorous hounds made it to the library or the modest gravestone in the local cemetery.

'Cultural tourism,' says Laura patiently, stretching her aching back, 'is tourists coming for arty farty things. Festivals, ballet and such. Not just Maoris or sport. We are cultural tourism.'

'These tables are dirty,' says Lisa, looking at her hands in distaste.

'Well, clean them,' snaps Betty. 'And get that child down off there.' Lisa, lifting Charlton down from the Garden Centre's wrought iron plant stand, doesn't expect much more from Betty, The Boss. Lisa knows she has a part-time job only because her mother's skills as the motel's long-standing housekeeper and occasional waitress are highly valued.

Besides, this arrangement suits Betty. It enables her to concentrate on making the guests feel at home. Betty believes she is good at this – asking where they come from in Canada, Japan, Germany, wherever; putting a single Belgian chocolate nightly on each pillow like they do in big city hotels. She is certainly a lot better at customer relations than Clarry, whose manner when guests ring on the office bell to sign in and get their key, can sometimes, even on a good day, be dour.

Better the devil you know, Betty thinks grimly, as she watches Lisa hauling Charlton down off the pot plant stand and knocking over only one peace lily. As a former teacher, Betty prides herself on knowing the young, and thinks that Laura giving her twenty-two-year-old unmarried daughter a home and a job is a mistake in the long term. She doesn't understand it. Betty's own three flew the nest years ago! Doing so well overseas! But after Charlton was born, Laura had made it clear that she and Lisa came as a package.

Laura, straightening up chairs, is wondering which unit the singer is in, and what she might wear tonight. The gold fitted jacket she bought in Sydney might be a bit over the top, even if she could get into it, doubtful after a long lazy summer. She wants a more New York sophisticate look. Black.

'Looking good.' After fifteen minutes of intense discussion and experiment, the two older women stand back. There are tables for the drink and the buffet and just enough space for the band, the freewheeling singer and all the gear. Betty will bring in some fresh flowers and candles for the tables. Laura will put out the programmes. Lisa can go home now.

Cows! Lisa is thinking, as she puts a grizzling Charlton in the stroller and wipes his nose. She checks the twenty tables she has just expertly set, despite this bloody baby and that hauling round of furniture and bloody boring chat.

What with the motel fully booked and its staff in a heightened state of readiness for a major arts event, Carmen dashing in to her studio unit to throw down her bags and change for the reception, and Lisa heading off home to give Charlton a sleep, it is entirely possible that Carmen and Lisa might not meet up at all on this perfect March afternoon, the weekend before Easter.

Better for all – and especially for Charlton, a peaky child given to volcanic tantrums – if they don't. But they do, because on such cruelly random coincidences do life's dramas depend, and Lisa is a conscientious worker.

Half way across the courtyard enclosed by the horseshoe of units, pushing her fractious child, she remembers she has left some cleaning gear in one of the bathrooms. Bloody hell – Charlton as usual, needing a poo, distracting her.

Bummer, she thinks. It's the unit the black Golf is now parked in front of. Good one! She'd heard the shrill voice of its owner earlier, bossing the driver of the delivery van. She sighs. For the sake of not involving Betty and Laura, and thereby in the cause of peace, she will deal with it alone. Hopefully, if she grovels sufficiently, it will not get back to Clarry, whom she regards as terminally anally retentive.

Standing at the open door behind the stroller, on the grounds that it might afford her some protection, Lisa calls softly, 'Excuse me, unit five? Hey, excuse me?'

'Yep?' The voice from within is followed a few seconds later by a gorgeous creature erupting from the bathroom: all legs below a very short black skirt; skinny arms and bare shoulders; long straight blonde hair and the mask achieved by too much foundation. Lisa recognises the type – Auckland Bulimic Chick personified – but she also recognises the person. 'Carmen?' she cries. 'Shit! Carmen! What are you doing *here*?'

'Do I know you?' She is gathering up a little black jacket, a tiny black and silver bag, car keys, cellphone, Pump bottle, clearly in a tearing hurry. She gives Lisa's stroller, old jeans, limp T-shirt and post-breast-feeding shape a quick once-over.

Lisa, feeling instantly put-down, ploughs on. 'Flat in Mt Eden, three years ago? I was second year varsity. Weren't you doing journalism?' And when the penny still hasn't dropped, 'Lisa Blowse. I got pregnant. This is it.'

She might yet need the protection of Charlton in the stroller, for different reasons. She gives it a little push forward, which she hopes conveys maternal pride. Something Carmen hasn't got, for all her shiny car and black designer suit.

'Oh *Lisa*.' Carmen laughs. 'Yeah, I remember, huge dramas, huge mystery about the dad, wouldn't have an abortion and went home to Mum. I'd forgotten it was here. Do you really live in this dump?'

Lisa recoils from this brutal summing up of her Auckland experience. Betty's brother Tony and wife Nance had given her a room and tried their best, but eventually had asked her to leave. She'd got into a wacky flat of sociologists and marketing students, succumbed to the prevailing culture of smoking, sniffing and drinking anything to hand, and eating too many potato wedges.

Failing all of her first year BA papers except one, she'd assured her mother she'd lose weight and get some exercise and try harder, she really would. But the second flat in Ponsonby was worse. For one thing, it housed too many actors; and it housed Carmen, a sixteen-year-old stick insect from Pakuranga who'd won a coveted place in a journalism course at Unitech. Bright, blonde, loud, gullible, ambitious, confident and stupid, all the things Lisa had been when she arrived in the city a year earlier.

But whereas Lisa's life had done a U-turn back to Mum and humdrum domesticity, her major weekly excitement a Lotto ticket, Carmen three years on was clearly doing well.

'I left some cleaning gear in your bathroom, sorry,' says Lisa.

'Do you *clean* here?'

'Yes. Sometimes. Mostly wipe tables.'

'God, you poor thing.' With unfeigned hostility Carmen looks at Charlton trying to wriggle out of the stroller. 'Look, I've got this wedding. It's my brother, though why he's bothering is beyond me – he's been bonking the bride for three years. No, it's because she goes with a farm. Where's the House on the Plains?'

'Turn right at the water tower.' She wishes Charlton would stop that whining. 'About five blocks down.'

'What water tower?'

'That tall grey thing like a medieval keep you see coming into town. Can't miss it.'

'Well I did miss it. What's a keep?'

Lisa is amazed that Carmen, a journalist, doesn't know what a keep is, and especially this keep. If you squint at it through half-closed eyes, especially on rainy, misty days, it looks medieval and mysterious, like something from a book of fairy tales. Rapunzel's tower.

'So which way do I go?' says Carmen, impatiently squeezing past the stroller. 'Fuck.' She bends down to examine where the wheel hub's sharp edges have scratched her tanned shaven ankles, swipes off the rubies of blood, licks her finger, and continues on to unlock the car. 'Hey, listen up, I'm only going for the reception, just the speeches. Meet you here for a drink later? Catch up? And come to the jazz tonight... Which unit is my bloody family in?'

'I don't know. And it's not that easy to...'

'Well, they're in one of them. Mum, Dad, two little sisters. I said I'd be independent, thanks. Couldn't *stand* it. The paper's paying, anyway.'

She revs up the Golf, sending a cloud of exhaust fumes across the courtyard. 'I'm doing a piece on New Plymouth on the way back, interviews and stuff. Can you pull that door shut? Thanks. See you tonight. Ciao.'

Charlton, frightened by the car noise, has begun to scream.

'Turn left into High Street and left at the water tower,' calls Lisa. 'Keep going until you see the sign. Can't miss it.'

She remembers, as she goes into the bathroom to retrieve the cleaning gear, that she must go and check last night's Lotto winners.


Carmen does miss it the first time, because Lisa, irritated by her wailing son and flustered by Carmen's skittish thought processes, had confused left with right, which she'd often done as a child.

By the time Carmen finds the House on the Plains, the two hundred guests are well into the champagne – only Deutz, she notes with satisfaction – and are standing round the verandas and patios of the gracious old homestead watching the bridal party endure a lengthy photographic session in the gardens below. The photographer has placed them under a splendid *Magnolia grandiflora*, heavy with creamy flowers, and behind is the mountain in its full glory, of course. If you're lucky enough to have a wedding in Taranaki with the mountain clear, you make the most of it.

She groans – the bridesmaids, *four* of them, are dressed in that old urban-chic cliché of black silk. *Strapless*, even. So *wrong* out here in the middle of nowhere. No taste at all. She feels almost sorry for her brother, who's losing his hair. Tracked down almost at once by her parents, she lightly dismisses their concerns as to why she wasn't at the church.

'I was the first car in the queue, honest…' she babbles, knowing that they don't believe a word and would have decided that she was simply late out of bed and late in leaving Hamilton, had no idea actually how far it was and doesn't actually care. Familiar territory on both sides.

The photographer, in unprofessional pastels, is drifting round her tripod, calling the groom's parents back into the picture.

'Why are these photos going on so long?' Carmen asks a passing waiter with a full tray of Deutz flutes. He has a radiant white shirt, a little black goatee, and is clearly gay, funny and trustworthy. She has a journalist's nose for these things. She replaces her empty glass with a full one. 'I think that's so rude, don't you?'

'I hear,' he says conspiratorially, 'I *hear* they first went to the Memorial Park gardens, and the photographer was snapping away when this bearded man in very short shorts comes dancing apologetically over and says he is *dreadfully* sorry but he is a bit short of man-power to get a big deep-freeze he is buying out of a garage and onto a trailer and *could* they possibly *help*?'

'They didn't!'

'It's second-hand, this freezer, a very good price. So yes, Hugo and all the blokes in their tails and silk cummerbunds go off to this run-down California bungalow in the street next to the park, watched by a sabotaged and twittering photographer, half of whose subjects have disappeared, and by some rather bewildered black frocks.'

'Oh dear,' says Carmen, amazed at this man's ability to speak in long flowing phrases and giggling with joy. '*Won*-derful.'

'Brenda throws a small tantie, and who can blame her! Gets back in the limmo and drives here. Announces to Daddy that Hugo will find her and her bridesmaids at the reception *when* he's stopped humping deep-freezes around the place and if he can be bothered. Hugo arrives panting, with more than a few fences to mend. But pictures have to be taken for posterity, hence…'

He nods at the bridal party, now augmented by both sets of parents, who are smiling fixedly into the wide-angle Nikon. 'Ooh, I just love black silk. Aren't they all lovely?'

'No, they're not,' says Carmen forcibly, the champagne on an empty stomach predictably making her voice sound disembodied. 'The groom is my brother and a prize wanker. He's been bonking the bride for three years.'

The waiter looks around, aghast. 'Shush your mouth, pet,' he whispers. 'He can't be a wanker if he can lift a whole deep-freeze on his wedding day, now can he?'

Carmen stares at his sweetly malicious smile, and starts laughing. Oh, it was worth coming all this way, just for this.

'Are you coming to the jazz in town tonight?' she asks, feeling expansive, just slightly giddy. 'The singer is a mate. And I'm meeting this other old friend who wipes tables at this ghastly motel. It's so *sad*, she was so into poetry and grass and E and stuff and had guys like you wouldn't believe, and then she had this horrible baby and now she's incredibly repressed and depressed and unhappy and... Is there somewhere I can sit down?'

The notion of a brilliant mercy mission is forming itself in her head.

The waiter, dextrously balancing his tray on one hand, leads Carmen to an unoccupied wooden garden seat flanked by massed lavender bushes. By good chance a large tray of club sandwiches is hovering nearby. Carmen finds herself sitting with a black linen napkin across her bare knees nursing a small heap of plump white sandwiches.

'Groom's sister gets pixillated at wedding. Bride's family say they will never forgive. Shock horror at Taranaki wedding. Eat.'

Carmen looks up at him gratefully. He knows her for a journalist who can write headlines, though God knows how. He understands that later on today the lovely talented Lisa must be rescued from a fate worse than death. He might even know the singer whom she met once recently and who, post-Jason-baby, will finish the night in her unit.

'I think you should come tonight,' she says, munching. 'Leave this bunch of drunks. Great jazz and a performance poet.'

'I am coming,' he says, twinkling. 'I'm the poet. This pays the rent.'

With the gleaming white homestead in its delightful rural setting and distant mountain all burnished gold by the setting sun, the reception grinds through its traditional programme. Hugo redeems himself with a terrific speech praising the gentlemen dairy farmers of south Taranaki, and especially his generous, indeed visionary, father-in-law Garry, father of his beautiful bride Brenda, husband of his gracious and equally beautiful wife Doris. 'To Garry,' he concludes.

Carmen, somewhat recovered, gets into animated conversation with three of the groomsmen about flying small planes. She lets them know that by the time this chick is twenty-five, she will have moved from the staid old print media – although hey, it's the *best* training – into television interviewing, like Susan Wood, though she'd *love* to do a reality television series like *Changing Rooms* for experience. She gets several invitations to go flying from the airfield tomorrow if the weather holds. Although, they say, when the mountain's clear like that – they all pause for a moment to drink in its breath-taking symmetry against a now pearly apricot sky – this usually means there's rain on the way. Taranaki sunshine.

Lisa, having waited tables for a while, is back in the two-bedroom brick-and-tile apartment two blocks away from the motel, which she shares with her mother. At 7pm she's on the lonely nightly count-down to getting Charlton into his small bed in the corner of Lisa's room, and asleep.

At least, she thinks, as she spoons Baby Four Fruits Yoghurt into him, daylight saving has finished. It would be dark by eight, thank Christ. Normally she doesn't care, really. One night is much the same as any other. Tea, bath, *The Simpsons*, book, bed, light out. Drink, another book, light out. Nursery songs, and finally sleep.

What sustains her is not the support of Laura, who's usually down in the bar in the Central at this hour, but the stern handsome face of Charlton Heston beaming down at her from every wall of their bedroom. A younger sterner Charlton as Moses, as Michelangelo; and older, smiling and distinguished, as himself.

Charlton had, by some miracle, actually come in person to Auckland while she was at varsity. He had launched his biography at Dymocks Bookshop. He'd sat Moses-like with Max Cryer, being interviewed before an audience of over two hundred. His wife had worn a hideous suit, lurid lime green long before it was fashionable, and Charlton himself was over seventy and mean people around her thought he'd had a face-lift. But Lisa knew she was in the presence of a Hollywood Legend and at the first words uttered by that rich, sexy voice, had felt quite faint. When Moses raised his muscled arms and led the multitudes through the Red Sea, that was what made her spine tingle, never failed. What other name could she give her son?

Tonight, however, she doesn't feel like *The Ten Commandments* on the vid. She is feeling unsettled, left out. And Carmen chick is going to the jazz night. Carmen has not followed up her suggestion for a catch-up drink. Lisa hadn't really thought she would. Weddings tend to go on a bit, and remembering Carmen's reputation in the flat, Lisa doubts if she'd be capable of driving herself anywhere.

But as the light fades from the sky outside, rationalising that Charlton slept for forty minutes in his stroller and now seems quite perky, Lisa decides that she will go to the jazz evening.

Her inescapable son Charlton will sit quietly on her lap listening to civilised jazz and poetry, and fall asleep. Then she'll put him in the stroller, to sleep in a dark corner of the hall until she is ready to go home.

It's the prospect of poetry that draws her, as it once drew her to Auckland and to events at the Dead Poets Café and to any poetry readings she saw advertised. In lectures she grew to be bored rigid by, and finally loathe John Donne and the rest of the metaphysicals, she detests the whimpy woolly Romantics; what she craved then and craves now is stuff that is being written right *now*, read out now, like Robert Sullivan, stuff that's raw, rude, sexy, political, that has energy and rap rhythms and really shocks people. She'd written a bit herself during that eighteen months before everything turned to custard, some pretty wild and powerful ramblings in her notebooks; she'd never had the courage to share them with anyone, let alone get up and read them.

Then there'd been that trendy book launch and an awful night in a Herne Bay apartment, and seven weeks later she'd bought a pregnancy kit.

Bingo! All hell had broken loose. She was still living in it, reminded quite often by a bland pleasant face on the six o'clock news, banging on about the economy. The man is stronger and more dangerous than he looks.

She lifts Charlton down from his chair and whips off his bib. 'Want to go to a party?' she asks.

The child stares at her, silent. 'Yes *please*, mummy,' she taunts. She roughly pulls a clean sweat shirt over his head, laces up sneakers, wipes his face, and plonks him in front of television while she dresses in her one best skirt and one of her mother's less hideous tops and clips up her long, blondish hair. She can't afford to colour it, and she gave up on make-up three years ago, as a sort of penance.

In the mirror she sees herself as a scruffy hard-up solo mum desperate for some decent music and adult company. Moses and Michelangelo stare disapprovingly down at her. She doesn't expect them to approve, or even understand.

To Mr Heston she says out loud, 'Give me a break!'


The tragic consequences of the jazz and poetry night at the Oddfellows Hall, a rare local arts festival event eagerly anticipated by those who'd wisely booked early, will not be truly revealed until late Monday night. Monday morning, just as the groomsmen predicted, will bring ominous grey skies obliterating the stately mountain to the north. By midday the showers will have become heavy. There will be no flying in two-seater planes for Carmen or anyone that day. Perhaps the suddenly autumnal weather plays its part in the decisions that create the unfolding drama, who can tell?

But here, at 8.30pm in the Oddfellows Hall, with the porch and side doors open to a still, clear Sunday night, the potted trees glistening in the candlelight and the well-fed audience settling back, the words and music are about to begin.

Betty is well satisfied. The chef, employing three extras in the kitchen, has risen to the occasion, amply justifying the $55-a-head (excluding wine) charge. The band has turned up sober and unstoned, as far as she can tell, and on time, which she had been warned – unfairly and scurrilously – might not be the case. They are professionals, gentlemen despite their ponytails and piercings. The singer is testing the mike for the benefit of the sound engineer at the back.

Clarry is satisfied. His units are full, mostly with the band and a wedding party from Hamilton and Auckland; his restaurant staff have done their job well; and an arts festival dignitary from New Plymouth has just thanked him for making this event possible. Praised him – and Betty – for their cultural leadership in holding fast to a name that, she understood, still caused controversy in the town. They and the proprietors of Morrieson's Café, who, marking the occasion, had closed their shop and were actually here tonight, were together making a unique and enlightened contribution to the nation's young literary heritage.

Laura is much less satisfied. An hour or so earlier, Betty had been called back to the motel to calm down a guest whose husband had gone for a drive and failed to return. What with the water tower fatality, setting up for an Arts Festival event and now a missing husband, it'd been one of those days. So Laura and the dopey barman had had to deal with the first stampede for wine and beer. Only then had she been able to slip out from behind the makeshift bar and persuade the singer to sit down and join her for a drink, though he sipped only mineral water. He wasn't eating, of course; never ate before a gig. When he excused himself to join the band, she felt she'd made considerable headway. He was attentive and charming – and, it turned out, only eleven years younger. He was really interested in her own early career as a backing vocalist with the Queen City Big Band.

Then two young women had unexpectedly arrived to throw her fantasies into disarray: a long-legged bimbo in black, possibly fifteen, who'd rushed up and air-kissed the singer with obvious, sickening familiarity; and worse, her daughter and grandchild.

Laura swore. She was in no mood to be in grandmother mode, nor did she approve of any young child, even Charlton, running round this late; neither did she appreciate Lisa borrowing her clothes. But the young thing in black also seemed to know Lisa, and before Laura knew it, both had helped themselves to the remains of the buffet and settled down on spare seats at the back to put their blonde heads together for a good girly chat. Embarrassed by her whining grandson, Laura had little option. Now, as the first set gets under way, she is behind the bar table holding the baby, hoping like hell that the singer is too preoccupied and dazzled by the spotlights to notice.

Lisa is having a night out – Carmen has just pointed out her friend, the performance poet, over there in the black shirt and goatee, such a *witty* man – and that is enough for her.

Carmen is on a high. She's done her sisterly duty at the wedding, got only a little drunk, and got her twin missions quite clear in her head: one, to persuade Lisa it's not too late to start again at varsity (she'd only have to pay a late fee, student loans were easy, Waikato had good hostels, and her mum could surely look after Charlton in term-time, for a bit), and second, to bed the singer before dawn tomorrow.

She'd focus on Lisa first, the singer later.


If only the performance poet had come on earlier. By the time the band has done three sets and the poet is about to rise to his feet, Carmen has shouted Lisa five vodkas and watched her staunchly resist her mother's every suggestion to take Charlton home. Lisa has decided, before it's absolutely too late, to go back to varsity. Like, tomorrow.

Carmen, glowing with alcoholic and altruistic satisfaction, has been perched on a table, her skirt barely covering anything, locked in steamy eye contact with the singer as he performs a set of Burt Bacharach: 'What the world needs now…'

Laura, seeing the singer irretrievably lost to an eighteen-year-old with not enough clothes on, has had enough. Tight-lipped with fury and resentment and knowing that a five-piece jazz combo is one thing but the hushed concentration needed for the spoken word is another, she puts Charlton in the stroller, takes him home and knocks up the fifteen-year-old next door to come and baby-sit because she has other fish to fry.


How Lisa, Carmen and nearly all the audience love the poet! How they applaud his energetic performance of 'Profit', about schizophrenics sent out into the community, and 'Stakeholders', delivered deadpan, about meaningless language. Some in the audience, including Clarry, ascertain that the poet's politics are a little too left of centre for their taste, but nevertheless acknowledge that it is a poet's job to be provocative and make you think, and applaud good-humouredly.

Lisa is thrilled when the poet, wending his way through the congratulations and outstretched hands of the predominantly female audience, comes to have a drink with her and Carmen. He is every bit as witty as Carmen said. Carmen urges him to tell Lisa the hilarious story of the deep-freeze.

As midnight and the scheduled end of the evening approaches, however, Lisa is not only a little drunk but rather loathe to go home, knowing the cold wrath of recrimination that will descend on her. This defiance, this neglect of her maternal duty, has never happened before. Laura will be sitting up in her pink satin pyjamas, face shiny with Turnaround cream, watching the infomercials and waiting to pounce.

There is only one other place she can go.


So it happens that Carmen, having first accepted an invitation to join the band in one of their units for a nightcap and a joint, at 4.10am leads the singer by the hand past the unit which, with the dark green Subaru parked outside, undoubtedly contains her sleeping family. They open up Carmen's studio unit to find Lisa asleep on the double bed among two Belgian chocolate wrappers and three empty cognacs from the mini-bar, out for the count. Blotto!

Swearing obscenely, stoned to the eyeballs, Carmen and the singer haul her onto the divan and cover her with a blanket.

But how it cramps Carmen's style! She loves sex in unexpected, really odd places and in this poky, sterile little unit with its concrete-block walls and shocking furniture straight from the seventies, had planned on using it *all*. She is just enough in control of things to scrawl on the back of her business card, 'Lisa baby, DON'T fucking wake me. See you in Hammy asap. DON'T BRING YOUR SPROG.'

There's a knock on the door. Carmen giggles: the poet, something a bit different.


Lisa sleeps until 11.40am and has disturbing dreams of climbing up a tower, up its narrow circular staircase, something to do with bunjy-jumping down on yellow plaits to a man on a horse. She is given to analysing her dreams. Remembering that she's just made a life-changing decision, she thinks the man on the horse is the man she's going to meet at varsity who will become her partner and loving stepfather to Charlton. A PhD student, because she knows lecturers, especially at very PC Waikato, are out of bounds.

She hears rain. Then she opens her eyes and dully recognises where she is, the familiarity of the hard divan beneath her. In real life, this is the very unit where thirty-seven months ago her waters broke as she was cleaning the lavatory, two weeks before her due date. She got no further than this divan, screaming at Laura that no *way* was she going in a fucking ambulance to Taranaki Base Hospital. Betty and a hastily-summoned midwife couldn't persuade her to move either. Clarry had had to turn away a booking for the unit and put up the No Vacancy sign. He'd had to pay for commercial cleaners to come in when it was all over.

Charlton had arrived after seventeen hours in labour, scrawny, puce and way too much like his father. She didn't love the child then and she didn't love him much more now. Hadn't bonded, hadn't contacted the dad. She must get off this bed of remembered pain, blood, screaming, anguish – hours of it. She should say goodbye to Carmen. She needs a piss.

In the absence of love and forgiveness, as the rain sets in and attitudes harden, this is what happens in Morrieson's Motel.

Lisa fails to see Carmen's card. What she sees is a room where it's obvious there has been a great deal of physical activity, and three naked people in the double bed. The place stinks. The bathroom is a mess of discarded clothes, used matches and puddles of water.

Disgusted, she retreats outside to see Laura coming out of the unit opposite, wearing her work gear and pushing the cleaning cart, trailing Charlton.

Betty and Clarry, wearily lugging potted trees from the Oddfellows Hall to a delivery van, are alerted to the row developing between mother and daughter in the courtyard. The family in the Subaru is just leaving and makes good its escape. They leave behind a note for their wayward daughter, whom they know better than to disturb.

Betty picks up the screaming Charlton and takes him into the office. Clarry fires both Laura and Lisa on the spot. Betty silently agrees with getting rid of Lisa, but not Laura. Already, she is working out how Laura can be reinstated without Clarry losing face. Well, he's always making dodgy innuendoes when she's around, it won't be hard.

Lisa runs home, sobbing, through the driving rain.

Betty soothes both Charlton and Laura. She tells Clarry to finish the cleaning, gets rid of a cultural tourist in the office who wants to do a PhD thesis on guess who, and drives Laura and grandson home. They should rest. She'll need them, at least for a while, in the restaurant tonight

She dries them all off, gives Charlton his lunch, and firmly instructs mother and daughter to pull themselves together. She'll work on Clarry – Laura will have her job back. But Lisa – you'd better start thinking of another job, another life. Get out on your own, out of your mother's hair. Join a playcentre, for God's sake. Despite everything, says Betty nobly, she'll give her a loan to tide her over.

Lisa retires, sniffing, red-eyed, sick to her stomach but resolute, to be soothed by Moses and Michelangelo.

After work that night, Laura goes down to the Central bar, where she intends to spend the night getting drunk, stiffening her resolve.

Little Charlton watches *Play School* videos until late afternoon, then he eats some macaroni and falls asleep in front of *The Agony and the Ecstasy*.

Lisa carries him to bed, kisses him, packs just her most essential clothes and one picture of Michelangelo. Lisa writes her mother a note for when she gets back from the restaurant. She needs some time out, she's got a brain, she wants to write, she's got talent, she wants a life. She lies down under the blankets fully dressed.


Laura comes unsteadily back at midnight, convinced that what she is about to do is for Lisa's good. It's the only way; rational discussion with the girl would be hopeless, get nowhere.

She looks into the bedroom where Lisa and her child sleep. The last three years have just about worn her out, and last night was the last straw. It'd been bad enough struggling for years to bring up Lisa single-handed; now, twenty-two years later, though she loves the little boy as much as any grannie, who wouldn't, she's not about to do it again. She has her own life to think about, her own yearning for a man, for companionship. She has a girlfriend in New Plymouth who'll give her a bed. Jobs in hotels come easily enough to someone of her looks and experience. Bugger Clarry.

Laura silently packs, grim-faced. She digs out her references, writes her daughter a note – *I just need a bit of space for a few weeks.*

*Love you* – and slips out of the flat. Lisa, sleeping fitfully, hears a car go, but assumes it's the man next door who works odd hours as an ambulance driver.

Lisa wakes just before dawn. She has always been able to give herself instructions to wake at a given hour. She kisses Charlton again, picks up her suitcase, fails to see her mother's note beside the kettle, puts her own note on the table, and silently leaves. It never occurs to her that her mother would not be in her bed, fast asleep behind the closed door.

Charlton stirs and wakes, a little fatherless boy in an empty flat, watched only by posters of his namesake. It will be nine hours before Betty, going round to the flat with a casserole as a peace offering, discovers him.

Carmen drives northward across the rainswept plains. No mountain now, just grey murk, a slippery road. She'd rung in sick yesterday. What a wicked little weekend!

She has a vague memory of some wild sex, watching horror vids during what was left of Monday, the singer's endless supply of stuff. She thought an extra player might have been involved somewhere, a body sleeping on the divan. She hadn't said goodbye to Lisa. Didn't know where she lived, did she. Bet she hadn't got the balls to leave her kid with her mum, to actually *do* it.

She speeds northwards, turns right to Waitara. It's only as she's again waiting in the Awakino Gorge for the stop sign to change – a different Maori, a slouching kid of thirteen in a yellow parka – that she remembers Lisa saying confidentially over their vodkas that if certain things got out, someone…

'You mean the bastard who's Charlton's father?' asked Carmen, thinking of recent scandals.

'Could be,' said Lisa, remembering the violent scene in the flat in Herne Bay only too clearly.

'A big, hunky, pro sports guy?'

'I don't think so.'
'Celeb, someone on TV?'
'Couldn't say.'
'Lecturer?'
'Don't even go there.'
'Politician — you could bring down the government?'
'Wow,' Lisa had said, laughing at her. 'I should be so lucky.'

Carmen also now remembers that she was supposed to be doing a story in New Plymouth. Fuck! She could nip back down to see Lisa, get her drunk again, get the story, sell it to the *Herald*, front page exclusive, television, fame, fortune. Thirty thousand from one of the women's mags. Yes!

She signals to the young Maori that she wants to do a U-turn, go back. 'Forgot something, dumb blonde,' she yells. Nine cars behind her have to back up to make it possible.

Is there a final irony in Carmen speeding south while the possibly famous Lisa is in an Intercity bus travelling north?

Well, no, there isn't, because Lisa, deciding that Carmen always did and always will mean trouble, has hitched a ride with a lonely sales rep travelling south to Wellington, where tomorrow she will enrol at Victoria. Wellington's closer than Hamilton, anyway. She'll be able to get back to see Charlton more often.

After all, Wellington's where Charlton's father is. And yes, from what she knows of politics from TV, she could quite possibly bring down a government. She wouldn't, for Charlton's sake, but it's quite a nice powerful feeling, really.

# The Authors

**Barbara Anderson's** first book of short stories was published by Victoria University Press in 1983. She has since published six novels, one of which, *Portrait of the Artist's Wife*, won the 1992 Goodman Fielder Wattie Award. A second book of short stories, *The Peacocks*, was published in 1998. She lives in Wellington with her husband.

**Catherine Chidgey's** first novel, *In a fishbone church*, won the NZSA Best First Book of Fiction Award at the Montana New Zealand Book Awards and was runner-up for the Deutz Medal. It won Best First Book at the Commonwealth Writers' Prize (Asia/Pacific region) and received a Betty Trask Award in England. Her second novel, *Golden Deeds*, was also runner-up for the Deutz Medal.

**Tessa Duder** trained as a journalist, swam butterfly for New Zealand, and had four daughters in three different countries before she began writing fiction. Her 25 books include eight novels, five anthologies, a play for teenagers, school readers and adult non-fiction, published in Australia, USA, UK and Europe. *Alex*, the first book of the multi-award-winning *Alex Quartet*, was made into a feature movie in 1993, and the first of a new series, *The Tiggie Tompson Show*, won the 2000 NZ Post Senior Fiction prize.

**Maurice Gee** is a Wellington novelist whose best-known books are *Under the Mountain* and *The Fat Man*, for children, and *Plumb*, *Going West* and *Live Bodies*, for adults. His new novel, *Ellie and the Shadow Man*, will be published next year.

**Kevin Ireland** lives in Devonport, on Auckland's North Shore. His thirteenth book of poems, *Anzac Day*, was published in 1997.

His fourth book of fiction, *The Craymore Affair*, appeared earlier this year. His memoir, *Under the Bridge & Over the Moon*, was published in 1998, and won the Montana prize for History and Biography.

**Stephanie Johnson** writes novels, short stories and plays. Her novels include *The Heart's Wild Surf*, *The Whistler* and most recently *Belief*. She lives in Auckland and was the 2000 Meridian Energy Katherine Mansfield Fellow in Menton, France. In 1999 she established, with Peter Wells, the Auckland Writers' Festival.

**Graeme Lay** was born in 1944 in Foxton, in the Horowhenua, raised in South Taranaki and educated at Victoria University. His first fiction was published in the late 1970s. He is the author of five novels, two collections of short stories and several non-fiction works. His latest books are the novels *Temptation Island* and *The Wave Rider*. He lives in Devonport, on Auckland's North Shore, where he is a full-time writer.

**Owen Marshall** has been a fulltime writer for about 10 years, and before that a teacher. He is the author or editor of 14 books, the last of which, a novel *Harlequin Rex*, won the Deutz Medal for Fiction at the 2000 Montana Book Awards. In the Queen's New Year Honours 2000, he was awarded the ONZM for services to Literature. He has spent almost all his life in South Island towns and has an affinity with provincial New Zealand. He lives in Timaru.

**Sue McCauley** grew up in the country (southern Hawke's Bay) and has lived in a number of rural New Zealand towns and cities including Dannevirke, Okaihau, Masterton and New Plymouth. She currently lives in Christchurch. Her writing includes novels, short stories, non-fiction, and drama for screen, stage and radio.

**Gordon McLauchlan's** first book, *The Passionless People*, was a social commentary on New Zealanders, and became an instant best seller after its publication in 1976. Since then he has become one of the country's best known journalists and broadcasters, has written a number of other books, and on two occasions has been literary editor of the *New Zealand Herald*. But his story in this book is his first attempt at fiction.

**Vincent O'Sullivan** is a poet, playwright, short story writer, novelist and critic. His last published fiction was *Believers to the Bright Coast*, 1998. A new volume of poems will appear early next year. He is the Director of the Stout Research Centre at Victoria University, Wellington.

**Sarah Quigley** is a writer of fiction, non-fiction, and poetry. She has a D. Phil from Oxford and has lived in England and the States, but like every good New Zealander she keeps coming home. She has held the Buddle Findlay Sargeson Fellowship and has recently been awarded the inaugural Creative NZ Berlin Residency, to write her third novel.

**Elizabeth Smither** has published three collections of stories: *Nights at the Embassy*, *Mr Fish and Other Stories* and *The Mathematics of Jane Austen*. Her collection of poems, *The Lark Quartet* won the Montana New Zealand poetry award for 2000. She lives in New Plymouth where she works as a librarian.